ALSO BY JAN TURK PETRIE

Until the Ice Cracks
Vol 1 of The Eldísvík Trilogy

No God for a Warrior
Vol 2 of The Eldísvík Trilogy

Within Each Other's Shadow
Vol 3 of The Eldísvík Trilogy

Too Many Heroes

Towards the Vanishing Point

The Truth in a Lie

Running Behind Time

Still Life with a Vengeance

Contents

"People like us, who believe in physics,
know that the distinction between past, present and
future is only a stubbornly persistent illusion."

Albert Einstein

A reminder of the story so far

In 2020, Tom Brookes is partway through a train journey from Cheltenham to Paddington when he accidentally slips through a time portal and ends up in 1982. Reaching Paddington, he's horrified to discover what's happened. He makes the return journey hoping to get back to his own time and bumps into Beth Sawyer. In the darkness of the tunnel, she grabs his arm as he goes back through the portal and finds herself thrown into the midst of the 2020 Covid pandemic.

Beth is slow to accept the reality of her new situation. Tom wants to help her to get back to 1982, but the crucial train – the Gustav Holst – is unable to make the return journey due to a landslip. Since her time leap has left her with no money or resources, Tom persuades his mother, Lana, to let her stay in their cottage in the Cotswold village of Stoatsfield-under-Ridge.

Though they come from very different eras, Tom and Beth begin to develop feelings for each other. Tom thinks up a plan for them both to make money on Beth's return to her own time. After some internet searches, he lists the winners of various sporting events in 1982/83 along with future high yield share investments.

Discovering the landslip has been cleared, Beth and Tom board the distinctive train intending to make the leap back in time together. They end up in early 1983. On the journey Tom begins to suspect they're being observed. Once they reach Paddington, Beth goes off to phone her aunty while Tom is confronted by Ford and others calling themselves Guardians. They make it clear they intend to force him to return to his own time.

Through subterfuge he manages to break free and flees with Beth before they can stop him. Having "lost" several months of her life, Beth has also lost her acting job and her flat share.

The couple book into a cheap hotel and, despite the circumstances, spend a passionate night together. Before they can enact any of their future plans, the Guardians catch up with them and force Tom onto the return train and back through the time portal to 2020. During the journey Ford inadvertently reveals Tom is able to time travel because there is something special about him. Heartbroken at his forced separation from Beth, he arrives back in Cheltenham and his own time.

Meanwhile, in 1983, Beth is reduced to sleeping on the sofa in her old flat. However, armed with the cash Tom acquired and the list of winners he gave her, she begins to make money betting on the outcome of various sporting events. Once she's accumulated enough seed money, she hopes to invest in the companies on his list.

All goes well until Beth is shocked to discover she is pregnant with Tom's child. Severe morning sickness prevents her from continuing her money-making activities. Her suspicious flatmate, Rachel, searches Beth's handbag and, on finding lots of unexplained cash, confronts her. Beth is forced to reveal the source of her new-found wealth and hands over the sheet of future betting and investment information. After initial scepticism, Rachel takes over the whole project and is soon making lots of money for herself.

Back in 2020 in Stoatsfield, following a casual chat with the woman serving in the local shop Tom discovers his mother, Lana, has had a very distinctive male visitor. Suspicions aroused, he rushes home to confront her and is astounded when his mother finally reveals her own extraordinary past. His ability to time travel is inherited from his absentee father – a man he'd previously known only as "Uncle Matt" who is one of the Guardians.

In 1983 Beth finally wakes up without feeling nauseous. It's a sunny spring day and she decides to go for a walk. As if she's being guided, she heads for Hyde Park and then Paddington station where the Gustav Holst is ready to depart.

Tom gets a phone call from his mother when out walking. After a hurried return, he is shocked and delighted to find Beth sitting in the kitchen drinking tea with his mother. When she stands up, he can see she is pregnant. Revealing that he is the father, Beth suggests the baby must have inherited Tom's ability to time-travel and that is how she was able to travel back through the portal.

Though happily reunited, the family face an uncertain future together.

Now read on…

PLAY FOR TIME

Chapter One

Gloucestershire, England.

August 2020

Beth

The cold goo on her stomach sends a chill through Beth. Lying on her back like a beached seal, she feels utterly powerless. Not the best angle to handle this moment of truth – for better or worse. Her sweaty hand involuntarily curls around the lifeline of her new mobile phone.

The woman draws the now slimy probe back and forth across Beth's enlarged belly. 'To answer your previous question, there's definitely only one baby.' At least that's some relief. Voice muffled by her mask, she adds, 'And certainly a good size.' Filling out the form in reception, the question about dates had made Beth's head spin – her guess a stab in the dark.

She can't see much of the midwife or technician or whatever she is. It's hard to understand why they need to wear quite so much protective gear – it's not as if the thing's about to burst out through her stomach wall like in that alien film.

The whooshing sound of a rapid pulse fills the small room. Beth's ears pulsate in time. The woman angles the screen towards her. Peering up at it, Beth watches a series of indecipherable ever-changing shapes and patterns in monochrome. With all their twenty-first century medical advances, she'd expected it to be colour.

The woman does something which freezes the image on the screen and then draws a circle around what could be a head. If Tom was here, he'd understand what she's doing. Though this is a private clinic and they're paying customers, covid regulations mean he's had to wait outside in the car park.

More than once, Tom has declared, 'I'm quite sure it's a girl' and, given his extraordinary abilities, she believes him. He's already referring to her as Vega – the name of the brightest star in the Summer Triangle of stars. 'Don't forget to film it all,' he'd shouted after her.

Beth asks, 'Is it okay if I record this for my partner?'

She deciphers the series of mumbles into the mask as, 'It's hard for dads. I'm sure we can bend the rules. Go ahead.'

Like Tom had shown her, Beth locates the camera icon and selects the video option. It's a struggle to keep her raised arm steady. 'You said just now that it's a good size – does that mean it's larger than a regular baby would be?'

This produces a frown on the small portion of the woman's face that's visible. 'No, not at all… I'd say everything looks pretty much what we'd expect for your dates.' Gloved hand on the probe, she appears to be measuring the distance between two points. 'Slightly more than average length for this stage of gestation.'

Beth is shocked when a bent leg appears out of the darkness – her baby asserting its presence. Looks like she's trying to kick the probe out of the way. Leave me alone, I'm sleeping.

'Correct number of toes on both feet.'

'But why is the heart beating so fast? Is this scaring her?'

Smile in her voice, the woman says, 'A baby's heart rate is always relatively fast – normally between 110 and 160 beats per minute. It can also vary a lot. Nothing to be alarmed about, I assure you.'

On the screen a shape recognisable as a face briefly emerges. Such a serene expression. Wow!

'Although there are no guarantees, your baby appears to be normal in every way.'

Staring at the screen, Beth sees movement – a perfect little arm materialises to scratch the profile of its face. Tiny chin jutting out. Little pert nose as clear as anything. A huge relief given that the baby's grandfather is a Guardian and at best they only resemble humans. She'd watched Rosemary's Baby late one night so is glad there's been no mention of a tail. And no sign of horns. She can't tell if there's anything wrong with its eyes – they appear to be closed.

'Would you like to know the sex of your baby?'

Beth's tempted to tell her she already does. Instead, she asks, 'Can you tell that for certain?'

'Not always, but in this case, I'd say it's very clear.' The woman holds her head to one side. 'These days, expectant mothers – or I should say *people* – can get a bit prickly about gender.' In a rehearsed way she adds, 'We simply offer to identify your baby's current biological sex for those parents who consider that to be significant.'

Beth feels a strong flutter. Simultaneously the onscreen image reveals the individual bones making up a kicking foot. It spurs her on. 'Yes – I think I would like to know.'

'You're quite sure?'

She nods. 'Yes – I'm sure.'

'Then congratulations, you're having a little boy.'

'Really? I mean you're absolutely one hundred percent certain about that?'

The woman freezes the screen. 'Pretty unmistakable I'd say.'

She's right.

The picture jumps back to real time. Now the angle has changed; the baby's moved away from the probe as if he's annoyed to have his private parts openly discussed.

'I'll see if I can get a close up of his face for your partner,' she says. A quick adjustment and then satisfied the woman stands back, arms folded.

And there he is filling the screen – her son. Their son. So much for Tom's psychic powers. Hi there. Raising a hand, she waves at him.

'Will you look at that.' The woman chortles. 'If I didn't know better, I'd say he's waving right back at you.'

All too soon the screen goes blank. The woman hands her tissues to wipe the goo off her belly. Once that's done, she pulls her top down and heaves herself off the bed.

One thing's for certain, there's no way she's going to call their son Vega. Far better to give him a common name, though that's bound to have changed since her time – back in the early eighties.

Chapter Two

Tom

The sun is trying to shine through wind-lashed rain. Beth's been in there far longer than he'd anticipated. Unable to sit still, Tom grabs his mum's umbrella and leaves the shelter of the car. He alternates between pacing and leaning against the short wall opposite the entrance; adopting a casual stance in a futile attempt to counteract his nervousness.

He'd found this private clinic online. A simpler solution given Beth's current undocumented status. It annoys him that after weeks he's still waiting for confirmation from Davy's hacker friend that what he's referred to as Beth's "legend" has successfully been installed onto various official websites.

The umbrella keeps trying to take off. He's about to close it when Beth finally appears. Pushing her way through the glass door her dark hair in wind-driven turmoil, she takes off her mask and stares up into the rainy sky. Despite her tan, she looks ill. Or utterly shell-shocked.

Shit!

He hurries towards her with the umbrella aloft, juggling

it so he can take her arm in case she's about to faint. 'Are you okay?'

'Apparently.' There's a slight edge to her voice when she adds, 'The woman said everything appears to be normal.'

He'd detected stress on the words *appears to be* but that was just her repeating the usual caveat. Relieved, Tom steers her towards the shelter of the car. Halfway there she stops walking to thrust her mobile into his hand. 'I filmed it like you wanted me to. It should be on there.'

'Great.' He slips the phone into his pocket. 'And everything's okay? Only it seems like there's something you're not telling me.'

She shakes her head. 'It all looks fine – at least that's what she told me.' The dark umbrella is casting its gloom over her features.

'And the baby – there's nothing wrong with her, is there?'

'Medically speaking we're both fine.' She hesitates. 'It's just – well it was a bit weird. I wasn't expecting…'

Reaching the car, Tom holds the door open, relaxes a little once Beth is safely sitting down. He slams her door shut then runs round to dump his mum's brolly in the boot before jumping into the driver's seat beside her.

Beth is staring at the rain-soaked windscreen. He persists, 'There something worrying you – I can tell.'

She opens her mouth to speak but then pauses to reconsider. Finally, she says, 'Like I said, the woman who did the scan said to tell you everything is progressing normally.' And yet her blue eyes remain troubled.

'Then why are you acting like you've just had a shock?'

Beth stares down at her swollen belly with an ambivalent look on her face. 'For a start your premonition was completely wrong.' Her freckles bunch up when she wrinkles her nose. 'There's a boy in here, not a girl.'

'Is that all?' He can smile at last. 'A boy, eh? I mean yeah, that's a bit of a surprise, but hardly a disaster. In fact, I don't know about you, but I'm equally thrilled we're having a son.'

'And another thing,' she says, 'you can forget about calling him Vega or any other weird sort of name. He'll have to be something common like Ben. Or George like the prince. Or even Tom junior – although that might get quite confusing.' The windows are already steaming up. Both hands on her bump she adds, 'We're going to need to protect him.'

'Of course – that goes without saying.' He frowns. 'Unless you mean against something in particular?'

She's shivering despite the humidity. 'It's hard to explain. If you watch the video, you might pick it up.'

'I might pick up what? Come on, Beth – out with it.'

'I wish you'd been there to see for yourself. The baby – our baby – well he looked straight at me. This may sound daft but I'm convinced he could see me as clear as anything.'

'But you must know that's utterly impossible.' He wipes his hand over his mouth to suppress a smirk. 'Ultrasound scans – they're a one-way thing. They let you see the baby but definitely not the other way around.'

'I know that – I'm not bloody stupid. They had scans in my day too, you know.' More head shaking. 'But he *could* see me – I'm sure of it. He even waved at me.'

Tom pats the back of her hand and by extension her baby

bump. 'They move their little arms and legs around all the time in the womb. It's quite normal.'

'But *he's* not normal, is he? I mean his granddad…' She lowers her voice, 'Is one of them.'

'Ah – you're worried about what he might have inherited from Matt. For goodness' sake, he might be a Guardian, but Matt also happens to be *my father.*' On the verge of losing his temper, Tom takes a deep breath. 'Does that make me abnormal in your eyes? Is that what you think? What you're saying?'

'You have to admit, you are a bit *unusual.* More than a bit, in fact.' She finds his hand, squeezing it before he has a chance to snatch it away. 'Not that I don't love you for who you are and all that.' Her face softens into a smile which she's quick to drop. 'But this isn't about you.' She nods at her stomach. 'It's about him in there. Watch the video – you'll see what I mean.'

'I don't need to watch it to know you're talking complete–' He stops himself. 'Look, Beth, this has been a stressful time for both of us. Especially you. Getting used to life in 2020 instead of the early eighties – well it must have been one hell of an adjustment to make. You're still finding your feet in this century. I get that. Being pregnant on top – well, it's no wonder you're feeling a bit overwrought. Surely you admit you might be imagining the whole waving thing?' In a gentler voice, 'He's *our* baby. The two of us may have done a bit of time-travelling – which I admit *is* fairly unusual – but aside from that we're relatively normal human beings. There's no reason to suppose our son will be anything else.'

'I've been thinking about that.' Again, she wraps her hands around her rugby-ball stomach. 'You know the way red hair or, I don't know, blue eyes can often skip a generation–'

'Hold on a minute. So, based solely on the fact that the baby momentarily looked as if he could be waving at you, you're suggesting our son could be…' He hesitates to say the word aloud. 'You think he might be *a Guardian*.'

'No – I'm not saying that. At least I don't think I am. Not exactly, anyway.'

'Then what the hell are you trying to say?'

'Look, think about it for a minute. If I hadn't been pregnant with him, I'd still be stuck in 1983. *He* guided me towards the station that day. *He* got me through the portal the last time, not you.'

'Okay, that's true, but–'

'So, I'm just floating the idea that our son might not be entirely normal.'

'Great – so even before he's born, you've decided the poor boy's a freak.'

'There's no need to raise your voice.' Her hands expand like she's trying to physically block the baby's ears. 'On the scan he *looked* perfectly ordinary. Besides, even if he wasn't, I'd still love him. And I would certainly never use a horrible word like freak to describe him.'

'Whatever word you use, you're already thinking it.'

'Tom, calm down. All I'm saying is I know what I saw – what I felt when it happened.' She reaches to pull her phone out of his pocket, waves it in his face. 'I could be wrong. On the other hand, it's possible he might have some…' She hesitates. 'Some *unusual* abilities. Why don't you watch the video?'

He snatches the phone from her. 'Okay, okay, I will but only to prove to you that…'

'Wait.' She grabs the phone back. 'You need to watch it with an open mind.'

'Okay, then let's view it together. Right now.'

Tom tries to hide his impatience when it takes her ages to find the app. About to press play, she says, 'I realise I could be wrong. I'll keep an open mind, as long as you promise you'll do the same.'

'I swear to you my mind is as wide open as Norwich City's defence.'

'This isn't a joke.'

'Sorry,' he says, 'it's just I'm really excited to see him for the first time.'

'Okay then.' She presses play.

After watching the footage, Tom wordlessly gives her back the phone and then stares at the rivulets running down the misty windscreen. 'I hate to say this,' he says, breaking the silence, 'but I see what you mean.'

Chapter Three

Pathways Cottage, Stoatsfield under Ridge

Lana

They've gone out and Lana is making the most of it, feet up, cup of tea by her side. She lets the notes of a Sibelius symphony soothe away her cares. A few short months ago she'd been contentedly living alone, her house settled and orderly around her. But time has moved on. Had other ideas.

She glances up from her book as the grandfather clock's mechanism whirs in preparation for the sonorous dong that sounds the half hour. Tom and Beth are bound to be back soon – and with reassuring news she hopes. No doubt the two of them will burst through the front door in the usual whirlwind of noise and disruption. Before the pandemic Tom had been more or less independent – an occasional, very welcome visitor but only that. She'd had all the time in the world to read, listen to her music, even take an afternoon nap without fear of interruption. These days solitude is a rare treat. Soon the baby, her first grandchild, will be making his or her presence felt and there will be little rest for any of them. A prospect that simultaneously dismays and delights her. Conceived in 1983 and yet he or she won't be born for several months. Ridiculous that such a thing is becoming a family tradition. Although she's only lived for a total of 61 years, she was born in 1923, so by rights ought to be 97. At times her bones like to remind her.

Out loud she scolds herself. 'Don't you go turning into a miserable old woman.' Hearing her voice, the dog opens one eyelid. Letting it drop again, Poppy rearranges her limbs and settles back as if exhausted by the effort.

Financially speaking, it's been a struggle at times. Ever since Beth's arrival, they'd talked about how they might gain access to the money in the savings account the girl had set up back in 1983. Beth favoured the idea of Lana impersonating her. The two of them would go into the bank together and distract the staff while Beth signed the necessary documents to unfreeze what must now be a dormant account. Tom suggested it might be better to use stage makeup to age Beth appropriately. The possibilities the money might allow were tantalising. High stakes. Given the current covid restrictions imposed by the banks, they'd all agreed to do nothing – at least for the time being.

Lana picks up her book to find she has no memory of the last few pages. Perhaps she'd turned over too many at once. Before she can piece together the thread of the story, she's distracted by a low, continuous noise. Shaking her head she dismisses it, puts it down to an overhead plane or distant thunder – though the afternoon's intermittent showers seem to hold no threat of such a storm.

The sound intensifies. It's coming not from outside but inside. In fact, from under the table. Where Poppy had a moment ago been flat out and snoring, she's now wide awake and emitting a deep, threatening growl.

Next second the old dog springs to her feet with unaccustomed speed to snarl and snap at the closed door. Lana kills the music. 'What in the world's the matter with you?' She tries to quieten her with reassuring pats, but the raised hairs along the dog's spine stay rigid. 'Why are you making such a fuss, you silly old thing?' Poppy takes no notice. Up on her hind legs despite her arthritis, her claws scratch at the wood in her desperation to get at whatever threat she imagines is on the other side.

She hasn't behaved like this since…

Oh God. There can be only one explanation – *he* must be back.

Lana grabs the dog's collar, is forced to wrestle her back into the room before she can shut her up behind the closed door. If it had a lock, she would turn it. She rushes over to the front window and, sure enough, the black Range Rover is out there blocking her in. She hears the knocker rap against the door. Heart beating out of her chest, Lana walks towards it.

There can be no escape. She has no option but to open up.

'Hello again,' Ford says. 'Hope you don't mind me calling round unannounced.' No face mask, of course. Unruffled by the rain and swirling wind, his dark suit and polished shoes as immaculate as always. His lips form an approximation of a charming smile. With his floppy greying hair and piercing blue eyes, outwardly he could be described as dashing. Tom had recently alerted her to his strong resemblance to the actor Liam Neeson, shown her the famous clip in which Neeson's character talks menacingly about his particular skill-set; fictional abilities that pale into insignificance compared with those Ford is able to muster at a moment's whim.

Lana has no choice but to stand aside and let him enter. Once he's over the threshold, the dog increases her scrabbling and snarling, sounding less like an elderly Labrador and more like some hellhound about to burst out to tear their visitor limb from limb.

'You really ought to keep that creature of yours under better control,' he says. 'I'm surprised it hasn't already come to a sticky end.'

To put another door between the two, she shows him into the kitchen where he sits down without an invitation. Ford appears to be sniffing the air – the lingering smell of the plum jam she'd made earlier. With a distasteful expression, he feels behind his back and withdraws her knitting – the tiny stripy cardigan she's just started on. He drops it, needles and all, onto the hard floor. Half of the stiches fall off the needle but she dare not attempt to pick it up – her hands are shaking too much.

'Poppy's usually as quiet as anything,' she says. 'But, there again, I've noticed before your unique effect on animals.'

'I consider it a gift.' Down the hallway the dog begins to howl loud enough to scare the neighbours. Then too abruptly, Poppy goes quiet. Lana hopes he hasn't put her in some sort of trance. Ford studies the ancient beams above his head, then frowning, turns his gaze towards the Aga pumping out heat that can no longer escape the room. 'I always forget how ex-traordinarily *quaint* this house is.' He injects the word quaint with a full measure of distain.

'I'd offer you a cup of tea,' she says, 'but then you'd only have to pretend to drink it.' She lets out a steadying breath. 'So, to what do I owe this pleasure?'

'Let's call this a courtesy visit, shall we?' He brushes some imagined speck off his jacket. 'I thought I'd call whilst the younger members of the household are otherwise occupied.'

She tries her best to look mystified, but this merely elicits that thin empty laugh of his. 'Spare me the amateur dramatics, my dear. Of course, I know Beth Sawyer is staying here with you and your son.' He holds up both hands. 'Which, granted, should never have been possible. Indeed, it would not have happened if we hadn't collectively taken our eye off the ball, as it were. I suppose one has to give the two of them credit for perseverance.'

'Then that should tell you something.'

His expression mutates to one of mild curiosity. 'And what would that be, precisely?'

She sits down before her legs lose their strength. 'Well, that there are forces in the universe you're not able to control.'

'Fascinating.' That laugh again. 'I'm all ears, as they say. Come now, Lana, don't be shy. I'm eager to hear more of your theory on *forces*.'

'Well for a start, there's the power of *love*,' she tells him. 'Something I doubt you know anything about.'

'It surprises me that you of all people should imagine we Guardians incapable of finer feelings. Especially given your own *personal* history.'

'Don't you dare bring Matt into this.' She feels her colour rising. 'He's nothing like you.'

'On the contrary – though I'll admit we have had our differences; I can assure you in many ways he is exactly like me. As for keeping him out of the current situation, biologically speaking, he's unfortunately very much involved.' A momentary pause. 'Which leads me back to our present conundrum.'

She musters her courage. 'If you try to send Beth back–'

'I assure you we would succeed this time.' He stands up so abruptly it makes her jump. 'However, in this instance, it has been decided that Miss Sawyer can remain here; on one absolute and unbreakable condition.'

She hardly dares to ask, 'And that is?'

Lips barely moving, his voice is inside her head now. 'Beth and her child will be allowed to live out their normal lifespan here *provided* they agree to do nothing to draw our attention to them. Let me make myself clear – we will not tolerate any further disturbances in… How to simplify the concept?' He looks up at the ceiling as if for inspiration. 'We insist there is no further interference in the natural order of unfolding events.'

In case he might change his mind, Lana quickly nods her assent. 'There won't be – I promise you.'

Relief overwhelms her as she stands up. Before she can elaborate, he points a warning finger in her direction. 'Under the circumstances, I felt a face-to-face confrontation with your son and Miss Sawyer was best avoided. I am trusting you to relay this message to them verbatim and with all possible *force*. You do realise what's at stake if our specified condition is violated?'

'I'll make sure they understand that.' She can't stop nodding. 'Thank you. And please thank the others for me. From us.'

'Hmm.' He spins on his heels, opens the kitchen door to an ominous silence. At the front door he turns. 'I hope there will be no need for me to call here again.'

Her own fervent hope. 'There won't be,' she tells him.

The wind tugs at the door then violently flattens it against its hinges. Unconcerned, she follows him down the path. Before reaching the Range Rover, he pauses. 'It may take a few hours for your pet animal to wake. Rest assured there will be no lasting effects.'

Before she can express her outrage, he stops her with a look. 'Spare me your protests. Be thankful I chose not to exercise any of the other options at my disposal.' That terrible smile makes its final appearance. 'Goodbye. Let us hope this is not *au revoir*.'

'I assure you it's goodbye.' Lana closes her eyes, wills him away from her family for good. The sound of spitting gravel is music to her ears. When she looks again, he's gone.

She stands quite still, luxuriates in the freshness of rain on her face. A movement draws her attention to the house opposite and the lace curtain falling into place at the front window. Elsie Kirby – the worst of the village gossips. Hands on hips, Lana stares right back at the old dear. 'Say what you like, for all I care,' she mutters. 'That's the last you'll be seeing of him.'

She wrestles to shut the front door then exhales as she leans back against it, already certain that they will agree to the bargain and the odious Ford will never darken her doorstep again.

Chapter Four

Tom

He turns off the television and goes to find Beth. Picking up on his mood, Poppy beats her tail against the floor then follows him along the hallway into the snug. She's dancing to Fleetwood Mac. Heading towards him, she sings the title, 'You make loving fun.'

'Nice to know,' he tells her turning it down to a level they can talk over. 'Some good news – we're still in Tier One. Well, for now anyway.' With the car packed and ready, he's mightily relieved the government hasn't lobbed a last-minute spanner into the works.

'So, you're saying we can still go?' Both hands in a praying position, Beth adds, 'Can't tell you how much I'm looking forward to us getting away by ourselves for a few days.'

'And now there's absolutely nothing to stop us. The whole of the southwest remains in the same tier and we're officially allowed to travel within it and, what's more, to stay overnight. No roadblocks to run. No border patrols to outwit.'

'And it's not like we plan to mix with any other households while we're there.'

'Seeing's we're mostly taking our own food, we shouldn't need to go shopping much. Which means there's little chance of us spreading our terrifying Gloucestershire germs to the locals.' He wiggles his fingers at her – a couple of spiky covid molecules ready to attack.

Stroking the dog's head, Beth laughs. 'You know you're making us sound like a couple of plague carriers. Far as I know, we're both fit and healthy – well apart from the fact that I'm about seven, or possibly eight months pregnant.' She shrugs. 'Give or take the odd forty years.'

'And you're quite sure you're feeling up to it?'

'I'm absolutely 100 per cent fine – honestly I'm feeling tons better than I did back when I was throwing up all the time.' She giggles. 'Although I suppose that was in '83.' She gives him a look he can't quite fathom. 'We need to make the most of our last child-free time.'

'Can't argue with that.' Tom turns the volume back up and takes her in his arms though her massive baby-bump makes the whole thing a bit more awkward than it used to be. Abruptly, the random selection moves on to "Go Your Own Way" – not quite the romantic note he was hoping for. 'Imagine just the two of us with the whole place to ourselves,' he whispers in her ear. 'It's going to be great.'

Though Tom's always felt a bit ambivalent about his mum's friend Sylvie, it was kind of her to offer them the use of what she calls her "cabin in the woods" for free. His mum had readily agreed to lend them her car for the trip. Thinking about it, he suspects his mum might have put Sylvie up to it in the first place. She's been remarkably accommodating, taking Beth in without hesitation, all the same she could be longing for a few days to herself.

Judging from the photos, the cabin looks terrific. Away from it all, but with a proper shower and a wood stove to heat the place and cook on. The weather's likely to be a bit different and yet it reminds him of a place he stayed in when he was in Oz. It was way up the Grampians though only a four-hour drive out of Melbourne. In the usual high-handed manner, the region was officially named by a Scottish surveyor who climbed there in 1836. Gariwerd is the First Nation name...

Beth breaks away. 'Are you even listening?'

'Why wouldn't I be?'

'I see what you did there. That whole answering a question with a question thing you do when I catch you out.' She holds up a hand to stop his protests. 'I only asked if you knew whether we're likely to get a signal there.'

'You know, I remember when you referred to my mobile as *my bloody device* and yet now you seem pretty damned reliant on that device of yours.'

'I was merely thinking I might need some distractions if all that isolation gets a bit too much.'

'But you won't be isolated – you'll have me for company.'

'Exactly.' She has the grace to chuckle after saying it.

It's a sunny-ish sort of day – not bad for mid-December. With no holiday traffic to contend with they make good time. Sylvie had warned them they wouldn't be able to park near the cabin. 'It's quite a trek,' she'd said. 'But then you're young…'

Tom parks the car in the layby she'd mentioned. Carrying

only their most valuable possessions, they follow a narrow winding path through increasingly dense woodland. Overhead, bare-branched trees whistle and groan in the wind. Bramble shoots snag their clothes and hair. They eventually come to a steep flight of steps formed by logs set into the bare earth. In places it's slippery underfoot. 'I can manage perfectly well,' Beth protests when he takes her arm.

'Yes, but *I* might slip,' he says to hide a sudden alarming vision of her losing her footing and toppling down the steps.

It's a relief when they make it up the wooden stairs and onto the deck. While Beth gets her breath back, he retrieves the key from a key-safe in an adjacent outbuilding that turns out to be the composting toilet. There's only a faint whiff of something agricultural; the little enclosure smells mainly of the sawdust they've been instructed to sprinkle on after use. As it's unheated, they won't be lingering in there for long.

Constructed in a clearing from timber extracted from its immediate surroundings, one bloke had singlehandedly built the cabin. He'd designed it for year-long use, had sandwiched layers of sheep's wool from a local flock between the inner and outer timber walls. Apparently, he'd lived in it for several years until he got married and had a kid; at which point he sold up to Sylvie and moved on to a more ambitious project.

Everything is handcrafted except for the gutters and pipes running into a water tank that's raised up on stilts. Tom half expects to see a Flintstones-style car parked outside.

'I absolutely love it,' Beth says as soon as he opens the door. 'It's magical – like something out of a fairy-tale. So much wood everywhere.' She's right about that. In addition to the floors, walls and ceilings, every stick of furniture is wooden. The entire kitchen is handmade. If you uncork a bung in a device fashioned out of bamboo, rusty-looking rainwater is directed into the wooden sink. In the bedroom area, it would be hard to pick out the bed from its background if it wasn't for the multi-coloured, hand-knitted bedcover.

The one electric socket – powered by a solar panel on the roof – is enough to charge a phone but not much else.

Loads of logs are stacked up next to the stove. While Beth gets a fire going, he goes back to the car to fetch their bedding and towels. It takes another couple of trips to transfer the last of their clothes and provisions.

Exhausted, Tom flops down into a surprisingly comfortable rocking chair. The place has warmed up already. Beth hands him tea in an enamel cup. 'I boiled it twice just in case,' she tells him.

'This is the life,' he declares. 'I've always fancied getting back to nature.' The cup burns his hands, and the tea tastes a bit odd, but he drinks it anyway. 'Did you spot the telescope? The stars must look amazing here with no light pollution.'

'You'll certainly get plenty of opportunity for it,' she says, 'Not yet four o'clock and it's already getting dark.'

'Then let's light the oil lamps. Just you me and the flickering fire – it'll be romantic. You'll fancy me all over again.'

'Don't go getting any ideas.' She strokes the vast curvature of her stomach. 'I hate to break it to you but even if you looked like Robert Redford and Clint Eastwood combined, I'd still turn you down.'

Beth's teasing smile hardly takes the sting out of her

remark. He says, 'You know they're both really old men now, don't you?'

'Anyway,' she says, 'the good news is I checked, and you can get 4G in the bedroom.'

'I'm not sure that's adequate compensation,' he tells her.

It rains. A lot. By day three they're getting a bit sick of tinned food and, at times, each other. It's Tom's turn to cook. 'How about I spice things up a bit.' He rubs his hands together. 'D'you fancy a lentil and coconut curry?'

Beth hardly looks up from her paperback. 'Sounds great.'

The food is surprisingly delicious – they both have two helpings. 'God I'm stuffed,' Beth places both hands on her space-hopper belly. 'I might need a bit of a pause before I do the washing up.'

Her happy face contorts. 'You okay?' he asks.

'Yeah – just a twinge. All this sitting around reading's given me backache.' She pulls herself onto her feet then leans back. 'I just need to stretch my spine a bit.'

Hand in the small of her back, she walks around the room. 'It'll pass in a minute.'

'What will pass?'

'The pain.' She shuts her eyes. 'Just a touch of indigestion.'

'I thought you said you had backache?'

'Yes well, I did but now it seems to be a bit more gener-alised than that.'

'You don't think…I mean you're not in labour, are you?'

'Course not,' she scoffs. 'It's way too early for that. No need to start freaking out every time I get a spot of indigestion.'

She winces again. 'I'm sure it'll pass in a minute or two. I just need–'

'What?' He's on his feet. 'What is It?'

She looks down. Following her gaze, he stares at the growing puddle of liquid on the floorboards. Tom hopes and prays it might only be piss.

'Fuck!' she says, a look of horror on her face. 'I'm pretty sure my waters just broke.'

'Shit a brick!' Tom strides off towards the bedroom door but can't think what he was planning to do in there. He goes back to Beth, attempts to take her in his arms but she pushes him away. 'There's no need to panic,' he says, breathing so hard he thinks he might pass out.

Tom tells himself he needs to slow down. To think straight. 'Plenty of time to get you to a hospital,' he tells her. 'I can Google it – find out where the nearest maternity unit is.'

Beth's gone a bit pale. She's shaking. Shock possibly. He runs into the bedroom, grabs the bedcover and comes back to wrap it around her shoulders. 'It's going to be okay.' He strokes her hair away from her face then puts his hands on either side of her cheeks, lifts her head to direct her attention to what he's saying. 'We'll get through this, Beth, I promise you. Our son will be born, and everything will be fine. There's plenty of time to drive you to the nearest hospital once I find out where it is.'

She's nodding along with him now. 'First babies always take ages to be born,' he assures her, though he's not entirely certain that's statistically correct.

Chapter Five

Beth

He says, 'Okay, so, um, are you sure you're warm enough?' She throws off the bedspread and winces as her stomach contracts and a wave of pain runs through her. It's easier to nod.

'Right, well, you stay, um, exactly where you are and I'll just pop into the bedroom and find out where the nearest hospital is.'

When she moves, more amniotic fluid escapes and trickles down her leg. It's definitely not pee; it smells quite pleasant in fact.

'Okay I've got it,' Tom shouts through the doorway. 'The nearest one's less than seven miles away. We've got more than enough petrol to get there.'

'You're telling me now we're short of petrol. Why the hell…?' She holds her breath and waits for it pass. Not so bad that time. 'Why on earth would you let the tank get that low?'

No answer, only cursing. 'I don't believe it,' she hears him say. 'What sort of rubbish maternity unit closes at five o'clock in the sodding afternoon?'

Slowly she makes her way to the bedroom doorway leaving a wet trail behind her. 'You need to phone for an ambulance.'

'Hold on a sec, let me find out where the next one is.' He pulls a face. 'Eighteen miles according to Google maps. Look, I'm pretty sure we can find somewhere to fill up on the way.'

'I can't…' This one makes her bend double. In films they tell the women to control their breathing though she's not sure how you're meant to do that.

As the pain slowly subsides, she exhales. 'Tom!' she shouts. He takes a maddening amount of time to stop fiddling on his mobile. 'I really don't think I can make it all the way back to the car,' she tells him. 'Face it, we're miles from anywhere. If we run out of petrol on the way… I'm not having this baby in the dark on the side of the sodding road.'

He looks blank. 'What am I supposed to do?'

'Phone for a bloody ambulance,' she says. 'If the worst comes to the worst, at least they'll be able to talk you through it.'

He shakes his head. 'You've got to be kidding. I might be able to advise people on travelling to exotic locations, but I have no idea how to deliver a baby.'

'Then maybe you should bloody well Google it – that seems to be your answer to just about everything else.'

With both hands he presses down the air in front of them. 'We need to focus. Keep our shit together.'

Beth can't argue with that. She takes long steadying breaths and actually begins to feel a bit better. She sits down on the nearest chair hoping it will help. Tom comes back with that bedcover and she lets him drape it over her even though she's not cold. 'You're right,' he says. 'There aren't too many petrol stations around here. I expect most of them close early outside of the holiday season.'

She's about to say it when he holds up a finger. 'I'm going to phone for an ambulance – that's a much safer bet. And don't forget I've got the What Three Words app on my phone which means they should be able to pinpoint exactly where we are from that.' He turns to her looking pleased with himself. 'They'll be here in no time.'

Tom seems a bit calmer – more in control. She swallows down her own panic. On the phone, she hears him explains the situation quickly and clearly. He repeats those three words several times to make sure they get it right. Beth can't hear the other side of the conversation. His answers are mostly 'ah-huh'.

Finally, he turns to her, 'She wants to know how many weeks gone you are.' She could be an unexploded bomb.

'Good question,' she says. 'Tell her what with all the time travelling and everything I kind of lost count.'

'We think about eight months,' he says, 'could be more, could be less.'

He turns back to Beth. 'She says I need to check how far dilated your cervix is. You'll need to lie down on the bed, so I don't lose the signal at the same time.'

Tom thrusts his mobile into her hand. 'Hold this while I find something...' It sounds like he's rooting around in the kitchen cupboards. 'Perfect,' he declares with a note of triumph. He comes back holding one of those retractable carpenter's tapes. The metal sort.

'You're not getting anywhere near my vagina with that thing,' she tells him straight.

'Course not,' he says, 'It'll just help me get my eye in. Gauge the distance. She says I need to be as accurate as possible.'

Tom grabs some towels and lays them out on the bed. It's an effort to take off her knickers and lie still on her back while he makes his assessment looking from her to the tape measure and back again several times. 'What the hell difference does it make?' she demands.

Into the phone he says, 'Five centimetres give or take a millimetre or so.' He nods several times. 'She says we need to time your contractions.'

'Too bloody often,' Beth tells him.

'Where's your phone? I need the stopwatch feature. She wants to know if they're happening approximately three times in every ten-minute period.'

'Tell her yes,' Beth says through gritted teeth. 'In fact, more often than that.'

'Are you sure?'

'Course I'm bloody sure. It's not like I can't feel them.'

'She says to stay calm; nothing's going to happen until you're at ten centimetres.' He listens for a bit before he says, 'The regular ambulances are all tied up because of covid and everything. Instead, they're hoping to get the air ambulance out to us.' He's beaming. 'That's exciting.'

'Is it, Tom? I should have thought the prospect of giving birth in a back-to-fucking-nature cabin miles from any-where... to a baby who could be premature was excitement enough without the ambulance equivalent of the SAS airlift-ing me to bloody hospital.'

'She says to tell you they're just regular medics and they'll land nearby and transfer you to the helicopter by stretcher.'

Beth waits for the next one to fade before she says. 'Have you told them how steep and slippery that sodding path is? I might slide off the end of the stretcher and give birth in a swamp.'

'She says they're trained to do cliffside rescues in stormy conditions so that's certainly not going to happen.'

They wait. Every quarter of an hour or so Tom gets her to lie down so he can check her cervix again. Each time he pulls a face like he's in pain and not her. 'Eight and a half,' he announces. 'Or possibly almost nine. I'm not too sure. Think I'll stoke up the stove in case they need to boil some water when they get here.'

'What the hell are they meant to do with that?'

'It's what they always ask for in cowboy films.' He looks around. 'Let's face it, the similarities are fairly obvious.'

'Then maybe you'd better see if Sylvie's got some whisky stashed away somewhere because I could certainly do with some pain relief right now.'

'I'm not sure getting pissed is such a great idea.'

She heaves herself off the bed, walks a few steps and then bends double as the pain builds to a peak. 'A slug or two might help take the edge off,' she says, once it's passed.

He says, 'Beth I really think you should lie down again or, you know, I might not catch him in time.'

Reluctantly, she does as she's told. 'Trust me, this baby's not about to shoot out like some...'

Tom's not listening because he's on his phone. A glance sideways tells her he's searching on *How to deliver a baby*. 'I just want check a few more details,' he says. After he does, he looks shell-shocked. 'You're almost at ten centimetres. I think I might be able to see his head.' He wrinkles his nose up. 'It's a bit hard to tell.'

He's consulting his phone again. She's tempted to scream. 'You know sometimes that thing doesn't have all the answers,' she says, 'Call them again and find out what we need to do next.'

'Shh! 'Tom holds up his hand. 'I think I can hear something.'

She listens. He's right.

'Yes!' he punches the air. 'Definitely a helicopter.' Eyes shining with a schoolboy's delight, he says, 'That hammering sound means it's coming towards us. You can hear the blades hitting the air as it slows down. Now the whine from the turbines is louder because it's circling overhead. Must be looking for a landing site.'

Beth grits her teeth. 'Fascinating.'

The noise fades as it moves away. She hears it wind down and then stop. 'They must have landed somewhere,' Tom mutters. 'Hopefully not too far away.'

It seems an age before she hears drumming – boots on the steps outside. Thank God. A tall black man and a short white woman, their faces obscured by surgical masks rush in, loaded down with all kinds of packs and bags – one of them looks alarmingly like a toolbox. 'Hello there. Found you at last,' the man says. 'Sorry for the delay – it's been quite a trek. How are we doing?'

Tom says, 'Hi. This is Beth. Her waters have broken and she's about ten centimetres dilated. I'm Tom – her partner in crime. That was just a joke. I'm the father. Potentially, that is. Christ I really thought we might have to go it alone. Thank God you're here.'

'Well Tom, that was quite an introduction. Beth, I'm Doctor Foster – like the nursery rhyme. You can call me Chandu if you like.' He waves a hand towards the woman. 'This is Greta Harris – paramedic and, I'm sure you'll be pleased to know, a fully-trained midwife. You folks can relax now – you're in safe hands.'

Doctor Foster, eh. She wonders if he actually lives in Gloucester. No, it must be too far away. Unless he flies to work every day.

From the eyes and pink hair, she guesses Greta is young – far too young.

Beth starts to cry and then finds she can't stop.

Greta takes off her muddy boots and then her padded jacket. 'It's certainly cosy in here.' She puts her arm around Beth's shoulders. 'You know the two of you have done really well to get to this stage by yourselves. When you're ready Dr Foster and I would like to examine you and your baby if that's okay?' Beth nods. Greta gives her a reassuring smile. 'After that we'll see about some pain relief.'

'This is Entonox.' The doctor taps a cannister. 'Otherwise known as gas and air.'

Greta puts on a plastic apron, sanitises her hands and then snaps on surgical gloves. All the same her hands feel cold as she prods and pokes. Dr Foster hands her a kind of ear trumpet. She presses it to Beth's stomach and listens. Her eyes seem to be smiling when she says, 'Your baby's heartbeat is nice and steady. No sign he or she is in distress.'

'*He*,' Beth says, 'It's a boy.'

The next contraction is a big one that leaves her panting for breath.

Dr Foster is now kitted out in plastic. His gloved hands hover in the air above her. 'D'you mind if I…'

'Go ahead,' she tells him. He goes through the same routine of prodding and poking. 'Your baby seems a good size.' And then, 'His head is in the correct position,' like he's passed some kind of pre-birth initiative test.

The two medics turn their backs to confer. They wait. 'Under these rather exceptional circumstances,' Greta says, 'we think it would be better not to try to move you at this late stage.'

Next thing the doctor is on the phone to the pilot who must be still in the helicopter. It seems they need more kit. Goodness knows where they're going to put it.

'And you're sure about this?' Tom looks worried. 'Wouldn't Beth be better off in hospital just in case?'

'All the signs are good,' Greta tells him. 'Beth's doing a great job and your baby's head is well down. I could even feel his hair.'

'Oh right. So not a baldie then.' Tom looks at the doctor. 'Not that there's anything wrong with that.' He comes over to take her hand. 'Wow – our baby is going to be here soon. When he's a bit older he'll be able to tell people he was born in a cabin in the woods.'

Greta says, 'I'm sorry Tom but seeing's it's so cramped in here, would you mind shuffling up a bit – nearer Beth's head.'

'Oh right,' he says. 'Let the fox see the rabbit, so to speak.' He nods towards the bedside shelf. 'Glad I won't be needing those.' On a clean flannel he's laid out a clothes peg, kitchen scissors and a large oven dish.

None of them can keep a straight face. 'I won't ask what that meat dish was going to be for,' Beth says wiping her eyes.

Looking down at her enormous stomach, she curses evolution for not providing some sort of Velcro flap instead of an opening that still seems way too small for the job. What about the mess they'll make of Sylvie's bed? They can't leave the place looking like an abandoned set from the Texas Chainsaw Massacre.

'I suppose you could always call him Woody,' Greta says.

'No chance,' Beth tells her between gulps of gas and air. 'His name is Oliver. Ollie for short. I looked it up – it's currently the most popular boys' name in the UK. I expect there'll be loads of other Ollie's in his class at school. They'll have to call him Ollie B or something.'

The medics share a look but say nothing.

Chapter Six

Pathways Cottage

Beth

Hair still wet from his shower, Tom breezes into the kitchen where she's currently doing battle. Her hand is drawn back, poised to swoop in with a spoonful of greying mashed avocado mixed with ground rice. 'Here it comes…' She makes steam-train noises, growing louder as the spoon nears to his face.

Looking straight at her, Ollie shakes his head; his cupid's bow mouth clamped shut and refusing to open despite the spoon-train getting ever closer. Today his eyes look darker – more like his dad's. She opens her own mouth hoping he will emulate her, but his lips remain firmly closed, determination written all over his face.

She remembers how, in the helicopter, the paramedics had carried out more checks on Ollie. She'd been so scared they'd find something wrong with him, but Greta had given her a thumbs-up. Into her ear she said, "He's passed with flying colours," like it was a joke.

Their words have stayed with her. 'Will you look at those eyes,' Dr Foster said. 'Taking it all in, aren't you mate? I know they can't focus at this age, but he really seems to be sizing us up.'

Greta agreed. 'Looks so knowing, doesn't he? If you ask me, this one's an old soul. I reckon he's been here before.'

'Earth to Beth – come in please.' Tom squeezes her shoulder – an affectionate gesture which, at this precise moment, she finds mildly irritating. 'D'you realise he'll be a year old soon?' he says. 'Hard to believe, isn't it? Amazing how quickly the time's gone.'

Turning her head, Beth narrows her eyes at him. 'You meant that sarcastically, right?'

He grins. 'Okay, things haven't been easy at times, but I'd like to think we're through the worst of it now and coming out the other side. Remember how you were worried about him being different to other kids; well I reckon he's turned out pretty average. He's not walking yet. And he's not saying a lot. There seems to be nothing very precocious about him.'

'You think so.' She purses her lips. 'Of course, there could be another explanation.'

'Which is?'

'That he's simply biding his time.'

Chuckling, Tom shakes his head at Ollie. 'Hear that, little man – your mother's expecting great things from you.' As if on cue, Ollie turns his head to look straight at her.

No. She's imagining things. The kitchen is overheated despite the open door. She looks over at the mess she's left by the sink, the dirty laundry piled on the floor next to the washing machine she hasn't summoned the energy to load yet. The baby's dark hair now has green food-tips. From the smell, she guesses his nappy needs changing.

He definitely spat out more than he's swallowed and now his pudgy hand is drawing an elaborate daube on the white plastic tray attached to the highchair.

Eyes wide, Tom pulls an exaggerated smile aimed solely at his son. 'Will you look at those chubby cheeks. He may have crud all over him, but he's still a devilishly handsome little chap, you have to admit. Takes after his father, of course.'

Reversing the train, she drops the spoon into the bowl with a clatter. 'Then perhaps *his father* would like to get him to eat something rather than playing with it.'

Tom looks down at the avocado mix and frowns. 'Not sure I'd want to eat whatever that is.'

'Homemade and nutritious is what it is.' She thrusts the bowl at Tom, giving him no choice but to take possession of it. He sniffs at the mixture, puts the bowl down so he can drop a spoonful into his open palm. Having swallowed it, he pulls a face. 'Tastes like something you'd be forced to eat if you lived in some Martian colony.'

Ollie starts to giggle – quietly at first and then he opens his mouth and, head back, emits a throaty chuckle like he's just heard the funniest of rude jokes. Always a pushover, Tom laughs along. Though she's cross about her wasted efforts, watching their shared hilarity, her resistance melts and soon she's doubled up with laughter; even the chaos around her seems funny now she comes to think about it.

The noise rouses the dog from her regular position beside

the highchair ready to pounce on whatever might come her way. Catching the collective mood, Poppy begins to bark with excitement.

Lana appears in the doorway. Her voice cuts across the din, 'Have you all gone stark raving mad in here?'

Silenced with the others, Beth wipes her eyes with the heel of a hand, no doubt smearing her face with green gunk. 'Probably,' she says. 'To paraphrase that slogan – you don't have to be mad to live here, but it helps.'

Sylvie is lingering in the hallway behind her, pointedly keeping her distance. It's possible she's still harbouring some resentment about the stains in her cabin. Tom had gone back there to clean up. Tried his best. What more could they do?

Ears pricked, Sylvie's trembling greyhound retreats to the open front door. Outside it's sunny – looks more like spring than winter.

'Ganny Lanny.' Ollie's small, food-smeared hands open and shut in a wordless invitation for Lana to join in the fun. Beth notices her stern face softens like it always does at the sight of him – her little prince.

'I can't get over how he's able to say your name so clearly at his age.' Sylvie runs a hand through her severely cropped grey hair. 'Harriet Browning's granddaughter is three months older than him and, by all accounts, still hasn't said a word.'

'Well, it's not a competition, is it?' Beth tells her. 'Those sorts of comparisons aren't very helpful. Babies progress at their own rates, in their own time.'

'Yes, of course,' Sylvie says. 'Not that I know a great deal about such things.' She shivers as if appalled at the very idea of caring for anything except a fur-baby. Angling her head, the woman's sharp, judgemental eyes range across the undone chores.

Lana asks, 'Can I tempt you to stay for a coffee and a piece of lemon drizzle?' Beside her stern-looking friend, Lana's expression is softer, kinder; her skinny jeans and sweatshirt less age-appropriate.

'No thanks,' Sylvie's quick to reply. 'I just called round to return that book. I really ought to be getting back.'

'I've been thinking about inviting the Brownings over next time their daughter and her baby are staying with them,' Lana says, though this is the first Beth has heard of such a plan. 'Young families are a bit thin on the ground in Stoatsfield these days. When Tom was a baby, there were a lot more children. I found it was quite a relief to meet other parents who were going through the same sort of thing.'

'Good idea.' Tom puts on a smile as he casts the food bowl aside. 'Can't do any harm. In fact, it might be good for Ollie. He needs to get used to being with other babies before he goes to nursery.'

Lana's lips narrow like they do when she's less than pleased about something. 'I didn't realise you were planning to send him to a nursery.'

Picking up the mood music, Sylvie says, 'Well, I'll take my leave. Come along, Bertie.' The dog moves aside to let her go by. Collarless, he always trots a few paces behind the woman, as if on an invisible lead.

Having seen her friend off, Lana comes into the kitchen. 'Poor Sylvie – she's really worried about the numbers being so high.'

Tom frowns. 'Sorry?'

'The covid figures,' Lana says. 'You must have seen it on Points West. All those nasty little red arrows going up in our region in place of the nice green ones that were coming down. Sylvie's not eligible for her booster yet – she's considerably younger than she looks.'

'Unlike the rest of us,' Beth points out. She's only ever seen Sylvie as old and disapproving. If fear of catching covid keeps her away, it's an unexpected bonus.

Before Lana can complain about the mess, Beth makes a start on clearing up, scraping the leftover mix into the food bin. Taking the hint, Tom begins to load the dishwasher. Since the subject's already been raised, she says, 'I'm hoping to get a job as soon as Ollie's old enough to be left.' Anticipating Lana's protest, she adds, 'We both think it will be good for him to get used to being around other children. After all we don't want them thinking he's some sort of oddity, do we?' She knows that will have struck a chord. They haven't yet mentioned their plan to move out once they can find a place of their own.

Beth waits. Instead of responding, Lana's attention has turned to the tray fixed to the front of the highchair. 'Goodness me, will you look at that. He's drawn a complete forest scene. My word – it's perfectly to scale. There's even a lake with a log cabin beside it.'

The three of them gather at the back of the highchair to study the surface from Ollie's perspective. 'Maybe we're all reading too much into it,' Beth says in hope. 'You know – like one of those ink-stain tests.'

'You mean a Rorschach test.' Tom shakes his head. 'No.

Mum's right. Look how detailed it is. There's even a boat on the lake with someone fishing from it.'

It could be a scene in North America or Canada – some places she's never been. Beth says, 'D'you think it could be somewhere he's seen on the telly and remembered?'

'Possibly.' Tom wipes his hand across his mouth. 'If he produces something like this at nursery, Christ knows what they'll make of it.'

'I expect they'll assume he's one of those savant artists,' Lana says. 'Like that boy who draws all those detailed buildings from memory. It's an extraordinary gift.' She gives a heavy sigh. 'Although I believe children like that tend to be non-verbal.'

Those mercurial eyes shining, Ollie's tiny finger points to centre of the drawing. 'Boat,' he tells them in case there was any doubt.

'Shit,' Tom says.

Ollie chuckles. 'Shit,' he repeats. Another fine joke.

Chapter Seven

Lana

Encountering Harriet Browning in the village shop, Lana issues the invitation. 'Splendid Idea but why don't you come to us instead?' the woman suggests, her black facemask doing nothing to soften her brusque manner. 'The tots will have far more space to crawl around.' A look of pride enters her faded blue eyes. 'We simply can't keep little Eugenie still these days. She's into everything. I'm sure she'll be taking her first steps any day now.'

Feeling slighted by the judgement that her cottage can't possibly be big enough to entertain them all, Lana nonetheless acquiesces – after all she won't have to rush around cleaning up.

As an afterthought and seemingly about to depart, Harriet asks, 'I assume you're all double-vaxxed?' She might as well have said housetrained.

'Of course,' Lana assures her. 'In my case triple, in fact. Although not the baby, of course.'

'Good.' Harriet nods her approval. Feeling it unnecessary to reveal her own vaccine status, she leaves the shop.

Unpacking her shopping later, Lana makes a note of the fixture on the kitchen calendar. Something for them to look forward to – although already she's having doubts.

Tom walks past with the baby in his arms. 'Afternoon tea at The Grange, eh? Thank goodness I'll be spared that particular encounter. Johnny's asked me to work extra shifts in the pub.'

'Pub,' Ollie repeats. 'Pub, pub, pubbly-pub.'

'That's right; clever boy,' Tom tells him. 'Your daddy works in the pub. For the moment anyway.'

Lana's tempted to tell him that's hardly something to be proud of but instead she turns away. 'I'm going to put the kettle on. Fancy a cup of tea?'

'I'd rather have a coffee.' Tom lowers the baby into his highchair.

'Co-ppee.' Ollie slaps the tray, frowning as if displeased with himself. 'Co-ppee.' Shaking his little head, he looks up at Tom.

'Co – ffee,' Tom repeats. 'With a fuh.'

Ollie shivers, his mouth silently rehearsing the sound before the word comes out loud and clear, 'Co-ffee.' There's a pause before his face crumples, 'Not tea.' They applaud him in unison.

Over the coming days more words arrive in a veritable tsunami. At first, Ollie concentrates on naming the objects around him. After each attempt, his outstretched finger points at the item in question. He gives them a quick glance to check he's pronounced it correctly.

By the end of the following week all praise has dried on their lips. Adjectives and verbs are added at an astounding rate. Goodness knows how he's picking it up so fast. When he combines them into ever more sophisticated sentences, the three of them exchange worried glances. It's now beyond a joke.

Lana decides she should ring Harriet Browning claiming some sort of illness as an excuse, but on the appointed day the wretched woman looms large through their kitchen window when they're having breakfast. Her gloved hand raps the glass. 'See you all later,' is accompanied by an uncharacteristic cheery wave.

So here they are standing in the rain presenting themselves at the appointed hour. Though Lana has walked past the house on countless occasions, this is the first time she's ventured inside the porticoed entrance of The Grange. It's a fine old building, its walls a mellow dressed stone. She rings the old-fashioned pull bell, half expecting a uniformed butler to emerge.

Harriet opens the door. The loose silk blouse she's wearing is a match for her iron-grey hair. Unsure how to greet them now that air kissing is verboten, she says, 'Come on in out of this bally awful weather.' Her impatient hand ushers them inside. 'We're in the small sitting room. I thought it would be cosier on a day like today.'

The hallway is designed to impress with a wide staircase leading up to a half landing and then on to the sort of galleried walkway you'd expect to find in a far grander house. The air is artificially scented to mask something staler.

'Is it okay if I leave the buggy in the corner here?' Beth asks, putting on the brake. Getting a nod, she unbuttons the transparent covers and run-off water begins to pool on the pale stone floor. 'Oh dear, I've made a bit of a puddle,' she says. 'If you've got a mop handy, I'll wipe it up.'

'No need,' Harriet tells her. 'The, um, pushchair won't be in anyone's way just there. Mrs Willis can sort the floor out later.'

Beth lifts the baby out to prop him on her hip. While stroking her son's hair back into passable order, she beams at their hostess. She's wearing blue jeans and an oversized navy jumper with a stain on the shoulder that looks suspiciously like baby sick. As for Ollie – instead of the hand-knitted jumper Lana had proposed, Beth's dressed him in a dark grey hoody top with matching jogging pants like some sort of would-be thug. She says, 'I'm Beth, by the way.'

'Yes, I know,' Harriet tells her. 'I've seen you in the village. Tell me, how are you taking to life here in Stoatsfield? I expect you find it rather quiet after the distractions of London.' The woman has obviously done her homework.

Lana cuts in, 'She's fitting in very nicely.'

'And this is Ollie.' Beth swivels her hip along with the baby in the woman's direction.

'Ah yes.' After a cursory look, Harriet gives him a thin smile. 'Quite a chubby little chap, isn't he?'

Instead of his usual sunny expression, Ollie raises one eyebrow and looks the woman up and down, as if noting her tweed skirt, stout legs and sturdy shoes. Having made his assessment, he opens his mouth and pokes his little tongue out.

'He's teething at the moment,' Lana's quick to explain.

'I see.' Harriet ushers them along the hallway past a line of po-faced ancestors to the door at the end. They're shown into quite a large room which looks comfortable despite having too many competing patterns. The piano in the corner is festooned with silver-framed photographs. She can smell the woodsmoke from the fire blazing in the hearth. With its polished brass rim, the fireguard around it looks decorative but hardly sturdy enough in Lana's opinion.

A smiling young woman advances with her hand held out before she thinks better of it. 'Hello, I'm Kitty.' Pretty – no sign of either parent in her regular features. She hooks a strand of her long fair hair behind one ear. 'I suppose handshakes are out these days. Should we elbow-bump or something?' She takes a step backwards. 'Anyway, it's so nice to meet you all.'

Her baby is sitting on a Persian rug, rocking back and forth as she chews on one of several plastic rings held together in a bunch. 'What with the various lockdowns and everything, Eugenie hasn't had a chance to meet any other babies, have you, my darling?' The little girl's pink dungarees have a fluffy rabbit sewn to the front bib. Must be hard to get food stains out of it.

Beth positions Ollie on the rug opposite the little girl. The two babies stare at each other gladiator-style. 'Eugenie's never experienced a close encounter with another baby before,' Kitty says. 'Look at that expression – her face is an absolute picture. I must take a snap. Her first ever playdate.' Before anyone can object, there's a flash and it's done. Lana hopes she won't post it on Instagram.

Another flash and Ollie's head swivels around. She prays he's not going to say *cheese* or worse still *smartphone*. When his hand reaches out towards Eugenie's toy, the dribbling baby wordlessly snatches the whole thing away. 'Of course, having no brothers or sisters, she's never had to share,' Kitty says.

'Same for Ollie,' Beth tells her. ''Spect it'll be a hard lesson to learn.'

'Let's not stand on ceremony,' Harriet instructs. They sit. 'Lucky I kept some of the children's old toys in the attic,' she says. 'Robert – he's off playing golf by the way – sends his apologies. Anyway, what was I saying? Ah yes – Robert wanted me to throw them all out, or give them to a charity shop, but I told him they were bound to come in handy one day.' Some of the toys look as if they haven't been given a good scrub in thirty years. 'Of course, we've had to wait far longer than we expected for them to be of use.' Out of her mother's line of sight, Kitty rolls her eyes.

'Anyway,' Harriet continues, 'they certainly help to keep the little one quiet.'

On the edge of her overstuffed seat, Lana hears rattling before the door opens and a thin, dark-haired woman comes in carrying a laden tea tray. At its centre is a pump-action thermos – the sort they use in budget hotels. 'Thank you, Mrs Willis,' Harriet says. 'If you wouldn't mind putting it down on the table over there. We can help ourselves later.' A Victoria sponge that's too perfect to be homemade.

Ollie's now turned his attention to the upturned plastic crate near the fire. He crawls over to inspect the toys scattered around it. Hanging on to a chair seat for support, Eugenie hauls her sturdy little body into an upright position. Wobbling, she lets go with one hand as if about to launch herself at Ollie. 'Wa-wa da,' she warns him. Clutching the chair, she takes a few more hesitant steps before giving up and flopping back down on her padded backside.

'She's so nearly got the hang of it,' Kitty says with pride. Meanwhile her baby has picked up a wooden hammer. She raises it above her head as if she'd like to hit Ollie with it if only he was a bit closer.

Beth slips out of her seat to kneel next to him on the rug. Also getting down to their level, Kitty picks up a toy and holds it out towards her daughter. 'Look darling it's a train. A choo-choo.' In the face of her mother's animation, Eugenie remains resolutely unimpressed.

Ollie crawls over to prise the toy from Kitty's hand. Frowning, he puts it down on the rug then picks it up again. 'See – it's a little choo-choo train,' Kitty tells him in a sing-song voice. 'They go whoo-whoo! Whoo-whoo!' No wonder he's puzzled – Lana can't recall when she last heard a steam train's whistle.

Kitty stares expectantly at Ollie and says, '*Traaain.*' They all wait for his response.

Ollie's frown only deepens. He tips the toy upside down, his little fingers turning the wheels one at a time before he puts it back on the rug the right side up. Looking directly into Kitty's face he says, 'Actually, it's a traction engine.'

Breaking the stunned silence, Lana tries to laugh it off. 'I expect he got that from Thomas the Tank Engine.' She prays Ollie doesn't contradict her. 'Tom's been reading the books to him at bedtime.'

Her smile increasingly desperate, Beth adds, 'They're proper little sponges at this age, aren't they? Pick up anything and everything.'

Unconvinced, Harriet raises her eyebrows. 'If you say so.' Gumming the corner of a wooden block, her granddaughter seems more pudding than sponge.

Chapter Eight

Tom

The fire Tom had struggled to coax into life is now blazing away in the massive old inglenook. At the table next to it, the usual trio of elderly men nurse their pints while playing cribbage, pleased to be *out of the way of the missus for a couple of hours*. Proudly announcing that they're triple-vaxxed, it's nonetheless taken a while for them to return to their old ways. Unfortunately, Mr Donaldson has enthusiastically resumed his habit of spitting into the fire – possibly just to enjoy the resulting sizzle.

Though Tom hadn't expected to, he's enjoying bar work. Just a three-minute walk from home, plus it's good to be officially employed again. Unlike his previous occupation, after finishing a chore here he can stand back and actually see what he's achieved. Admittedly the regulars tend to prattle on about next to nothing, but the pandemic has taught him to appreciate human contact in all its forms.

Besides the usual smell of woodsmoke and spilt beer, the aroma of today's lunchtime special – curried parsnip soup with garlic bread – hangs in the air.

Time drags when trade is slower like this. Having skimmed one of the free newspapers they provide, a suspiciously friendly customer comes up to the bar for a refill. Deep tan, well-trimmed grey beard, he checks there's no one else at the bar before informing Tom that he happens to be the owner of The Pig and Piper over at Marshy Bottom. The man looks around the half-empty pub. 'Unlike this place, we're rushed off our feet even on weekdays.'

Tom recalls passing through the tiny, picturesque hamlet of Marshy Bottom on one of his long-distance walks. He'd stopped to eat his sandwiches on the bank of the river that dissects the village green, taken photos of the pub along with the dozen or so picture-perfect cottages it looked down on. A hot day and yet not a single window was open in the whole row. Upstairs curtains were pulled across. No cars parked outside the houses although every garden looked freshly primped – all the tell-tale signs most were second homes rarely visited.

'You certainly know your way round a bar, young man,' the bloke says. He hardly breaks eye-contact as he sips his half pint. Hospitality workers are in great demand; Tom's spotted numerous blackboards propped outside pub entrances more or less begging people to give it a try.

After a couple more sips and a bit more general chat, the pub owner lowers his voice. 'As it happens, I'm looking for a new bar manager.' They're interrupted a couple of times before the man – 'call me Pete, please' – adds, 'The job comes with a two-bed flat above the pub, which is not something to be sniffed at these days. Place has all mod cons, though I must admit the last chap was a bit of a slob. Be easy enough to make something of it with a lick of paint and a bit of imagination.'

Like some drug dealer, he looks about him before surreptitiously slipping Tom his business card. 'No pressure. Give me a call if you fancy popping over and taking a look around.' With a conspiratorial wink, he drains his glass and leaves.

By late afternoon the place is empty except for the cribbage players. Rain is lashing the windowpanes and looks to have settled in for the night. Outside the temperature is dropping fast; inside every light is blazing. Remembering his earlier conversation, Tom fingers the edges of the card in his pocket – a tempting offer for sure.

When the door opens, he half expects it to be an irate wife come to drag one of the elderly cardplayers home. Instead, it turns out to be Beth pushing the buggy, followed by his mum. The two look decidedly glum as they hang their dripping coats by the door. He's reminded of that old joke, is tempted to ask: *Why the long face?* but thinks better of it.

'Daddy! Daddy!' Ollie calls out despite the fogged-up plastic covers shrouding his view.

'Hello, little man.' Tom lifts the counter hatch and goes over to join them. He's keen to tell Beth about the possible job, but now is not the time. Better to wait until they're on their own. 'So how did the state visit go then?' he asks. 'Are the two of them betrothed yet?' This doesn't begin to raise a smile.

'I could do with a gin and tonic.' His mum hands him a tenner. 'Better make it a large one.'

'Before the sun's over the yard arm, Mother?' He chuckles. 'I'm guessing the afternoon went well then.'

Beth says, 'Think I'll have the same.' While his mum

struggles to remove the wet covers from the buggy, she follows Tom over to the counter. He lines up a couple of glasses. Before he can raise the first one to the optics, Beth whispers, 'We have a problem.' Her blue eyes are full of concern.

Tom stops what he's doing. 'What's wrong?'

'Well for a start, I don't think we'll be able to send Ollie to a normal school.'

Tom scoffs. 'You're not serious?' Across the room the baby is happily kicking his newly freed legs and waving. He waves back all smiles. Leaning over the counter, he says. 'What the hell happened up at The Grange?'

'Long story. It was awkward as hell. Things started to go really wrong when Lana was forced to tell them Ollie was fond of those Thomas the Tank Engine books.'

She raises her hand to block his objection. 'Before you say it, I know we haven't got any of them and I'm pretty sure he's never seen the programmes on telly. But that's not the point. As soon as Lana says it, Mrs Browning goes dashing off to fetch the damned books – turns out she has a load she'd saved from when her kids were young.'

'Okay. But that sounds absolutely fine; rather sweet of the old bat, in fact.'

Beth lays a hand on his arm. 'Hear me out.' He nods. 'So anyway, the books smelt ever so fusty, but that didn't stop the woman handing one to Ollie and giving another one to her granddaughter. As you might expect, little Eugenie just starts to chew on one of the corners. Of course, our Ollie's different. He studies the cover for a bit, then he carefully opens the book.'

Frowning, Tom says, 'So what? It's a book – you're meant to open them. Presumably there were lots of colourful pictures inside.'

'Yes, but Ollie's not content with that, is he? He puts it down – no, I should say *carefully positions* it on the rug in front of him and starts to chuckle at all the engines with their weird human faces. Then he lifts his little finger and runs it underneath the words. They were all watching when he opens his mouth and reads the story out loud. And I do mean word for bloody word. He hardly stumbles over the difficult ones.' She shakes her head. 'I had to pretend he was only reciting it from memory. Told them you'd read that book to him so many times it wasn't surprising he knew it off by heart – although that would be pretty amazing in itself.'

Tom doesn't like where this is leading. 'Anyway,' she says, 'they start to nod and that, like they're beginning to accept my explanation.'

'Well, kids do recite stuff...'

'Ah, but then Ollie goes and turns the book round so we can all see the pictures. "This train's called Thomas" he tells them. "Like my daddy".'

'Wow – clever of him to make that connection.'

'Oh, it's clever alright, but you seem to be missing the point.' She squeezes his arm rather too hard. 'Tom, our son is barely a year old, and he can sodding well read. As far as he's concerned it's a terrific new trick. He was even reading the road signs on our way here. Kept repeating *hump backed bridge, hump backed bridge. I* couldn't shut him up.'

Tom rubs his chin. 'Then I suppose we're going to have

to come clean at some point. We'll tell people he's a sort of prodigy. Everyone knows Mozart could play the harpsicord at three and wrote his first symphony when he was eight.'

She shakes her head. 'I didn't know that.'

'There must be loads of other examples.' He shuts his eyes trying to think. 'Then there's that, um, South Korean bloke – Kim Ung-Yong. I know his name sounds quite similar to the mad despotic leader of North Korea. Anyway, *this* other Kim has the highest IQ ever recorded. Not that IQ is necessarily the most accurate way of assessing intelligence. It's claimed he could hold proper conversations at six months old and do complex calculus by the time he was five.' He grins in the hope that she will see the funny side. 'In fact, by his standards, our Ollie's lagging behind a bit.'

'Maybe this Kim bloke is a Guardian. Have you thought of that?'

Behind her back Tom can see Mr Donaldson struggling to his feet to begin the usual slow shuffle towards the bar. In Beth's ear he says, 'There's no proof our son is anything other than a bit cleverer than most kids his age.' Responding to her look, he says, 'Okay, a lot cleverer. We'll tell them he gets that from his father.'

'He's not just clever,' Beth spits back, 'he's an out and out bloody genius.' Her breath warming his face, she whispers, 'Remember what *they* said about us not drawing attention to ourselves. What if people find out about Ollie and what he can do already?' Her hand goes to her mouth. 'Imagine if the papers get hold of the story.'

He takes her point. By all accounts Mrs Browning isn't

exactly renowned for her discretion. He grimaces. 'It's possible the cat's already out of the bag.'

'Yes, and Stoatsfield is a very small bag. Maybe the cat and his family need to slink off somewhere before anyone else notices.' She chews her lip. 'Some place where nobody knows us.'

Before old Mr Donaldson comes into earshot – which is about half a metre if you shout loud enough – Tom says, 'How d'you fancy living in Marshy Bottom?'

'Never heard of it.' She pulls a face. 'Sounds like a damp sort of place.'

'Possibly, but it's really pretty.' He scrolls through the photos on his mobile, holds up the evidence for her consideration. 'See what I mean. And the best thing about it is that, apart from having a destination pub, it's pretty much a ghost village.'

Chapter Nine

Lana

Lana recalls the times she'd bitterly resented not having her home to herself; now with only silence and order, she could weep. For the umpteenth time she scolds herself for being daft – it's not like they've emigrated; not yet anyway. The Pig and Piper's not much more than twenty miles away. All the same, the house feels forlorn without their discarded shoes crowding the porch or a line of tiny drying garments draped along the Aga rail to dry.

Not having a daughter, she misses the rapport she built up with Beth. Often they would sit up chatting with the telly off and the fire's heat dwindling to nothing. Hearing of the girl's feckless mother, she still feels aggrieved on her behalf. Tears of sympathy had filled Beth's eyes when Lana told her about her own mother's tragic death just before her fifth birthday. With no photos to remind her, she can no longer picture her mother's face.

Such maudlin thoughts will never do. To liven the place up, she marches into the snug, selects Tchaikovsky, and turns up the volume in a way she's seldom been able to over the last year. The familiar music starts slow and sad. As it builds, she spots one of Ollie's toys stuffed into a gap in her carefully arranged shelves as if it had been done deliberately. Reaching between the volumes, she prises out his well-chewed rabbit – his beloved Bobbity. How could they have left him behind? She brings the stuffed animal to her nose and devours the lingering scent it holds.

In spite of her arthritis, for the past week Poppy's been restlessly roaming the house and now she wanders in, plonks herself at Lana's feet and looks up at her with red-rimmed, accusing eyes. 'It's not my fault,' she tells her out loud; though once again she wonders if things might have turned out differently if she hadn't arranged that fateful visit to The Grange. Rolling her shoulders, she does her best to shrug off the thought, reminding herself that Tom might have taken the new job in any event. They're a young family – it's only natural they should want a place of their own.

Today the beauty in the music is lost in its volume and bluster. In the quieter moments, she picks out an underlying tone of foreboding. No wonder the composer had come to hate his own creation.

A flashing blue light draws her attention to the house phone and an apparent missed call. She mutes the music to play the new message. Tom begins by reassuring her all is well. He must be down in the bar because various conversations are going on in the background. 'We'd love to show you around the flat' has a forced jollity about it.

A pause. 'So anyway, Mum, I was wondering if you fancied

coming over on Saturday afternoon? Ollie would love to see Poppy – well and you, of course. We all would.' He clears his throat like he does when he's building up to something. 'I'll be honest – I was hoping you might do us a favour. We've got this big party booked in on Saturday night. If you wouldn't mind babysitting for a few hours, Beth can give me a hand in the bar. No worries if you're busy.' He must know that's highly unlikely these days. 'Oh, and did I mention there's a spare bed in Ollie's room if you'd rather not drive back in the dark? Only a single but, you know, comfortable enough I expect. We'll make it up ready in case. Okay – so, um, let me know how you're fixed. Bye Mum.' A short pause. 'Love you.'

Lana's not sure if she ought to be offended at the strings attached to the invitation – the implication that it's only her usefulness that's prompted their desire to see her so soon.

It's a struggle getting Poppy into the back of the car these days. Too heavy to lift, the manoeuvre involves awkwardly support-ing the dog's back legs while pushing hard. Resenting the indignity, the old girl circles her blanket several times before finally flopping down with a sigh that could be indignant.

As a joke, Lana straps Bobbity into the passenger seat beside her. He stares straight ahead, that one good ear trem-bling with every bump in the road. As she glances sideways, she could swear the little rabbit's mouth is more downturned than usual – like he's apprehensive about something. Chang-ing gear, Lana quickly banishes such a fanciful notion.

Around the next corner the wheels lose their grip on a mush of dead leaves forcing her to wrestle back control and then concentrate on the road ahead. From the boot, Poppy grumbles her distain for this mode of transport.

'I'm babysitting at the weekend,' she'd told Sylvie on their recent walk, a certain pride at being needed. Babysitting – an odd word. It's hard to know who's meant to be doing the sitting when by all accounts Ollie has now decided to walk. She's looked after him for the odd hour or two by herself, but never been called upon to amuse him for an entire evening. At the last minute, she'd grabbed a handful of Tom's old books and stuffed them into the carrier bag now sitting in the footwell next to her overnight bag. An eclectic, possibly eccentric, mix of stories. Given his astonishing progress, it's hard to guess which ones are likely to amuse Ollie. Now his speech is more advanced, will she still be *Ganny Lanny*?

It's a dull afternoon, relieved here and there by the twinkle of festive lights wound around bushes and over front porches although it's way past twelfth night. The weak sun is already streaking the sky orange and on the point of giving up. She flips on the headlights. As the road ahead empties of traffic, she switches to high beam.

A mile or so further on, the landscape opens out to a scale that makes her feel small. Clumps of trees gather along the horizon, waving their bare black branches in sync like so many arms lifted in prayer. Shouldn't she be feeling happier given she's visiting her family? To lighten her mood, Lana turns on the radio and the car fills with choral music.

The lane winding down into Marshy Bottom is narrow and bordered by high hedgerows that offer few passing spaces. Around every blind corner she anticipates meeting a horsebox or Ocado van but, this time, she's lucky. Nearing the bottom of the hill, she passes an outlying cottage and then there it is in front of her – the picturesque collection of stone cottages familiar to her from a photograph on the cover of one of her walking maps. Once the modest homes of working country folk, these houses have since become trophy acquisitions for city dwellers. Grinning to herself, she recalls the local paper reporting the unsuccessful attempt by a group of homeowners to have the place renamed Marshy Dale.

There's a noticeable absence of parked cars. A few low lights shine out from windows where no one has pulled the downstairs curtains. She spots a lit up red phone box to one side of the village green and is surprised to see this one still has a phone inside. She passes the war memorial and then, wheels spraying water, drives across the swollen ford – the spot where, for countless centuries, the river has continued to flow unhindered over the cobbled roadway.

The Pig and Piper comes into view. Set up on a small rise, its strung-out fairy lights trace the contours of a large awning under which a collection of tables and chairs have been provided for those still too timid to risk infection inside. It's swaying sign shows a fat pink pig following a boy with a penny whistle. She spots the car park entrance off to the left.

Surprisingly spacious, at this hour it's almost empty. Tom's tiny Fiat 500 with its mismatched panels is parked at the far end by overhanging trees. It's covered in bird droppings. She positions her own car away from the trees, where she hopes it will be in no one's way.

After liberating Poppy from the boot, clutching Bobbity

along with her bags she makes her way around to the rear entrance as instructed. Seconds after pressing the bell, she hears footsteps descending and then the door is flung open. 'Mum.' Tom hugs her close in a way he never used to before he had a family of his own. She breathes in her boy's familiar smell. Poppy's tail beats their legs in her determination to be included.

Despite the thick new rug, the din from below intrudes through the floorboards – insinuates itself in the steady drone of numerous conversations punctuated by shrieks of laughter or indignation. Can she get Ollie to sleep with all that racket going on down there? So far, so good – he's freshly bathed, dressed in his pirate pyjamas and lying in his cot clutching Bobbity to his chest like a long-lost friend. She wonders again why the toy's absence hadn't been noticed before. It doesn't surprise her that over the last week or so Ollie has decided to walk. Earlier, Beth had informed her that he now refuses to wear a nappy and has learnt to use the toilet by himself with the aid of a plastic step.

Like the rest of the flat, his room smells of fresh paint. Tom and Beth have done a good job making the place comfortable given the rather strange collection of furniture and fittings they've inherited. Like the rest of the flat, the baby's room houses an unlikely mix of new and old. Squeezed beneath the window – where she's likely to get a draught down her neck – is the iron-framed bed they've made up for her. Vintage some would call it. Spartan would be her word. She hopes it proves more comfortable than it looks.

Amongst Ollie's neatly stacked toys and jigsaw puzzles, a chess set is laid out ready to play. Fancy teaching him such games at his age. Tom ought to know better.

Ollie has calmed down after his earlier exuberance. She's pleased to see his eyelids are beginning to droop. Lana sorts through the carrier bag she brought with her and pulls out a few candidates for his bedtime story. She holds them out like a pack of cards for him to choose. After a quick appraisal, he points, 'That one.'

His 'Please' is an afterthought.

The dog snoring across her feet, Lana settles back into the easy chair they've managed to squeeze in beside the cot. Button backed and Victorian, she believes they call this a nursing chair. It creaks a little but is quite comfortable. She vaguely remembers buying the book Ollie's chosen – probably because of its illustrations. Set before the first World War, it's a story that would normally be too advanced to interest a child of his age. The pages are in pristine condition because Tom had never really warmed to it. With any luck, it'll send his son to sleep, and she'll be able to watch the travel programme she's been looking forward to.

Except Ollie is looking a lot livelier than he did before. With surprising ease and before she can stop him, he climbs right out of his cot and launches himself into her lap. She's tempted to scold him for such a trick, but instead she retrieves his lambswool blanket and wraps it around him.

He squirms on her lap. 'Read me the story, Granny.' Sadly, she's no longer *Ganny Lanny*. Making herself more comfortable, she slips off her trainers. 'Open the book,' he tells her.

'Don't be so impatient, you little scamp.' He responds with giggles and a look that would melt any heart. As she reads, he bends his head to study every page in detail. Like an echo, he whispers the words a half second after she says them, his determined finger tracing people and buildings and then the waves of red, white and blue coronation bunting strung between old-fashioned lampposts.

Chapter Ten

Ollie

He giggles. The people in the book have funny clothes on. Granny says the story is about something that happened more than a hundred years ago when everyone was dressed that way. She says, 'What they're wearing only seems strange and old-fashioned to our modern eyes.'

Puzzled, he checks her face and then compares it to the faces of the people in the book. Her eyes and theirs look about the same, except Granny's are real and the picture-people are only painted by someone and aren't really real.

It's nice to be sitting on Granny's lap again, once more wrapped in her warmth and the familiar smell of the shampoo she always uses. Poppy is snoring at her feet just like she used to before they moved. He's clutching Bobbity. Ollie had hidden him by the books so she would find him and have to bring him to their new house.

It worked. Granny is reading the story too slowly and now he's ahead of her. While he waits for her to catch up, he looks up at the pretend stars stuck on the ceiling. His daddy had to balance on a ladder to arrange them into special shapes called constellations – which is the name for the patterns they make in the real sky outside. They only shine when the lights are off. This room is meant to be his special one. His mummy used white paint and a giant brush to cover all the purple flowers someone had stuck on the walls. When the paint was dry, she put up lots of pictures of animals and birds. Then she screwed a sign on the door with his name written on it. *Oliver* it says, not Ollie because Oliver is his proper name though no one ever calls him that.

Smiling, Mummy said, 'So now, what d'you think of your new room?' He told her it was nice. He didn't say that he misses his old room in the other house. He misses everything about the other house. 'We needed a fresh start,' Mummy told him when he asked. 'A place of our own, as a family.' Which seems odd to him because in the other house Granny was there too and Poppy – who counts as family although she's not a person. In the other house they didn't have to hear lots of people talking and laughing downstairs, the sound buzzing in his ears like a ginormous insect that won't go away.

'Are you listening young man?'

'Yes.'

'Hmm.' Granny can usually tell when he's fibbing. Instead of carrying on with the story, she points to the coloured triangles on long strings that hang from the front of the tall houses in the book. 'They call that bunting. See how they've hung it up on the front of the buildings to show they're happy to have a brand-new king and queen. This is meant to be his coronation day. And before you ask, a coronation is a big and important ceremony where they play music and sing lots of hymns and the top vicar in the land places the crown on the new king or queen's head.'

'Why?'

'Well, they do it to show everybody who the new king is. Of course, it can also be a queen like Queen Elizabeth – the one we have now. Anyway, it's a joyful occasion. See how the people in the crowd are all happy and smiling? On the real coronation day they would have held celebration parties the length and breadth of the country. Even here in Marshy Bottom, I shouldn't wonder.'

'What happened to the old king?'

'Well now…' Her smile isn't the ha-ha type. 'The old king – who was called Edward the something-or-other – he was quite old and got ill; and then he died.'

'Why aren't they sad about the old king?'

Her face falls and wrinkly skin collects around her mouth. 'I expect they were sad for a while, but life goes on, as they say. Much better to look forward and be happy than to look back to the past and be sad.' When she smiles, the creases in her skin shoot up again. 'And now that's more than enough of your questions for one evening, young man.'

'But Granny–'

'Uh-uh!' She shakes her head. 'That's your lot.' She lays her finger across his lips. 'Now let's just get on with this story, shall we, or we'll be here till midnight.'

He wants to know more about what happened to the old king. Is everybody happy about having this new one instead? And why do some of the people in the picture have really

72

pretty clothes on, when others have dull ones with holes in them? What was it like to live here more than a hundred years ago?

While his granny reads, his imagination wanders in other directions. Her voice becomes a soothing drone blocking out the noise from downstairs. Ollie yawns then puts his thumb in his mouth. Eyelids growing heavy, he drifts off to sleep, his thoughts already escaping the confines of their new home.

Chapter Eleven

Lana

The cold wakes her. Total darkness – so black it sends a shock-wave through her. First thought – she's died in her sleep. No, she's still breathing; she can hear her pulse whooshing in her ears. She can't have gone blind so quickly and yet there's not the faintest glimmer of light through the window or underneath the door.

Of course, there are no streetlights in the village and most of the houses are empty. There's no sound from downstairs, or upstairs for that matter. Had she herself turned off the lamp? Tom and Beth must have gone off to bed without looking in. Why hadn't they woken her up, for heaven's sake?

Lana's stiff from the chair. Snuggled up against her, his breathing slow and steady, Ollie provides the only warmth. Her hand finds his head and she gently smooths his fine hair down. He remains asleep and yet must still be clutching Bobbity – she can feel the little rabbit's body digging into her breastbone.

Fighting pins and needles, she takes Ollie's weight in one

arm as she cautiously levers herself upright. He's certainly a lot heavier than he used to be. The dog's no longer at her feet, possibly not even in the room. Who let her out? It really is freezing – she imagines her unseen breath frosting the air in front of her.

As soon as enough blood has returned to her legs, Lana takes a tentative step forward, gropes with her free hand but fails to locate the wooden bars of Ollie's cot, which oughtn't to be more than a yard or so in front of her.

Instead of the smooth new rug, she feels something soft and yet lumpy under her feet. Shuffling awkwardly with her burden, Lana advances one careful step at a time until, at long last her outstretched fingers make contact with something. In every direction its smooth surface continues uninterrupted. A wall. Papered by the feel of it. She shakes her head. This makes no sense – where's the rest of the furniture? Heart leaping, for a second she thinks she can smell smoke before she recognises the waxy aroma of recently extinguished candles. Must be coming from downstairs.

Is she still dreaming? No – Lana's certain she's awake with her grandson and his toy rabbit clutched to her chest. She's reassured by the sudden echoing call of an owl. A moment later there's an answer from another owl; fainter this time; must be further across the valley.

She takes a few steps in the direction of the door and stubs her toe on the cold metal of the bed frame. Her free hand finds what she thinks is a coarse woollen blanket. What's happened to that nice duvet she saw earlier? Did they want it back?

It's a relief to sit down on the bed, hear its springs squeak and sag beneath her. Ollie's legs and arms begin to twitch like he's running from something in his sleep. Lana pulls back the blankets and lays him on the sheet. She could have sworn this bed was underneath the window earlier on. Who could have come in and moved it? Wouldn't the noise – all that scraping – have woken her up?

No one goes senile overnight. Besides, now her eyes have adjusted she can just make out a grey square on the opposite wall which has to be the window. There's no sign of the thick penguin print curtains she'd drawn across earlier. How could they have disappeared?

Blundering around in the dark in the freezing cold isn't sensible – that much at least is obvious. For now, the most rational thing for her to do is to climb into the bed next to Ollie. Thank goodness she's fully clothed because two meagre blankets are barely adequate against the iciness of the room. The bed's so narrow she hardly dares move as she snuggles close to him. He's still wrapped in the lambswool throw and, when she checks the back of his neck, he feels warm enough to the touch.

Facing the wall, she feels vulnerable so, by careful incre-ments, she turns over until she's lying on her back. Breathing in Ollie's familiar smell, a terrifying explanation presents itself and won't let her rest.

Chapter Twelve

Tom

The two of them fall into an easy rhythm as they work side by side behind the bar. Whenever there's a brief lull, his eyes are drawn to Beth. He notices the way she serves even the most demanding customers with a genuine smile they can't help but respond to. As the evening goes on, more of her long dark hair escapes the elastic band meant to be holding it back, falling to frame her face in a way that perfectly enhances its contours. Tonight, the two of them are in harmony, and she is his beautiful Beth again – someone he's often missed over the months since they became parents. After another quick glance, he shakes his head in disbelief at the thought that at the end of this shift he will go to bed with this luminous creature.

Reaching for the same optic, their hands touch, and they share a quick smile that's enough to set his heart racing. In the next pass, she winks at him – an unmistakable come-hither. Tom struggles to contain his mounting excitement. The pandemic changed everything. It derailed his life in so many ways. And yet before he would never have believed he stood a chance with a woman like Beth. And now there's Ollie too. His son. How lucky could one man get?

One persistent customer – a posh bloke flashing a gold Rolex – is hanging around the bar and blatantly flirting with Beth. He's probably clocked there's no ring on her finger. Though she's handling the situation, Tom's tempted to intervene – tell the bloke where to sling his hook. If he did, she'd rightly accuse him of behaving like some caveman.

They're rushed off their feet. It's warm work and Beth's skin is shiny with perspiration; she keeps wiping her brow with the back of her hand. All the same, he wishes she'd do up a couple of buttons on the front of her shirt. Since she's no longer undocumented, legally there's nothing to prevent them from tying the knot. Of course, he'd need to find enough money to buy her a proper ring before planning a suitably romantic moment to offer it to her. She deserves something classy.

He glances at the clock – only half an hour left till kicking out time. He can hardly wait to have her all to himself.

The kitchen staff have already left. The hat the customers pass around is presented to him stuffed full of banknotes and pound coins. He thanks them loudly for such a generous tip. After multiple goodbyes, they stagger out in groups to fall into the line of waiting taxis. Diesel fumes are clouding the air as he stands on the threshold to wave the last of them off.

With a sigh of relief Tom slides the final bolt across. Beth has cleared the last of the glasses and is now mopping up spillage on the polished countertop. 'Enough,' he declares. 'As your employer, I insist you put that cloth down and call it a night. I can sort everything else out in the morning.'

He leans in to kiss the back of her neck, breathes in her unique aroma – his woman. When she offers no resistance, no plea of tiredness, he caresses one of her breasts – smaller now she's no longer feeding the baby. She swivels around until she's facing him, strokes back his hair to look deep into his eyes before kissing him with such passion it robs him of his breath.

Tom wakes with a start, the terror of his dream slow to fade. It's dark. Everything's quiet – too quiet. His head is heavy from sleep and the alcohol various customers had pressed on him. Uninterrupted for a change, last night they'd made love in a way they hadn't in a long while. He grins at the memory; at the way the sheets now smell of sex.

His smile fades. There is something else – something niggling away at the edge of his consciousness. In trying to pin it down, he realises with a growing conviction that something isn't right.

Hoping to be proved wrong, he finds Beth's shoulder and shakes it. Muttering, she turns away. Another shake before she half opens one eye. 'What?'

'Something's odd.'

'That's not what you said last night.' Her arm extends to stroke his chest; she presses her warm naked flesh against his. It would be easy to give in to temptation, but he knows he mustn't. 'Think I'll just go and check on Ollie.'

'Why? He's quiet – sleeping dogs and all that.' Her fingers are exploring his stomach – inching their way down. 'Stay here.'

'Hold that thought,' he says. 'I'll be back in a minute.'

'But you'll only go waking him up. Or your mum. Or the dog. Probably all three.'

'I'll tiptoe in. It won't take me a sec.'

'Then at least put some clothes on. Not sure Lana will appreciate a full-frontal at this hour.' Beth rolls over. 'What time is it anyway?'

'No idea.' It's cold. The heating hasn't come on so it must be before six. 'Go back to sleep,' he tells her. When he stands up, the dim light of the security monitor comes on. Although he was somewhat distracted, he's fairly certain he remembered to set the alarms on the lower floor and both stairways before he came upstairs.

Tom gropes around until he locates his hastily discarded underpants and t-shirt. In the hallway, his movements trigger the censor light from another monitor to blink on. Shivering, he treads carefully on the old floorboards as he makes his way towards Ollie's room.

As he's opening the door, he hears footsteps coming towards him. Something soft brushes against his bare leg; a wet tongue rasps his skin. He bends to stroke Poppy's head. 'Shhh!' Her hot smelly breath is directed at his face. The dog groans as she finishes a yawn.

There's barely enough light to make out Ollie's cot. Tom steals further into the room expecting to see his son lying there fast asleep. But he can't make him out, can't see properly without turning on the main light and waking him. Instead, like he has so many times, he listens for his regular breathing. Of course, Poppy chooses that moment to start whining – demanding to be let out or something. When he doesn't respond, the dog gives a sharp bark. 'Quiet,' he whispers, 'or you'll wake them.'

Poppy begins to bark louder; she won't shut up. He can't imagine how either of them could sleep through the racket she's making. Fear creeps across Tom's scalp like a cold hand. He gropes for the light switch and flicks it on. Eyes smarting, he finds himself staring down at his son's empty cot. The bed his mother should be sleeping in looks undisturbed. Her overnight bag is on the bed. It hasn't even been unpacked. Looking up at him, Poppy's whining sounds like an I-told-you-so.

What the hell…?

Reeling backwards, he steps on something hard. An open book. His mum's discarded trainers lie right next to it like a clue she might have left for him to follow. Instinct tells him not to touch either in case... Oh God – his imagination's running too far ahead.

Tom shuts his eyes while he tries to construct a logical explanation for their absence. Could they have gone for a walk? Hardly likely barefoot. Pulling back the curtains only confirms that it's still pitch-black outside. Perhaps Ollie couldn't sleep, and his mum's taken him along to the kitchen to give him a bottle or something. Yes – the two might have dropped off on the sofa.

As far as he recalls, the kitchen door was open when he came out of the bedroom. Wouldn't he have heard them, seen a light?

The same instinct that guided him earlier causes Tom to crouch down and study the picture book's illustrations. Holding it to the light, he sees a street of narrow townhouses – the sort that still exist in parts of London. And in the foreground two figures – a woman and a young girl dressed in old-fashioned clothes. Wide-brimmed hats, their skirts hovering well above their ankle over sturdy boots. The lamppost looks Victorian, but he guesses this is meant to be later – probably before the first World War.

Turning his attention to the more immediate situation, he switches on more lights, rushes down the hall to check first the bathroom and then their kitchen-cum-living room. There's no sign of either of them. The dog barks at the outer door. When Tom checks he finds it's still double locked with both inside bolts across. None of the windows are open.

Desperate for an explanation, he begins to wonder if Lana could have disturbed burglars. No, if someone had broken in downstairs after the takings, it would have triggered the alarms.

Poppy is aimlessly rushing around, her paws skidding on the floors they so recently polished. These days most customers pay by card, so thieves would target the stock. Used to deep silence at night, he's pretty sure he would have heard people moving around, bottles clinking, an engine left running outside.

Before he can check, Beth comes out of their bedroom tying the belt of her dressing gown. 'What's all the noise? Why's the dog making such a fuss? Where's Ollie?'

Answers die on his lips. None of this makes sense. Beth is looking up at him expectantly. 'Ollie – he's gone. He and Mum seem to have disappeared. Vanished into thin air.'

She looks up at him in disbelief. 'Don't be daft.' She jabs

an angry finger at him. 'Not funny, you bastard.' Seeing his expression, her mouth crumbles. She shakes her head. 'You're talking utter crap – just trying to scare me.'

Beth runs to Ollie's bedroom while he remains rooted to the spot, trying to clear his head. Think. No one's broken in. If they'd left via the stairs, the door would be unlocked, the bolts certainly wouldn't be across. Anyone on the stairs would have triggered the alarm.

Beth's anguished cry twists his stomach like a knife plunged. He hits the side of his head against the wall. 'Think, damn it.' He hits it again – harder this time. How could his mother and his son have vanished into thin air?

'No, no, no. This isn't happening.' She pushes past him to check the other two rooms. Her howl is primal; agonised. He headbutts the wall; this time it hurts so much his legs give way. Why would something like this happen to an ordinary family like them?

But they aren't ordinary, are they? Ollie is extraordinary in every sense. As he sinks to the floor, Tom lets himself imagine the one explanation that makes any sense: somehow, the two of them must have travelled to another time

The burglar alarm goes off. Beth has charged down the stairs without first un-setting it. Ears pulsating with the noise, he scrambles to his feet to go after her. He remembers to grab a torch. He lets the alarm carry on ringing knowing it will have alerted the security firm by now. When he doesn't respond, they'll call the police.

Poppy is outside running around and barking like a dog possessed. The noise is loud enough to wake the whole village

– not that there are many to wake. Beth keeps calling Ollie's name over and over. More desperate each time. The dog breaks off to investigate every bush.

Barefoot, Beth's running around the village green screaming out their names. Maybe she's right to try. Perhaps his mum has had some kind of strange turn and, disorientated, taken the baby for a walk in the dark. Venturing further, he joins in with her calling hoping to defy his own logic, praying there could still be a less terrifying explanation for their disappearance.

Chapter Thirteen

Lana

Daylight confirms her worst fears. Her gaze falls on a wash-stand in the corner with an old-fashioned china jug and basin set on top. Beside it, a deep-seated wooden chair that must be a commode – the sort many still used when she was a child in the 1930s. The same armchair she'd sat in last night is on the other side of the room next to a small fireplace. It's now covered in brown velvet. Kindling and screwed up paper is laid ready to ignite in the cast iron grate. And there's wallpaper – a busy flower pattern on an eau-de-nil background, bleached to palest green where the sunlight must hit it. No personal items anywhere except a framed embroidery of a bunch of pansies and roses above the words: *GOD is our refuge & our strength*.

She's still taking it all in when Ollie stirs in his sleep, mutters something indecipherable. His cheeks are red – could just be where he's teething. She gently checks his forehead and finds it cool to the touch, thank goodness.

Not wanting to wake him until she fully understands what's happened, Lana's shivering as she slides out of bed, her feet finding a rag rug made from multicoloured scraps – the sort her mother used to work on in the evenings. She creeps over to the front window. The thin outer curtains are tied back from the frame leaving inner lacy ones that obscure the view. She lifts one corner to get a better picture of what's out there and is relieved to see the distinctive row of stone cottages Marshy Bottom is known for. Everything looks peaceful and orderly. Ducks are waddling unconcerned across the village green. As always, the river continues to flow over the cobbles of the ford.

It's quiet. No planes or contrails up in the sky, not a single car to be seen. The red phone box is gone. Standing roughly in its place is an iron pump alongside a carved stone trough. Instead of tarmac, the road surface is rough and pitted. In place of gravelled parking spaces, the front gardens of the cottages have been transformed into rich brown stripes; here and there she sees lines of leeks and winter cabbages, the stumps of Brussel sprouts. Further back, each cottage has a stone built outside privy. Drying clothes billow like drab bunting from washing lines supported by wooden props.

She starts at the sound of approaching hooves – the heavy clip-clop of two magnificent white shire horses, the brasses on their bridles catching fire in the low winter sun. They're reined to a halt directly below the window. From her vantage point she can see the cart is loaded high with wooden barrels. The man in charge calls out something she can't decipher. He jumps down from the bench seat, drops the end board of the cart, and begins to offload barrels.

The top of someone's head appears in response – a grey-haired man in shirtsleeves has come out of the pub's front door to roll the unloaded barrels over to the open trapdoor that must lead down to the beer cellar.

While this is going on, a figure emerges from one of the doorways opposite – a man, clouded breath obscuring his features. He's wearing a long dark coat and a flat cap. Could be any age from young to old. He's walking at a pace, rubbing his hands together for warmth, hobnail boots ringing out as they hit the stony ground. He gives a low cry she interprets as a greeting. His arm goes up to wave at a figure in one of the gardens – a chestnut-haired woman scattering feed for an assortment of pecking hens. The woman calls back, her reply indistinct. She wipes her hands on the skirt of a full apron that's protecting her dull brown dress with its almost ankle-length skirt. Her thin ankles end in stout leather boots similar to the ones Lana's granny used to wear.

She gasps, steps back from the window shocked by the realisation that their clothes are the same style as the people in the book she'd been reading with Ollie before she fell asleep. No coincidence – she's sure of that. She checks the seat of the armchair then underneath it, but the book has disappeared along with her discarded trainers. The story was set at the time of George's coronation which, from memory, must have been around 1911. Wherever Lana looks, the physical truth of their situation is undeniable – somehow, they've been transported back more than a hundred years.

The Guardians have the ability to do such things, but she can't imagine why they would want to since they'd explicitly forbidden it. How else could it have happened?

There are only two of them in this room and she's most

definitely not the one with extraordinary abilities. Struggling to control her heart, her breathing, she tells herself that, if she's right and Ollie has somehow made this happen, there ought to be a way she can get him to reverse it.

A dog barks. Someone is chopping wood, she can make out the fall of their axe, the crack of splintering wood. And now there are other sounds coming up from downstairs. Shouting that heralds the start of a longer conversation. A man and a woman clearly engaged in an argument, though she can't make out the words. It occurs to her that, in this era, this probably wasn't just a village pub – more likely it was an inn offering accommodation to passing travellers. Which must be why this bedroom is so impersonal – it's one of their letting rooms.

'Why's it so cold, Granny?' There's a wobble in Ollie's voice. He's thrown off the covers and is sitting up in the bed rubbing at his eyes. In his thin pirate pyjamas, he's shivering and clutching at himself. 'I need a wee-wee.' He slithers down the side of the bed, landing on two feet like a miniature gymnast dismounting.

She goes over to the commode and lifts the lid to reveal a blue and white chamber pot – the sort people put plants in these days. Well, not *these days* obviously. She beckons him over. 'Look there's a potty inside this chair. Isn't that clever? You don't even need to go to the bathroom to have a wee-wee.' He stares at it in wonder. 'I'll lift you up.'

'I can manage by myself.' A determined expression on his face, he climbs up to balance with his feet on either side of the rim and successfully aims into the pot. Climbing down again, he says, 'Mummy says I should always wash my hands after a wee-wee.'

There's a cake of carbolic soap by the basin but no water in the jug – no means of washing his hands, though right now that's the least of her worries. 'Just this once you don't have to,' she tells him.

He eyes her with suspicion but doesn't argue. Instead, he looks around seemingly taking in all the changes. He must wonder where his cot and toys have disappeared to. She expects him to ask about the changes, or the whereabouts of Beth and Tom. Instead, he points an accusing finger. 'Look, Bobbity's right under the bed.'

While he's crawling around under there, Lana makes use of the commode and then, feeling guilty, drops the lid on its brimming contents. Ollie emerges. 'Don't worry, you're quite safe now,' he tells the toy rabbit, brushing fluff from his one-and-a-half ears.

In as casual a tone as she can muster, she asks, 'Do you remember the book we were reading together last night – the one about the little scullery maid back in the olden days?' He nods. 'Did it make you want to go there?'

She waits. He finally speaks but only to say, 'I'm really, really thirsty, Granny.'

'Okay, we'll get you a drink in just a minute.' She tries again, 'Ollie, did you dream about that book when you were asleep last night?' She holds her breath.

He gives her a puzzled look. 'Is it breakfast time?' Patting his stomach, he giggles. 'My belly sounds really cross.' He's right – she can hear it complaining.

A different approach. 'Ollie my love, if you close your eyes and try really really hard, can you picture this room like it was before, with your cot just over there?'

He shuts his eyes for a couple of seconds before blinking and emphatically shaking his head. Perhaps he will be able to concentrate better once he's had something to drink and eat? With only the clothes she stands up in, she has no way of paying for breakfast. Maybe the pub landlord, or one of the villagers, will take pity on a small child in need – although Ollie hardly looks underfed.

The two of them can't stay up in this room, but as soon as they venture downstairs, people will wonder where the hell they've sprung from. Dressed as they are, they'll stick out like blowflies on a wedding cake. Ollie might not be too much of a problem – she can wrap the lambswool throw around his printed pyjamas and warn him not to utter a word.

Looking down, she takes stock of her own outfit – grey t-shirt under a black and white overshirt, black skinny jeans, owl print socks and no shoes. Shit!

If she does up her shirt buttons, she can hide the Greenpeace slogan on her t-shirt, but she's fairly certain women wouldn't have worn tight trousers in this era. In fact, most of them were still constrained by corsets.

Perhaps she could try wrapping one of the curtains around her waist. Eyeing them up, Lana can tell they're too short for the job. It would look like she's wearing a weird sort of tutu. Besides, they have a distinctive print – someone from the pub might recognise the material.

If they sneak down the back steps, she could maybe grab a few appropriate items of clothing off a nearby washing line. They always do that in films. Although with everyone up and about, she could easily get caught red-handed. At this time of day, the clothes would probably still be wet. Even if they aren't, with so little clothing to their name, it's likely the owners will spot their missing items and accuse her of stealing.

Would it be easier to disguise herself as a man? In her best gravelly voice she says, 'Hello. Nice to meet you.' Ollie laughs out loud – loud enough for someone to hear. 'Shhh!' Not to alarm him, she winks like this is a big wheeze he's in on. If she took a pair of scissors to her hair, she'd probably still need a bit of stage makeup to pass as a man. She searches the couple of drawers on the washstand but there's no scissors or knife, nothing that could help with the transformation.

Which means that if they're going to venture downstairs her only option is to brazen it out. Being so far off the beaten track, there's a slim chance the villagers might conclude that her outfit is all the rage in London. Her lack of shoes is an obvious worry – though if she was wearing her trainers, on-lookers would be even more astounded. The socks look way too modern, but will they even notice a detail like that? It might look more suspicious if she ventures out barefoot in this weather.

Lana takes a deep breath. 'Right Ollie – we're going to go and get you some breakfast.' She does her best to smile away signs of her mounting anxiety. 'I just need to wrap you up first. Oh – and this is really important – you mustn't talk to anybody we meet.' She lays a finger across her lips to illustrate. 'D'you understand? You mustn't say a word. Not one. Can you do that for me, Ollie?'

He nods several times but not in a serious way; more like this might be the start of a fun new game.

They emerge into daylight. Wrapped in his blanket Ollie should be warm enough but without a coat or jacket the bitter wind penetrates to her skin. At every step the soles of her feet discover sharp stones, her socks seem to be drawing moisture from the damp earth.

She can hear voices, the sound of snapping twigs. In the rough woodland that now runs down almost to the back of the pub, a couple of boys are collecting firewood. They too are wearing flat caps; the dull browns of their clothing camouflaging them perfectly when they stand still. They look to be around eight – nine at most.

Seeing her, the two children stop what they're doing and stare open-mouthed. Before she can say anything, like startled deer they take off at speed, shedding branches and twigs as they head towards the surety of the village green and the cottages beyond. Not an encouraging start, for sure.

Chapter Fourteen

Beth

Out of the darkness she sees blue lights pirouetting. A police car screeches to a halt, its ear-piercing siren abruptly dies. Like she's watching a film, she follows the two uniformed officers as they rush towards the lit-up pub and its open front door.

Tom yells at them. 'Stop!' Almost colliding, their heads swivel round. 'There hasn't been a robbery,' he shouts across the green. He gestures in her direction, 'Beth here triggered the alarm.'

In one of the cottages an upstairs light comes on – a ghost waking up. A slanting shaft of light falls across the grass, picking out the taller of the two officers striding towards them, his chequered hat casting a shadow over sharp features. 'And who might you be, sir?'

Coming to her senses, Beth cries out, 'For God's sake help us, our son – our baby – someone's taken him.' Overcome and icy cold, she sinks to her knees on the wet grass. Immediately a deadening damp creeps over her skin, sucks at her bare feet and legs, pulling her palms back towards the earth when she tries to lever herself up. Dread hollows her out.

The two of them tower above her. She stares at the raised hairs on Tom's bare legs. 'Let me get this straight, sir – the alarm was triggered but you're saying there's been no burglary?' The officer's voice is loaded with suspicion. 'And now you're telling me your son's gone missing?' He looks down his long nose at her. 'Is that right, madam?'

'Yes – Ollie. He's only a toddler.' She jabs an accusing finger in the direction of the pub. 'He's not in his cot... Go and see for yourself.'

'Just hold on a minute.' Legs apart, Tom blocks the man's way. 'My mother – our son's granny – she's, um, also missing. The two of them seem to have disappeared together; but, you know, if we all just try to stay calm for a minute, there could be a logical explanation...' Tom throws her a look she can't fathom.

'So now we're talking about two missing persons.' The policeman takes out his stupid pad, flips it open and angles it towards the light. 'I'm going to need some details. Why don't we start with your name, sir?'

'But you're wasting time–'

'Please madam, we can't authorise a search without more information. So, let's get a few things straight first. Your name, sir?'

'Tom Brookes. I'm the bar manager of the pub.' He points at the building. 'We – my family and myself – live in the flat up above. This here is Beth – Elizabeth Sawyer. She's Ollie's mum.'

'Short for Oliver is that?'

Tom nods.

'And the baby's last name – would that be Brookes or Sawyer?'

Wanting to scream, Beth beats the grass with both hands. 'You're wasting time. You need to help us look for him.'

'And we will, madam, just as soon as we have more information. So, your son – is he Brookes or Sawyer?'

'Brookes.' She drops her head in despair.

'And your son's date of birth?'

'Eighteenth of December 2020,' she tells him.

Tom puts both hands under her arms and hauls her to her feet like she's a sack of coal or something. 'Beth and I – we've searched the whole flat,' he tells the copper. Dressed only in her mud-caked dressing gown, she's shivering violently. When Tom puts an arm around her, he weighs her down. She shrugs him off. 'We need to spread out.' Before she can set off, Tom grabs her arm.

The policeman puts a hand on her shoulder. 'Please try to calm down – Beth isn't it?'

She nods.

'Has either of you searched the rest of the premises? Downstairs – the bar, toilets and so on?'

'No, we haven't,' Tom admits. 'But the alarm was set down there, so no one could have gone in that part of the building without it going off. And there'd be no reason why Mum would have taken Ollie down there.'

The other policeman – the short stocky one – has moved closer, head cocked to one side, he's talking into his radio. Calling for reinforcements she hopes. He jerks a thumb towards the pub. 'I'll go and take a look around. Can you give me the code for the alarm so we can shut it off, sir?'

Tom shouts out numbers. 'It's pointless,' he says. 'Beth's right – we're wasting time.'

The alarm falls silent though she can still hear its echo in her head. The first policeman hasn't moved. 'We find it's best to start with the most likely explanation. As the saying goes: if it looks like a duck–'

'For Christ's sake, you're not winkling out communists.' Tom's fists are curled. 'Our son is missing. A vulnerable infant.'

'Along with his grandmother as I understand it. And her name would be?'

'Lana,' Beth supplies. 'Lana Brookes – that's Brookes with an e, not that it makes any sodding difference.'

The officer turns to Tom. 'How old is your mother, sir?'

'It's hard to be accurate,' Tom tells him.

A heavy sigh. 'Then approximately.'

'Early sixties. 62 or 3 – something like that.'

'And would you say your mother is of sound mind, sir?'

When he hesitates, Beth intervenes, 'Yes, of course she is. Lana loves our Ollie to bits. She'd defend him with her life.' She's fighting tears at the thought. 'She'd never ever do anything to harm him.'

The officer clears his throat. 'You say she's protective towards him. Is it possible…? Please don't take this the wrong way. Is it possible Lana may, rightly or wrongly, have felt it was in Ollie's best interests to remove him from your home?'

She grabs Tom's arm before he can take a swing at the man. 'That's utterly fucking ridiculous,' he spits. 'Mum would never think that for one second.'

Her own anger rising, Beth squares up to the man. 'Our

child goes missing in the middle of the bloody night and instead of helping us look for him, you point the finger at us and suggest we're somehow to blame.'

'Ah yes, blame the poor parents.' Tom looks like he's about to headbutt him. 'Is that the sort of logic they teach you these days, Police Constable whatever-your-fucking-name-is?'

'It's Fraser, sir. PC Arnold Fraser. And please try to moderate your language.' He's about to say more when the other copper comes out of the pub shaking his head. 'Place is empty.'

'Do you have a recent photograph of the baby?' PC Fraser asks. 'We'll also need a recent one of your mother, if you have it.'

Deflating in front of her, Tom says, 'Yes, of course. My phone's back in the flat, I'll go and get it.' He breaks into run.

Beth stands her ground. 'Can you tell me what your son was wearing when you last saw him?' the policeman wants to know.

She shakes her head. 'Lana put him to bed. We were downstairs working in the bar, rushed off our feet all night.'

PC Fraser narrows his eyes. 'Is it possible the two of them went missing earlier in the evening?'

'I suppose so,' comes out as a whisper. Beth shakes her head over and over. 'I should have checked on Ollie before we went to bed. I thought, you know, that it was fine because it was quiet in there. Lana was sleeping in his room – so there was, you know, no need to worry or…'

'Does Lana have a car?'

'Yes – she came by car. An old Golf – Tom can describe it better than me.' Into his radio he says, 'Check the car park,

Jim. See if there's a VW Golf parked up registered to a Mrs Lana Brookes.'

'I'm not sure if she calls herself Mrs or Miss,' she tells him.

'You look freezing,' he says in a kinder voice. Despite her protests, he takes off his jacket and hangs it around her shoulders. 'Why don't we go inside, Beth? I need you to check whether any of your son's clothes or toys are missing.'

By dawn there are police everywhere. Urgent, serious eyes above their black face masks, they talk into radios. In a line, bent over staring at the ground, a dozen of them fan out calling Lana's name.

Two more – a man and a woman – are checking the neighbouring cottages, working their way along the row, rapping on front doors that remain unanswered.

Tom is heading her way. 'You've still got mud in your hair,' he says attempting a smile. Though she's now fully dressed and wearing her thickest coat, Beth can't stop shaking. Their son is missing, but they aren't allowed to join in the search; they don't say as much, but she knows it's all to do with preserving evidence the two of them might otherwise contaminate.

The two officers are down to the last but one cottage when an old man appears in the doorway scratching his head. The policewoman steps forward to show him something on her mobile phone. Must be that photo Tom had chosen – the one of Ollie and Lana laughing because that goat was trying to eat her wellies.

The old man leans in inches from the screen. After studying the photo, he certainly has a lot to say – though for all she knows he could just be complaining about the noise from the pub.

While he's still talking and waving his arms about, both officers begin to back away. She hears them call out their thanks as they make good their exit. The policewoman keeps shaking her head. 'Well, that has to be a first,' Beth hears her say. The two are quick to hide their smiles when they walk past her and Tom.

Beth steps into their path. 'Did that old man tell you anything?'

'Nothing of use I'm afraid,' the policeman assures her. 'We thought it might be a lead at first, but it turned out to be nonsense. Alzheimer's, I shouldn't wonder.'

'Are you sure?'

The woman nods. 'Mr Tanner. Well, he started off by telling us how his mother had seen an older woman with a baby standing right here on the village green. Said she'd told him they were dressed in peculiar clothes and as far as his mother could tell, they'd just popped up out of nowhere.'

The other one takes over. 'Given his age, it seemed unlikely his mother could still be alive. When we asked if we could have a word with her, he said, "You'll be lucky, she died a good twenty years back". So anyway, we thanked the old boy for his help, and then he says, and I'm afraid it was hard to keep a straight face, "Course our mam was only a youngster herself at the time".'

Chapter Fifteen

Tom

As soon as the two officers are far enough away, he grabs Beth's hand and pulls her along with him. 'We need to talk to that old man right now.'

'What, you think he might have been telling the truth? Wouldn't that mean…' He stops when she stumbles and nearly falls. She's worryingly pale, looks like she might faint at any minute.

'Beth, take a deep breath. Now another. That's it. Listen to me, we both need to keep our shit together if we're going to help them. Let's start by finding out what this man might know. It might be a complete red herring, but we have to check it out. Agreed?'

She nods.

'Good.' He hooks an arm through hers and, more or less in step, they head for the cottage – distinctive as the only one with a rusting gutter and peeling paint on most of the windows. The gate swings back and forth having lost its catch. The concrete front path is cracked and pitted. Tom raps on the front door knocker with some force. When there's no response, he tries again – even harder this time.

A strained voice from inside says, 'Hold yer ruddy horses, will ya?' The chain is still across when a single, suspicious eye peers through the gap. 'You're not coppers.' That watery eye looks them up and down. 'What d'you want?'

Tom tries his best to sound calm. 'Mr Tanner, we're actually neighbours though we haven't met. I'm Tom Brookes – the new bar manager at the Pig and Piper over there.' Leaves it a moment for that to sink in. 'And this is my, um, Beth. I expect the police told you that our baby son and his grandmother have gone missing.'

'They did.' His head swivels in Beth's direction. 'I'm sorry to hear it.'

'The thing is,' Tom says, 'we think you might be able to help us, so we wondered if we might have quick chat.' He glances back at the growing commotion behind. More cars. Fuck, it looks like the press have arrived. 'Can we come in and have a chat, just for a moment? Please.'

'Like I already told them coppers I haven't seen a soul since yesterday.'

'All the same, we think you might be able to help us.'

'Hmm.' Those rheumy eyes rove over them once more before the old man gives a heavy sigh and, after a couple of unsuccessful attempts, he unchains the door. The metal end of his walking-stick rings against the worn brick floor as they follow at a glacial pace along a short hallway into a kitchen straight out of the 1950's. Hipsters would drool over the mid-century melamine cupboards, the standalone larder unit, the sunburst clock in pride of place above the beige tiled fireplace.

Worn out from the effort, Mr Tanner lets his cane fall with a clatter. He leans both hands on the edge of a sturdy wooden table and works his way round it until he lowers himself into an upright chair – the only one with arms. His scalp is visible through his thin white hair. One arthritic hand pulls together the front of the droopy green cardigan he's wearing over pyjamas.

Bending down to retrieve the fallen stick, Tom notices his bare ankles, tartan slippers that have seen better days. He hooks the handle of the cane on the back of a chair that ought to be within the old man's reach.

Noticing, Mr Tanner says, 'Ta.' And then, 'My carer's bin held up. Rang to say she can't get here till lunchtime. Ruddy nuisance. I'm all over the shop without her.'

'Why don't I put the kettle on,' Tom suggests, 'I expect you could do with a cuppa, eh?'

'Good idea. And make one for yer missus while yer at it – poor girl looks shrammed. Oh, and I could do with a couple of bits of toast, if you wouldn't mind doin' the honours. Just a scrape of butter mind – too much grease plays havoc with me insides these days.'

Kettle boiling, Tom finds a sliced white loaf and sticks two pieces into an ancient toaster with a dodgy-looking flex. The plug on the end is an old Bakelite one. At arm's length, he plugs it in, is relieved when there's no bang. 'D'you mind if we sit down for a minute, Mr Tanner?'

'Fill yer boots.'

Tom pulls out a chair for Beth, waits until she's seated before continuing with his tasks. He makes two mugs of tea, finds butter, a pot of jam, a knife and plate for the toast and brings it all over on a tray.

The old man feels the need to give detailed instructions concerning the buttering. He taps the jampot. 'I'm not supposed to have any of that 'cause of me diabetes.' A toothless smile. 'Don't suppose a smattering would hurt though.'

Tom obliges. Patience exhausted, he begins, 'Mr Tanner, I believe you told the police that, many years ago, your late mother saw a woman with a baby seemingly pop up out of nowhere on the village green?'

A gummy mouthful has to be washed down with tea before the old man finally speaks. 'You know it's funny how yer memory works when you get to my age.' A slow smile. 'Can't remember what you had for tea yesterday, but things from yer childhood sort of float back into yer mind like it happened last week.'

They're forced to wait while he takes another bite followed by another slurping swallow. Beth's clutching the warm mug – her trembling hands making the surface choppy.

Tom tries again. 'Your mother – what exactly did she see?'

'Well now, our mam used to tell us this tale about a strange thing that happened when she was only a young'un herself. In them days, her mam would set her to beating the rugs out over the washing line in the garden every Saturday morning without fail. Course, that was only the start of her chores…'

Tom steers him back. 'Can you tell us what she told you she remembered about that particular morning, Mr Tanner?'

'Mam said it was early – not long light. She's busy beating away at them rugs and the dust's flying in clouds when an odd-looking person she'd never seen in her life before comes out from behind the pub over there and starts walking towards the green. As this person gets closer, Mam can make out it's a woman though she's got a most peculiar hairstyle and these skin-tight trousers the like of which Mam's never seen before. And there's no shoes on her feet though it was perishing cold at the time. Mam can see she's carryin' summat mysterious – a bundle wrapped in a blanket that turns out to be a chubby little babby.'

Beth gasps. Tom shakes his head at her. They're forced to wait while the old man takes a couple more slurps from the mug. 'Where was I?'

'You were describing the woman and the baby...'

'So I was.' His tired eyes look directly into Tom's. 'Mam said this woman was such a queer sight to behold, the rest of 'em comes out of their gardens and cottages to gawk at her thinking she might be some apparition or suchlike. Presently, the strange woman smiles at them showing a pearly set of teeth, and in this posh voice, she says, "Hello. It's nice to meet you all". Well now, Alfie Jenkins who used to live next-door but one, had been turning over his garden and still has the fork gripped in his hands. He was a grumpy old bugger, by all accounts and ugly as sin. So anyhow, old Jenkins, he steps forward and says to her, "Who the ruddy hell are you?" Seein' his angry red mug close up was enough to frighten any bugger and straight off the babby's little face crumbles and he or she cries out as clear as a bell, "I want my mummy". Our mam starts wondering if this woman could be a sprite or some sort of elf or pisky that had stolen this poor babby away from its real mother. I doubt she was the only one harbouring the exact same suspicion. Next thing, seein' them gathered in on all sides, the babby takes fright, opens its mouth and wails. Finally catching its breath, the little thing cries out, "I want to go home". And with that, the two of them disappear into thin air. Not in a puff of smoke like a conjurer might summon up. No. Mam swore blind that one minute they're standing there as solid as you or me, and the next they're gone.'

The old man's attempt to snap his fingers fails. 'The only trace left behind to prove it had happened at all was the trail the woman's footsteps had made through the wet grass. That was it. By all accounts, no one ever saw hide nor hair of either of them again.'

'Oh my God!' Beth leaps up from her chair and rushes out. Tom remembers to thank the old man before running after her. He finds her outside on the green staring transfixed at the pub. She's beaming, excited. 'They're back! Look, they're right there at the window.' Tom can only see the heavy sky reflected in the glass.

Before he can caution her, she runs across the grass, dodges around all the people gathered in front of the pub and disappears inside.

Hard on her heels, he mounts the steps two at a time, races along the corridor to Ollie's bedroom where Beth is now on the floor doubled up and howling.

The room along with Ollie's cot is still empty. Tom quickly checks all the other rooms before he sinks down to his knees and take her in his arms. Rocking back and forth, the two of them can only weep.

Alerted by shouts from below, he opens his eyes, stares at the picture book he'd found earlier – the one they must have been reading together. Terrible images crowd his mind of the two of them irretrievably lost in another time.

When the phone in his coat pocket rings, he ignores it. It stops only to immediately start up again. Wiping her face, Beth says, 'You should probably get that. It could be important.' They've lost their son – what could anyone say to make things better?

All the same, he pulls the damned thing out and checks the screen. The words, MUM – HOME send a shockwave through him. The phone continues to vibrate in his hand. He hardly dares answer.

'Tom, it's me.' Recognisably his mother's voice. 'I'm back at home – in Stoatsfield. Ollie's here with me. Don't worry – he's quite safe.'

Questions can wait. He leaps up, pulls Beth onto her feet. 'We're on our way now,' he tells her.

A glance outside confirms the small obstacle of the police and reporters surrounding the pub. Shit a brick!

Chapter Sixteen

Lana

The phone rings again. Beth this time. 'Like I told Tom, he's absolutely fine.' Lana is determined to sound calm and reassuring; the room would slip sideways if she let it. Her voice falters, she can only repeat, 'Yes, honestly; he's right here in my arms. No, we won't go anywhere... I swear.' A hollow promise – it's not like she's the one controlling events.

Barking – Poppy must be in the car with them. The engine note alters as he changes gear for the long steep climb out of the valley. Now they're both speaking at once. She rubs her brow. 'I don't understand,' she admits.

'We've been worried out of our minds.' Beth's tone suggests it's her fault.

Lana braces her legs like she's onboard a ship in a storm; inhales then exhales slowly. 'Yes, we'll be staying right here.' Against her, Ollie is pale and trembling, his little hand clamped around Bobbity's foot.

She resists the urge to shut her eyes for fear they might be transported straight back to those hostile villagers closing in, the spikes of a raised garden fork glinting, all of them staring with a shared certainty that, for her and Ollie to be standing there at that moment, some fundamental law of nature must have been violated.

The signal breaks up. In the silence Ollie's desperate cry repeats in her head. *I want to go home.* He must have spotted the woman in the grey apron with her hands outstretched – the intention to snatch Ollie away so clearly written in her eyes. They were sizing her up too. It's possible that, in the more remote villages back then, some still believed in witches – evil whores doing the devil's bidding. They sensed the natural order needed to be re-established and quickly.

'… told police we had covid symptoms and we were off to a test centre,' Tom this time. 'Doctored a lateral flow with cola to get a false positive.'

'Clever of you,' she tells him.

'Yeah, I read about kids doing it to get out of school.'

'Shit – there's a car right behind.' Panic in Beth's voice, 'I think someone's following us.'

Tom, 'Is it the police?'

'The car's not marked,' Beth says. 'Could be reporters.'

Remembering that sheer drop with its broken barrier, Lana raises her voice, 'You need to stay calm. Concentrate on the road.'

Tom says, 'Ironic coming from you…'

Silence. They've gone.

Then the line crackles. She lets out her breath. The connection's clearer. 'Put Ollie on,' Beth demands, like it's that easy.

'Mummy wants to talk to you, sweetie.' His expression

is still worryingly blank. 'Just say something into the phone, sweetheart. Anything.'

Ollie moves but only to shake his head. She holds the handset closer to his ear. Over the sound of crashing gears and Tom's swearing, Beth asks, 'Are you okay, little man?'

Lana nods hoping it will encourage him to respond. In his other ear she whispers, 'Say yes.'

'Yes, Mummy.' His jaw clamps shut after that.

Beth between sobs and renewed static, 'Thank God. We've been so worried…' Lana moves the receiver away from his ear while his mother elaborates; hearing about their anguish isn't going to help.

What if they're right about reporters following them – they could be leading them straight here. She cuts in, 'Please don't do anything silly.'

The reply is inaudible.

Trapping the phone between her jaw and shoulder, she frees a hand to check Ollie's feet. As she feared, they're icy. Her own not much better. She's weakening, musters all her strength to say, 'I'm sorry, but I'm going to have to put the phone down now. We both need a drink and something to eat.'

Beth's still talking when she hangs up and moves closer to the Aga's warmth. When she tries to put Ollie down, his grip on her tightens. She leans against the range for its heat to permeate. One-handed, she finds milk, pours some into a saucepan spilling a few drops onto the hot plate where it sizzles and spits. The sweet stench of it fills her nostrils.

Lana does her best to ignore the phone though its incessant ringing gets inside her head. Eventually it stops and she can concentrate on heating the pan. 'What we need is some nice hot cocoa,' she tells Ollie. An effort to find the right tin and then a teaspoon to prise off the lid. 'This'll soon sort us out.' Banishing other thoughts, she concentrates on spooning powder into the milk along with some sugar – meant to be good for shock.

'Would you like to stir it, Ollie?' He's always loved doing that. She tilts him forward, tries to pass the spoon handle to him but he turns away, buries his head in her chest. If *she* can't begin to process what's happened, how could a baby make sense of it?

Once it's warm enough, she pours some into a sippy cup they'd left behind; finds a mug for herself and empties the rest into it. One at a time, she transfers their drinks to the kitchen table.

The grandfather clock dongs the half hour and Ollie jumps in fright. 'It's only that silly old tick-tock,' she says. 'We don't take any notice of him, do we?'

It's a comfort to lower herself into her usual chair with its cushion, to feel those solid arms surround them both. She shifts Ollie and his toy further into her lap then pulls the blanket around his legs and bare feet.

Her arms finally relieved of their burden; she gives a long sigh of relief.

Lana opens her eyes in panic, appalled she could have allowed herself to fall asleep. Ollie is still there in her lap, thank God. He's much warmer than before. Around her the room comes into sharp relief. It holds the same indefinable smell, the same crowded shelves; the usual view through the window of the cottages opposite. The clock's baritone tick continues undisturbed. When she looks up, she notices the familiar backbone of ancient beams, the usual cracks and marks along the blackened timbers.

Ollie could be asleep – given the angle, it's hard to tell. Taking care not to disturb him, she leans forward to wrap her hand around the mug then raise it to her lips. The cocoa has cooled and tastes sickly sweet as it slithers down her throat. She almost gags but, needing the energy, swallows more of it. Aware that Ollie is watching her, she says, 'Mmm, delicious.' Eyes wide, he's studying her face for clues to the truth. She picks up his little cup with its jolly dancing teddies and offers the spout to his lips. He shakes his head. 'Try some – it's yummy,' she tells him. Fighting nausea, she sets the example by draining her own cup and smacking her lips. 'Delicious. Everybody loves cocoa, don't they, Bobbity?'

Ollie frowns at his toy rabbit as if expecting him to answer; after all, in a world with no fixed rules, anything might be possible. Lana lifts his cup up and, this time, he grabs it with both hands, brings the spout to his lips and drinks.

Tyres crunch the gravel outside. They burst in, bitter cold air swirling through the kitchen before the wind slams the door shut again. Beth snatches him away from her with such force he loses his grip on the cup along with Bobbity and starts to wail. His mother hushes him. 'It's okay now; everything's okay now…' Stroking his head, Beth continues to rock him until his sobs peter out. Tom folds them both into a hug so tight it's a wonder that, at the centre, the baby still has room to breathe.

Relieved of duty, Lana stares at the opposite wall while time passes – seconds, possibly minutes – impossible to differentiate. They're talking, their mouths moving with urgency though she struggles to make sense of it.

She's roused by Tom – his arms encircle her. 'Mum, I have no words,' he says – though those are words, aren't they? Like a politician, or the pope, he bestows kisses on the top of her head, tearfully telling her, 'Thank you for keeping him safe,' as if she needed thanking for heaven's sake.

Somewhere outside, Poppy is barking and whining like she's possessed. Probably still trapped inside the car. If Lana could muster the strength, she'd get up and let her in the house.

Unless.

Fear congeals in her stomach. They've drawn attention to themselves, violated the agreement with the Guardians. She grips the chair arms. They've broken the agreed rules; there are bound to be consequences.

Though she's never been religious, she needs to do something to ward *him* off. Under her breath, Lana starts to recite the 23rd psalm. *The Lord is my shepherd; I shall not want…*

'Mum!' Tom's shaking her shoulders. 'Are you alright? Mum, you're not having some kind of stroke, are you?'

Beth is cooing, lost in the restoration of her son. Looking past her to the front window, Lana thinks she can see a shadow lurking there. *he leadeth me beside the still water.*

Tom's kneeling in front of her, stroking her hair, blocking her view with his head. 'Mum, it's alright. I know you've had an awful shock but, like you said yourself, you're both back safe and sound. No harm done.'

Wishful thinking. Up close, those same dark eyes gazing into hers. 'Everything's okay now, Mum.' His off-centre smile takes her back to when he was a boy. He says, 'We need to sit down together and figure this whole thing out.' Overhead a low plane rumbles like approaching thunder.

A sharp rap on the front door cuts through everything. No one moves. Outside, the dog has stopped barking. Lana presses on with more urgency, *He restoreth my soul...*

Chapter Seventeen

Tom

Their visitor could be a reporter. Or, worst-case scenario, the police are out there on the doorstep demanding answers. He should prioritise – set other concerns aside for now while he concentrates on extricating them from the immediate danger that they'll end up in serious trouble with the law for wasting police time. Having lied to them about the whole we're-off-to-get-a-covid-test thing, will they swallow any new story he comes up with? Not that one readily presents itself. He's fresh out of ideas.

The situation is certainly not helped by the fact that, having kept it together admirably until now, his mum appears to have lost it completely and is rocking back and forth in her chair, mumbling some sort of incantation like a woman possessed. He's experienced the disorientation caused by time travel but even so… Tom tries reassurance, even shaking her. Momentarily she stops only to start up again.

Beth's ministrations seem to have done the trick with Ollie – he's perked up at last. Stepping back from the others, Tom treads on something. He picks up his son's toy rabbit. Bobbi-ty's smart blue outfit is now covered in something brown that, thankfully, smells like chocolate.

Three determined raps on the door – the sound echoes through the house. Whoever it is, they're not going away. With every curtain pulled back, there's nowhere to hide. They're sitting ducks. Given the lack of options, it might be best to face whoever it is head on.

Beth digs him with her elbow. 'You'd better go and see who that is,' she says, as if it's likely to be the postman or some in-nocent door-to-door salesman – if they still exist and/or were ever likely to venture as far off the beaten track as Stoatsfield.

Clutching their son to her chest, she's staring at him like this is the natural division of labour and it's his job to sort this whole bloody mess out. He shakes his head. They're in deep shit – does she seriously imagine he can come up with an explanation that will make it all go away?

Three more raps. Louder this time.

If it's reporters out there, he'll tell them he has no comment to make and then shut the door in their faces. Although the danger is that he'll sound like a criminal. Doorstepping is part and parcel of their profession. Given how cold it is, they're likely to get fed up after a bit and bugger off.

If it's the police, it's more serious. He'll need to concoct some version of events that explains everything as some sort of elaborate misunderstanding. A farcical mix-up of various comings and goings. He doubts they'll see the funny side.

Alternatively, he could say his mother is a confused, essen-tially harmless, elderly woman, who for reasons only known to herself and showing extraordinary resourcefulness, had made off with her grandson in the middle of the night. At this precise moment she would easily convince them she's demented. No – he can't throw his own mother under a bus.

Given the scale of the search party, if he can't persuade the police to take a lenient approach, they could be facing criminal charges for a gross waste of police time and resources. A stark choice. He lays Bobbity down on the table. Horribly besmirched, two glassy eyes stare up at him expectantly.

More knocking – this time long and insistent. His mind still in flux, Tom bows to the inevitable and walks out into the hallway to face the unknown music.

Just as he's reaching to unlock the front door, his mum rushes out, grabs his arm and pulls him back towards the kitchen. 'No, don't answer it, Tom,' isn't exactly sotto voce.

On the other side of the door a dark shape is looming – a solid figure pixelated by the glass. Tom hears frantic scratching like some wild beast wants to enter.

They both jump when there's a clank and the letterbox is prised open. Part of a cleanshaven chin appears; a normal enough mouth fills the gaping hole in their defences. It falls into a smile. 'Open up, will you. I've come here to help.'

'Oh, good Lord…' Blanching, his mum's hands fly to her face. 'I'm not sure but I think it might be… No, it can't be.'

Tom grabs her shoulders. 'Can't be who, Mum? Tell me.'

'That voice… it does sound a lot like Matt.'

'Matt?' Tom narrows his eyes at her. 'As in Uncle Matt? As in my actual biological father?'

'Tis I – the very same,' the letterbox mouth announces.

'Instead of standing there repeating my name, could one of you please let me in before this daft old dog of yours licks me to death.' As if on cue, Poppy sets up a whine like a lost soul in desperate need of shelter.

The letterbox snaps back into place. His mum touches his arm, holds up a finger in a silent sign to give her a moment. Facing the hall mirror, she rakes back her hair and tries to pump it up at the back. He hears her inhale as she pulls back her shoulders then nods her assent.

A bitter wind blows through the house. Poppy rushes in ahead of their visitor, slobbering and jumping up despite her arthritis. Tail beating against every hard surface, the dog then runs back to the threshold where Uncle Matt hasn't moved. Giving him a throaty grumble, Poppy nudges at his leg with her snout as if he's a stray sheep to be rounded up and ushered inside where he belongs.

Framed like a photograph, Matt appears almost unchanged. A smirk plays on his still handsome face. As smartly dressed as Tom remembers, his dark hair is touched with small patches of silver around the temples. An identikit of a mature man at home in any era – someone they might choose to model knitwear at the back of the Sunday papers.

'Tom, my boy,' he says, 'look at you all grown up.' He extends a hand but then changes his mind and steps closer to pull him into a bear hug. His father – the mysterious figure he built so many elaborate fantasies around when he was growing up. Against his own, Matt's chest has none of the softness of old age.

They're now of a similar height – if anything Tom's a

fraction taller. A very minor victory. Enveloped in the man's forgotten smell, he wrestles with competing emotions. 'Yeah, time flies,' he says over his shoulder, lacing the words with irony. 'More so for some of us, it would seem.'

'My son,' he declares, more like a priest than a father. Tom feels a wave of resentment for the years this man has chosen to be absent from his life. What right has he now to claim their biological ties when he'd masqueraded as "Uncle Matt" – an occasional fleeting visitor his mum always described as "an old friend".

Pulling away, Matt gives him a long, close look, brown eyes as dark as his own. It occurs to Tom he could be reading his thoughts. To avoid such close scrutiny and mindful of the dramatic drop in temperature, he mutters 'excuse me' and shuffles behind his father to close the front door.

Matt's attention shifts to his mum who for some reason is retreating towards the kitchen as if in fear. 'Lana, my dear,' he says. 'How many years has it been now?' A strange question – he doubts Guardians experience time in the same way normal people do.

His mum gives Matt an appraising look, no doubt taking in the shiny brogues, creaseless grey trousers and the sort of gaberdine coat old movie stars used to favour. Handy, Tom imagines, if you need to nip back to that era at a moment's notice and yet simultaneously appear acceptable in the modern age.

Finally, his mum shakes her head. 'Look at you – you've hardly aged.' It sounds like an accusation. She bites her quivering lip – could be fighting back tears.

'It's so good to see you, Lana,' he says. 'I've missed you more than I can say.' He takes a step nearer, holds out both arms in an invitation for her to come forward and embrace him – the prodigal partner come home at long last.

Declining the invitation, her face settles into an expression that's far from favourable. 'So, you've finally deigned to grace us with your presence,' she spits. No subtly there then.

'I would have come sooner–'

'But…' She scoffs. 'Ah yes, I remember there was always a but.' Her eyes blaze at him. 'I suppose you've been too busy playing God or whatever it is your sort get up to.'

Matt purses his lips. '*My sort*?' He glances at Tom. 'I suppose the resentment you both feel is understandable. Although, as I recall at the time, Lana, you professed to understand why it was necessary, even desirable, for us to part.' Tom is close enough to witness the slight shudder that runs through him. 'In any case, I'm here now – and as I think we can all agree, on a matter of some urgency.'

The anger on his mum's face is replaced by an unfathomable look. Hearing a noise, he notices Beth standing at the kitchen door with Ollie in her arms.

'You must be Beth,' Matt says. 'I'm delighted to make your acquaintance.'

She gives him an uncertain smile.

'Whatever else you may think, we're undeniably family,' Matt says. 'And in times of trouble, families need to stick together.' A long, almost exasperated sigh. 'You spoke of *my sort*, Lana, and yet you must be aware that Tom here, and more especially,' he nods towards the baby, 'young Oliver, are also *my sort.* Welcome or otherwise, I've come here due to recent events. As you might imagine, none of it has gone unnoticed. The situation is potentially…'

When he looks at Ollie the baby stares back at him unafraid. Matt clears his throat. 'Not to put too fine a point on it, the situation could readily get out of hand if we don't contain the damage – and do so quickly.' His eyes range over them one at a time. 'Like it or not, I'm afraid you'll have to trust me.'

Chapter Eighteen

Beth

Now he's moved further into the light, the resemblance between them is obvious. Very like Tom around the eyes, Matt's quite good looking in a sort of black-and-white-film-star kind of way. Considering he's *one of them*, he seems friendly, charming even. Although Lana and Tom are both giving off such negative vibes, she could be mistaken about that.

Ollie's reaction, on the other hand, is to beam at him, wave both arms and then just stare speechless as if utterly transfixed. From her previous run in with the Guardians, Beth begins to suspect her son's been mesmerised. Could he literally be under his grandfather's spell?

Matt bends down, pulls a funny face at Ollie and is rewarded with a deep chuckle. He says, 'Much as I'd love a chance to get better acquainted with my little grandson here, we need to discuss more urgent matters.' Those dark eyes swivel to look directly at her – a piercing gaze that's utterly disconcerting. 'I suggest we do so out of the child's hearing.'

Beth stares back, is damned if she's going to be ordered

about by him. 'My son – our son – is staying right here.' She's not about to relinquish her hold on him.

'In that case, I'll make sure he's sound asleep.' As soon as the words are uttered, Olli's breathing slows, he gives a big yawn, stretches both arms and shuts his eyes.

'Now just hold on one second.' Tom squares up to his father. 'You can't go around doing things like that. Look at him – he's fast asleep. I demand you wake him up this minute.'

Matt is unmoved. 'I assure you it is in his best interest.' Talking over Tom's objections he says, 'Listen to me all of you; what I just did is nothing in comparison with what's likely to happen to the boy if we can't agree on a course of action here today.'

Lana steps forward and lays a hand on Tom's shoulder to silence him. 'Is Ollie in some kind of danger?'

Matt nods. 'I'm afraid he is.' Seeing their horrified reactions, his face softens. 'Look, why don't we all sit down for a start. Like I told you, I've come here to help.' He goes over to the table, pulls out a chair, sits on it and waits for them to do likewise. Beth's the first to comply. On her lap, Ollie is breathing steadily but doesn't stir.

Once they're all seated, Matt puts his hands on the table so they can see his open palms like a magician before a trick, trying to demonstrate he's hiding nothing. 'First things first – I'm pleased to say I've been able to successfully neutralise the situation in Marshy Bottom.' He looks around like he's expecting applause or something.

Tom frowns. 'What d'you mean neutralise?'

'The police officers and reporters gathered in the village

now believe they've gone there to search for illegal drugs hidden by a county lines gang. In fact, such a cache exists and is buried in woodland less than half a mile from the pub.'

'Nice one.' Tom's attempt at a high-five misses its target.

'Hang on a minute,' Beth says, 'You've actually gone and brainwashed all those people into believing they've gone there for an entirely different reason?'

Matt throws up those empty hands. 'A standard containment tactic.'

'But that means you're messing with people's brains again,' she says. 'That's unacceptable.'

'Needs must.' Matt's shrug is more of a twitch. 'As a bonus, once they find the drugs – and trust me they will – they'll be delighted, and of course one step closer to apprehending the vicious little gang who hid them there in the first place.'

Lana frowns. 'You're saying the police and everyone else… that the whole lot of them have now completely forgotten about Ollie and me being reported missing?' Matt nods at her, his smile broader, more confident.

'That's brilliant.' Tom beams at his father. 'Problem solved.'

'However.' When his face falls, Matt looks older, graver. 'I'm sure by now you've all worked out that the story Lana was reading with Ollie last night induced an unexpected reaction. It triggered a particularly lucid dream which, because of his remarkable abilities, caused him to violate the temporal laws and travel back in time approximately a hundred and ten years.' His face softens when he looks at Lana. 'Fortunately, since he was in your lap at the time, he wasn't alone.'

Beth tries to banish thoughts of the alternative – the

possibility of her son, by himself and lost in a place they could never reach him.

Matt clears his throat. 'The hostility you met with from the villagers was enough to induce a strong desire in Ollie to return to this own time and place. However, once you were back, he saw that the pub was surrounded by cars and strange people and became frightened; that fear drove him to hop to a different location in which he felt safer – this cottage.'

Lana says, 'That's exactly what happened. One minute we were back in your flat and I could see Tom and Beth out there on the village green; the next the two of us were here in this kitchen.'

Beth turns to her. 'I saw you both at the window. When you weren't in Ollie's room, I assumed it was just wishful thinking.'

'Wow – that's amazing,' Tom says. 'So, let's be clear, not only did Ollie manage to time travel there and back without any kind of portal, he also sort of *teleported* you both over here afterwards.' He seems thrilled – like he might already be considering the cool places they could travel to with Ollie's help.

Matt says, 'Before you get carried away, Tom, I must warn you that many of my fellow Guardians are horrified that a child of his young age was able to demonstrate such outstanding powers. Whilst recognising that Ollie has inherited these unusually strong abilities, they fear that if allowed free rein, he could potentially cause catastrophic temporal anomalies; unbridled alterations that might, to put it in layman's terms, ultimately threaten the stability of – well just about everything.'

Tom scoffs. 'What – they seriously think a toddler is capable of destabilising the universe? Why not the multiverse?'

He looks over at her for support. 'No offense, but that idea is totally preposterous. Totally over the top.' A throaty chuckle. 'Sounds to me like they could be just a teensy-weensy bit jealous of what Ollie can do – never mind his mind-blowing potential.'

'None of this is cause for jocularity.' Matt gives them each a long look. 'The collective view is that Ollie is currently too young to exercise control over his whims and thus poses a substantial threat.'

'Really?' Tom shakes his head. 'Look how small he is. How can our son be a threat to anything?'

'You've all met Ford,' Matt says. Beth nods along with the others. The mood instantly darkens. 'Ford argued most vociferously for the need to intervene. He now has an enthusiastic new enforcer who styles himself Nikolai – an over-privileged, utterly ruthless individual who nonetheless garnered some support for his suggestion that Ollie should undergo a procedure that would, at least in theory, neutralise certain parts of the child's brain.'

Above the collective outcry Beth wails, 'Oh my God – they want to lobotomise him.'

'Try to stay calm,' Matt says. 'I'm pleased to say it was a minority view against a greater number of ethical objections.' He attempts to lay a hand on her arm, but Beth shrugs him off, stands up to physically distance her sleeping son from the outrageous power he and his kind possess.

'Hear me out.' Matt leaps to his feet. 'Of course I argued forcefully, and I have to say persuasively, against the very idea of any such a barbaric intervention.'

'I should bloody well hope so,' Tom tells him. 'The sick bastards…'

'How could they even suggest doing something like that to a baby?' Beth demands.

'They're frightened.' Matt lets that sink in before lowering his voice to something smoother and more mellifluous. 'I'm confident I can persuade them to sanction an alternative course of action – which is to place Ollie out of harm's way until he's old enough to act with greater restraint and maturity.'

'Hang on just one fucking minute.' Tom gets up to close the gap between them. 'Are you suggesting we lock our son up?'

'Good Lord no.' Matt looks shocked.

'So, how in hell are we meant to keep him *out of harm's way*?' Beth asks.

'And this business of him reaching maturity,' Tom adds. 'Are we talking months? Years?'

'Hard to predict with any precision.' Matt rubs at his chin in the same way Tom does when he's thinking. 'Given the extraordinary rate of Ollie's physical and mental development and, with your help, it could be a year. Possibly longer.'

'So, the truth is you have no idea.' Beth's shakes her head. 'And in the meantime, where and how do you suggest we live?'

'Somewhere you're able to go about your lives in a quiet way,' Matt answers. 'I'm afraid you'll also need to block Ollie's access to further potential triggers.'

'You mean some place off-grid?' Tom asks. 'Are we talking Greenland? Tibet? The sodding North Pole?'

All eyes on him, Matt appears to think before he answers.

'Those locations are physically remote and yet, even in such places, Ollie could still encounter potentially disruptive narratives. Also, for all your sakes, some continuity of language and culture must be considered desirable.'

'Well then, Marshy Bottom isn't exactly a buzzing metropolis,' Beth says. 'Suppose we carry on living above the pub and get rid of our telly. Well, and most of our books and stuff like that.'

'But children need stories and books,' Lana argues. 'They're vitally important to their emotional development. Poor Ollie shouldn't miss out on all that.'

'True,' Beth says, 'but suppose he picks up one of those Horrible Histories books. Or, worse still, if it had dinosaurs.' She shudders. 'We'll just have to get rid of any book we think might set him off.'

'A good start.' Matt is like a headmaster talking to some particularly slow-witted students. 'However, bearing in mind Ollie's extraordinary ability to learn, you will need to ensure he has no access to computers, smartphones and so forth.'

Tom flings up his arms in protest. 'Now hold on just a second. I find it hard to believe we need to go quite that far.'

'No, Matt's right,' Beth says. 'We can't take the risk.'

Tom clutches his head. 'Okay so we need to flog the telly, but can't we simply hide our phones? Well, and my laptop and gaming console.'

'Given his proven abilities and increasing ingenuity, I doubt that would suffice.' Matt gives Tom a curious look. 'He's your son. The two of you must decide what sacrifices you're prepared to make to keep him safe.' Those dark eyes are on them both. 'I don't wish to frighten you, but if a similar incident were to occur…'

'The Guardians will intervene whether we like it or not,' Lana says.

Beth slaps the table, 'Then it's a no-brainer. We can use the landline when we need to make phone calls, and we get rid of all our electronic stuff. Don't you agree, Tom?'

Face like a sulky teenager, he says, 'It's a lot easier for you.'

She frowns at him. 'Oh, and why's that then?'

'Being without all those things is a lot harder for us digital natives.'

'You know we had television and radio back in the eighties.'

It takes Tom longer than she would have liked to say, 'If it's the only way to keep him safe, I guess we'll have to bite the bullet and do it.'

Chapter Nineteen

Ollie

Since *it* happened – the thing they don't like to talk about – everything's changed. He has to sleep in their bed now, which is hot with too many arms and legs in the way. They only go into the room that's meant to be his to get things.

He's not allowed into the bar downstairs where the customers are but through the window he watches them climb out of their cars before they go inside. Sometimes the children run about on the green, splashing in puddles or chasing each other, which looks fun.

Mummy says Daddy's lucky because he gets to talk to new people every day while she's stuck in the flat all the ruddy time and it's driving her mental.

The man who cooks the food has a motorbike, which makes a loud noise when he comes or goes. Ollie knows he's called Jake and he's a chef – not a cook – and likes to stand outside smoking even though Mummy says cigarettes are very bad for you. When he's cooking, Jake wears a white top and a blue apron. He has lots of drawings which are called tattoos on his arms and up his neck that don't wash off. If it's not raining, Jake stands outside by the bins sucking in smoke and staring at his mobile phone. Ollie can tell he's talking to his girlfriend Naomi, but he can't hear what they're saying.

Daddy still has his mobile phone, but now he keeps it hidden on the top of the bathroom cabinet where no one can see it. He's in the bathroom a lot. Always whispering.

The woman who helps Jake in the kitchen is called Lin. Ollie doesn't spot her very often. She's pretty with brown skin and curly black hair which is shaved off above her ear on one side. He tries to guess from the smell what Jake and Lin are cooking each day – which is hard because it mostly smells of frying onions.

The woman who cleans the bars downstairs is older and rounder. She's called Delores, which is a lovely name. Delores comes every morning except on Mondays. She's got bright red hair, which on sunny days looks like it's on fire. He's noticed the way she keeps jiggling the big bunch of keys inside her overall pocket. When she's finished cleaning downstairs, she carries her bucket and mops across the green and lets herself into one of the cottages. He's worked out the pattern, always knows which house she's heading to.

If it's raining outside, his mummy sighs a lot. She can't drive their car because she hasn't passed a test – which is something you must do to be allowed to drive. Without Daddy they can't go anywhere but around Marshy Bottom.

On the mornings when it's dry they walk over some of the fields and back again – which Mummy says is good for them both. She lets him walk on his own for a bit and then puts him in a carrier on her back when he gets tired. The sheep are fatter now because they have lambs in their bellies. Mummy says soon the lambs will be big enough to come out of a special place on the sheep-mummy and that's called being born. Some of the sheep have poo round their bums.

He likes it when they take bread outside to feed the ducks that live in the village but aren't pets because they don't belong to anyone. Once they have ducklings, they mustn't give them bread because it could swell up in the ducklings' throats and choke them. Most of the ducks are a sort called mallards, but the prettiest ones are a sort called Mandarins – which come from a long way away even though they're always out there with the others.

His mummy's promised that he can go and feed the ducks all by himself if it ever decides to stop flipping raining. Flipping isn't a naughty word so she can say it out loud.

The sky is lighter. Ollie checks the pond to see if rain is still making little circles on the water. It's not.

He finds her ironing. 'Mummy, the rain's stopped.'

'Halleluiah! God be praised,' she says in a loud voice. 'Would you ruddy Adam an' Eve it?' She checks out of the window to be sure. 'Look at that Ollie. You might not remember but that big yellow thing up in the sky is called the sun.'

'I know.'

'I know you know, Mr Serious Face.' She hands him a bag of bread which she says is *stale*. That means it's not nice for people to eat but is okay for birds and other animals because they have different digestive systems, and so it doesn't matter. The pieces she gives him seem exactly the same as the sort they can eat, except maybe they're a bit harder on the outside – though not nearly as hard as toast, which is perfectly fine for humans to eat.

He breaks it up inside the bag exactly like Mummy does so none of the crumbs can escape. Outside the tree branches are swaying a lot. He can tell it's still windy out there.

Ollie goes and fetches his quilted jacket – which is hung on the special hooks Daddy has put there so he can reach by himself. He puts on his wellies because of the rain.

Mummy's now stuffing dirty clothes into the washing machine so her voice echoes into it when she shouts, 'You're going to need –' Seeing him standing there behind her. 'Oh, I see you've thought of that already.' She shoves the washing into the machine and slams the door. Then she starts to do up his buttons even though she knows he can do it by himself. She says, 'We don't want you getting another ear infection, do we?' Before he can tell her he really liked that banana medicine, she pulls the hood up over his head. 'There we are. You're all set and good to go.'

Daddy comes out of the bathroom. Seeing him, he laughs. 'For goodness' sake, Beth, he's only going out to feed the ducks, not setting out on some artic expedition.'

'What's an *artic expedition*?'

Her smile drops and she looks at Daddy like she looks at him when he's done something naughty. 'The Arctic's a really, really cold and horrible place,' she says. 'Trust me, Ollie, you don't want to even think about going there.'

'Perish the thought,' Daddy adds.

'So anyway,' she says, 'You've got the bread and you're

wrapped up warm.' She pats his bottom. 'Off you go then, Mr Explorer. Oh, and remember not to give it all to that greedy drake – he's big enough already.' She smiles but her eyes don't. He can tell when she's worried because her voice has a different sound to it.

Daddy isn't. He chuckles. 'That drake's fat enough for the table. Reckon he'd be delicious with a few cherries swimming around him. We could put him on the menu.' This makes Mummy giggle and swipe at him with one of the dirty towels so Ollie knows that must have been one of his funnies.

Daddy comes down the stairs with him. He opens the outside door and says, 'Now remember you must always look both ways before you cross any road, even a tiny quiet one like this.' As if he might forget – which he never would, because a car could easily come along and squish him, and he'd be flat and dead like the bird that fell down Granny's chimney once.

Ollie's glad he has wellies on because the grass is muddy and slippery, and the ducks come running and slithering towards him quacking and making a fuss.

'Stop!' He points a finger at them the same way Mummy does. It works. 'You won't get any bread if you don't behave yourselves.' He holds the bag high so they can't snatch the food before he's ready. Their black eyes watch his every movement.

They go bonkers once he throws the first handful on the ground. Wings flapping, they scramble and scrabble, quack and push to get more than their fair share. They have to scoop it up with their bills – which are spoon-shaped on the end and not pointy like the beaks most other birds have.

Shaking the bag, he spreads the crumbs out, so the shy

ones can get the same chance as the others. When the bag's empty, he folds his arms to show there's no more.

A robin redbreast starts to hop about by his feet looking for his or her share of the crumbs. The ducks all carry on peering and poking at the mud for a bit before they realise they've eaten all of it and waddle off towards the pond he's not allowed to go anywhere near because he could fall into it and drown – which is when your mouth fills up with water so you can't breathe and then you choke and sink to the bottom and die.

Ducks and ducklings are safe on the water and never drown. They can mess about with their heads right under the surface for ages with their bums sticking up. Which looks very funny.

When he turns around, Mummy's standing on the green behind him. He can tell she's been there for ages watching him. She smiles, but he doesn't smile back.

A door bangs and then Delores comes towards them swinging her yellow bucket and carrying a mop-man with rope for hair. 'Morning,' she says, which is short for good morning – though *good* doesn't take very long to say.

'Morning,' Mummy answers.

'You're going to Briar Cottage today,' he shouts after her.

Delores stops walking and turns round. 'How in the blazes would you know that, young man?' Her curious eyes are on him. They're an odd colour somewhere between grey and green.

'Because it's Wednesday,' he tells her. 'Yesterday was Tuesday – when you go to River View – that one over there.

134

Tomorrow's Thursday, so you'll go to the one with the big tree – Honeysuckle Bank.'

'Goodness me you're a bright little spark and no mistake.' Her lipstick almost matches her red hair. She shakes her head. 'You've got a pint-sized Miss Marple on your hands there, Beth.'

'Yes well, Ollie's older than he looks,' Mummy says. She leans towards Delores and whispers, 'Tom might have told you about his medical condition…' Ollie can't hear the rest, but he knows she's fibbing.

Delores nods a lot. 'I didn't know. Tom never said a word.' Her face grows a bit sadder.

'Who's Miss Marple?'

She bends down and looks into his eyes. 'A very clever old woman off of the telly.'

'We don't have a telly.'

He can see Delores is shocked. 'Never mind,' she says. 'When you're a bit older you'll be able to read about her in books.' When she smiles, he notices her front teeth have a thin line of the red lipstick along one edge.

'What does the old lady do?'

'Solves mysteries. Ones other people can't. She lives in a village a bit like this one only a lot bigger and busier. Nobody really notices her, see, 'cos she's only this old lady. But Miss Marple she's got a lively mind and a keen eye and makes a note of everything that's going on around her.' She chuckles. 'In this village it wouldn't be a lot. Reckon you'd be hard pressed to make a decent story out of what happens around here.'

'Well, we mustn't keep you, Delores,' Mummy pulls on his arm. 'I'd better get Ollie here out of this bitter wind.'

'What's a keen eye?'

'Think I'll let your mum explain that one.' Red hair flying, Delores waves her mop. 'Be seeing you again, young man.'

Chapter Twenty

Tom

It's well past closing time when Pete, the pub owner, makes one of his unscheduled visits – his none-too-subtle way of checking up on everything and everyone. From various things Delores and Jake have let slip, Tom's worked out the previous manager's departure was due to the fact that he was on the fiddle.

'I'll take the evening shift – you get off home,' Pete tells him. 'Good to keep my hand in once in a while.' Tom 's pretty sure he'll spend most of the time checking stock levels against invoices.

'Well, if you're sure.' He's already halfway out the door.

'Tom. I didn't expect you back so soon.' Beth looks exhausted. Now he thinks about it, she has done for the last few weeks. He's not the only one who could do with a night off. 'Why don't you go and put your feet up?' he suggests.

'And do what exactly?' Beth sighs. 'What I wouldn't give sometimes to be able to slump on the sofa and watch crap on telly. Or read a book with an actual story.' She touches his arm.

'Why don't I make us something to eat while you keep him amused?'

Ollie is sitting on the floor clutching Bobbity. The expression on his face suggests he doubts his father is up to the job. It's a miserable day – cold and rainy and getting dark. He doesn't fancy kicking a ball around on the green.

Tom looks about the room hoping for inspiration. Kitchen knife in hand, Beth comes to the rescue. 'You could play one of the games your mum brought over the other day.'

'But they're all a bit simple for him.'

'Maybe simple is good sometimes,' she says.

They start with draughts. Tom sets out the board then gets Ollie to choose a side. He's hardly finished explaining the basic principles of the game before Ollie says, 'Okay, I get it,' sounding more like a disaffected adolescent than a toddler.

The game has hardly begun before it stalls. Each time one of them makes a move the other anticipates it. On this basic level at least, they can read each other's minds. 'I know why they call these bored games,' Ollie says. A pun. Quite a good one, in fact. Tom grins – his son might be human after all.

The smell of frying chicken is making him hungry. Beth seems to be making better progress with her chore than he with his.

'I know, why don't we play chess,' Tom says. He gets up to look for the box. They haven't played in quite a while. Not since Beth had admonished him with, 'Your son is still *a child* remember. Plenty of time for that sort of thing when he's older. Preferably much older.'

When she sees what he's carrying, Beth gives him a dirty look and shakes her head.

Ignoring the pawns, Ollie studies the other pieces one at a time, running his little fingers over them in the process of becoming re-acquainted.

Tom reminds him about the different moves each is permitted building up to the royal pair. 'The queen is the key piece in any game,' Tom says. 'To begin with at least, it's a good idea to protect your queen so she doesn't get taken by the other person.'

'Why?'

'Remember the king has limited mobility – he can only move one square in any direction unless of course it's already occupied. The queen, on the other hand, is brilliant – she can move any distance in any direction.' Tom puts her on the board to demonstrate.

Smiling up at him, Ollie says, 'She's clever – she can do anything.'

Walking past them with an armful of clean clothes, Beth says, 'Which is something you should always remember about us women.'

It's early and the two of them are alone in the main bar. Delores has a tendency to rabbit on, but since chatting to Ollie on the green, she's like a dog worrying away at a bone.

'He's a bright little spark that boy of yours.' Straightening up from the table she's polishing, she nods towards the ceiling as if heading a ball. 'Must be hard on him with no one to play with all day long. Like they say – only is lonely.'

Irritated, Tom reminds himself she's a good worker and he needs to remain civil. 'Yes well, fortunately, Beth's great at keeping him amused.' He pretends to be concentrating on emptying the day's float into the till drawer. Takings have dipped a lot though nothing out of the ordinary for the time of year. A bit of spring sunshine and people will soon venture further afield.

Out of the corner of his eye, he watches her rub away at a surface that's already shiny enough. 'Beth told me how your boy's older than he looks,' Delores says. 'Can't say's I've heard of such an illness before.'

'Ollie's not ill, I can assure you,' he tells her. They've had time to rehearse Beth's impromptu lie – have even given it a name. 'Custos Lucis is more what you might call *a condition*.' He hopes his lofty air will disguise the fact that he's spouting utter nonsense. 'An *extremely* rare one. Aspects of it even baffle the world expert – who's based at Johns Hopkins over in Baltimore.' A nice little touch he's quite proud of. 'Even Doctor, um…' He grabs a name from the shelf in front of him. '*Professor* Hennessy doesn't fully understand the condition because, like I said, it's so rare. In fact, when I say rare, I mean I very much doubt you'd find any mention of it if you were to do a Google search.'

'Is that so?' Rub rub. 'Still, he must find it a bit hard with no other kiddies in the village.' She takes a purposeful breather from her task. 'You know, when I was younger, there were proper families living here. Big ones despite the size of these houses. One by one they pretty much sold up to the highest bidder. Did very well out of it, I shouldn't wonder.' She sighs. 'Seeing's it keeps me in work, I s'pose I ought to be the last bugger to complain; but to me it seems daft them London folk are happy to pay me over the odds to clean their empty houses every week when they can hardly be bothered to visit. A few days at Christmas and Eastertime. Not that they're here much in the summer, come to that. Too busy flitting off abroad.' She makes abroad sound like Mordor.

He says, 'I suppose they need you to check everything's okay inside. Apart from keeping it clean, you keep an eye on their valuable investment.'

'Maybe, but I tell you this – I'd far sooner work here where I got me work cut out at times than go mopping an already clean floor for no blimmin' reason.' She shakes her head. 'Seems to me them cottages are a waste of good homes.' A sigh. 'But then, what do I know, eh?'

When he doesn't answer, she tackles the next table. 'Anyway, like I was saying, I reckon it does kiddies the world of good to run around with other little 'uns of their age. Bein' the youngest, our Josie was a different child altogether once she'd started nursery. Though it 'ent for long, I was glad to finally get a bit of time to meself. S'pect your Beth would welcome a break.' Having made her case, she rests her hands on her hips and waits for him to respond.

Tom slams shut the till drawer.

Delores hasn't budged. 'My lot went to The Funday School – the one up on the main road just outside Eastridge. You must have noticed it – can't miss it with them giant butterflies painted on the outside wall and strung up in the bushes.'

'I've passed it,' he concedes.

'Can't say's I've heard a bad word about the place – which is rare given how fussy some parents can be these days.'

'Yes well, for the time being at least, Ollie's more than content at home with his mother where he belongs.' He strides off towards the kitchen.

'Just so you know,' Delores calls after him, 'they're more than happy to take kiddies from two upwards.'

Chapter Twenty-One

Customers are sparse but it's still early. Thing might pick up. With time on his hands, Delores' words niggle away at Tom like she's still standing there in front of him. Putting aside the considerable additional danger it would pose, Ollie might welcome contact with other children. Unfortunately, it's likely they'd pretty soon sniff out just how different he is. His own experience of being an oddity amongst his peers would pale to insignificance by comparison.

Then there's Beth to consider. Used to city life, how can she be content here? A girl in her early twenties is entitled to a bit of fun; instead, she's marooned in a small flat in a dead village miles from anywhere. And with little chance to make friends of her own age. She wouldn't be human if she didn't regret the loss of her old life at times. Her acting career had only just begun when they met and now it's on hold for the foreseeable future. Foreseeable future – now there's a concept to reckon with. In Hyde Park before he left 1983 behind, Ford had outlined Beth's alternative life – the huge success she was destined to enjoy as Elizabeth Trevino. Lately she's looked anything but happy. Across her nose the band of freckles he's always loved has faded to almost nothing. A cold tide of guilt steals upon him. God, is it any wonder she smiles less often than she used to these days.

By lunchtime Tom is resolute – things have to change for everyone's sake. Exactly how isn't something he's figured out yet.

He's collecting empty glasses when he catches a glimpse of his son's familiar blue coat through the window. Beth won't be far away though he can't immediately see her. After a cold start, it's turned into a sunny day out there. He stops to watch Ollie and is heartened to see the simple delight on his little face as he darts around scattering food for those ever-squabbling ducks.

'We know Ollie's far beyond his years,' Beth is always reminding him. 'It's our job to make sure he has a proper childhood. A good foundation for when he's older.' She's right. The truth is they have no idea what their son is already capable of. Beth recently conceded the need to allow the boy a few token freedoms. 'The last thing we should do is make him feel like a prisoner in his own home.' The same could be said for both of them.

Watching him, he takes heart. Ollie could be any small child out there enjoying himself. In many ways the scene appears idyllic. Buds are bursting on the trees; daisies have spread out like a carpet beneath him. His appears to be a picture-perfect life – if you didn't know any better.

The door to Mr Tanner's cottage opens and the old man emerges with his walking frame. He shuffles down his path one hard-earned step at a time only to be thwarted by the new catch on his gate.

Next minute Ollie is over there and up on his tiptoes undoing it for him. He holds it open while the old man passes through. Tom looks on with pride as he skips alongside Mr Tanner freely chattering away. The most unlikely of companions, they progress in their contrasting ways towards one of the benches positioned on the sunnier side of the green. Having reached this modest goal, Mr Tanner slowly lowers himself down onto the seat. Emerging from Mr Tanner's house is a young woman he hasn't seen before. She's dressed in a blue carer's tunic with matching face mask. He sees her call out and wave before she marches over to the bench to wrap a plaid blanket around the old man's lower half. After a brief chat, she strides back into his cottage where presumably she will continue her chores.

Jake has come out of the kitchen to complain at length about the potatoes. He holds one under Tom's nose. 'They're all like this. How am I meant to make decent-looking chips with these?'

Tom sees his point. 'I'll change the menu,' he tells him. 'Cut out the bad bits. We'll offer them mash. Maybe pommes anna would go better with steak.'

When he looks again Ollie and Mr Tanner are sitting side-by-side on the bench. The old man appears to be doing most of the talking. He raises a feeble hand and points to various parts of the green. Ollie is open-mouthed and listening avidly to whatever tale he's telling. An elderly man, most likely he's reminiscing about how things were like back in his day.

His day. Holy shit.

Where's Beth – why hasn't she gone over there just in case?

145

Fear crawls through the hair on the back of his neck. Abandoning his duties, he weaves a hasty but polite path through incoming customers to the outside door. On the threshold, he pauses to survey the situation. A car pulls up in front of him, blocking his view. People pile out forcing him to step aside and dodge past them.

The green presents a peaceful scene. Past the phone box at the far end, the old man is still sitting in the sunshine though his eyes appear to be shut, but the space on the seat beside him is empty.

Trying not to jump to the worst conclusion, Tom sprints across the road. Hand shading his eyes, he scans the line of cottages, the grass, the pond and its surround. With growing desperation, the open fields and trees beyond. There's no sign of Ollie.

He casts a shadow over the old man and those pale watery eyes open. 'Hello again, Mr Tanner,' Tom says as casually as he can. He sits down next to him. Though his pulse is racing, he masters his breathing. 'I happened to see you talking to my son a few minutes ago.'

'Aye.' A gummy smile. 'Nice little young'un you got there. Very helpful. Polite too – not like some these days.'

'Ollie – my son – he really does enjoy a good story.' Tom forces a smile. 'Can you remember what you were talking to him about?'

'Course I can.' He squints at Tom. 'I may be old but I 'ent senile – least ways not yet. I was telling him how, in the old days, they used to hold a fair on this green every Easter. After a long hard winter, everybody in the village looked forward to it.'

'I bet.' He keeps his voice calm. 'This might sound like a really strange question, but did you mention a particular year?'

Narrowing his eyes, the old man considers. 'I was tellin' him how in them days most people round here kept a few pigs in the back garden to help see 'em through the winter. Whatever our parents said, us kids couldn't help but get fond of them mischievous little piglets. And a course they soon got tame as you like. Didn't your little lad chuckle when I told him how our dad won first prize for the best piglet one year only for the little blighter to sprint off into the woods before anyone could catch him.' The old man's eyes sparkle. 'Our dad raised merry hell when they wouldn't give him the rosette. He'd already spent the prize money in the boozer so they couldn't take that back. On the quiet, us kids were delighted the little bugger had escaped the spit roast later that evening.' A fond smile. 'They never did find that piglet.'

'Great story.' Tom continues to glance around hoping Ollie will pop up but there's no sign of him. He leaves a beat before asking Mr Tanner, 'Do you remember what year it was when the piglet escaped?'

'Mmm. Now there's a question.' The old man scratches the white down on his chin. 'Our youngest, Jenny, was a babe in arms so I reckon I had to be about six or seven at the time.' The carer has come out of his house and is making her way towards them. The last thing Tom needs right now is a distraction.

'If you don't mind me asking, how old are you now, Mr Tanner?'

'I'm ninety-two – going on a hundred some days.'

How to narrow it down? 'This might seem an odd thing to

ask, Mr Tanner, but do you think that particular fair took place before or after the king's abdication?'

'Now that *is* a question.' Frowning, the old man shakes his head. 'You got me there, son. Like I said, I was only a youngster at the time; can't say's I paid much heed to that sort of thing. Got nothin' against our present queen, but as for the rest of that shower…'

The carer is almost upon them. 'Well, it's been nice talking to you.' Tom stands up. 'Better get back to work.' With a nod to the carer, he strides off towards the pub.

He's wasted crucial time talking to the old man while his tiny son is lost, defenceless and alone.

To ward off such thoughts, Tom shuts his eyes, tries to clear his mind and think logically. They share the same blood. His infant son clearly has the ability to open up his own time portal. Perhaps he's capable of doing the same thing. After all, Ollie must have inherited his extraordinary abilities. Hadn't he sensed on several occasions he was on the threshold of doing the same thing?

The pub is getting busy with the start of the lunchtime trade. Another car pulls into the drive. Any number of people might be watching him. The last thing he needs is witnesses to what he's about to attempt. The old red phone box lies directly in his path. Good enough for Superman. With no other option, he's got to try it.

Chapter Twenty-Two

Beth

Ambushed by the cooking smells being pumped out by the kitchen's extractor fan, she doesn't even make it to the outside steps before throwing up on a small patch of wasteland behind the bins. Revisited, her breakfast is not a pretty sight.

Breathless and sweating, Beth wipes her mouth with an old tissue from her pocket before she straightens up. At least she missed her dress – the first summery thing she's worn in a long while. Despite the sunshine, she pulls her thin cotton cardigan around her.

The car park is already quite full – Tom will be pleased. Hopefully no one saw her vomit – such a sight wouldn't do a lot for business. She kicks some decomposed leaves over the evidence. You wouldn't know it was there.

When she turns, her son is standing right behind her. The last she'd seen of him he'd been on the village green happily ensconced on a bench chatting to old Mr Tanner. 'Are you alright, Mummy?'

'I'll live.' Then seeing his anxious expression, 'Honestly I'm absolutely fine – it's nothing to worry about.' An understatement if ever there was one.

His little face is still serious. 'Something's just happened,' he says. 'Something really bad.'

'Is Mr Tanner alright?' Surely in so short a time the old man can't have taken a turn for the worse.

Ollie goes to speak but, before he can spit it out, Jake emerges from the kitchen. 'Don't mean to bother you, Beth, but the front bar's starting to fill up and there's no one to serve them. I've been looking everywhere for Tom, but he seems to have disappeared. Lin thinks she saw him out on the green a few minutes ago, but there's no sign of him now. I tried calling your flat but there was no answer.'

Has Tom had an accident? Is that what Ollie was about to tell her? Horrified, Beth stares at her son. 'Do you know where Daddy is?' His nod is solemn. Confessional. 'What's happened to him?' she demands. 'Tell me?'

Glancing at Jake, he says, 'I can't – it's a secret.'

'What d'you mean it's a secret?' She grabs his shoulders. 'Ollie – what's happened?'

''Spect the poor lad's a bit confused. He's only a little tot after all,' Jake reminds her. Not meeting her eye, he rubs away at something on his thumb. 'No worries. Why don't I get Lin to cover the bar for a bit 'till Tom shows up?' He nods at the Fiat. 'His car's still here so he can't have gone very far, can he?' Before she can respond, he heads back into the kitchen.

'So, what's this big secret?' she asks again.

'Daddy's disappeared.'

'Yes, I know that already. Jake told me.' Softening her face, she bends to his level. 'But you know where he is, don't you?'

Ollie nods vigorously. 'He went through the big red phone box.' It's unusual for him to make a mistake and say *through* instead of *in*. He grabs her hand. 'We have to follow him.'

'All three of us cram into that old phone box? Why would we want to do that? Is this his weird idea of a joke?'

Ollie pulls on her arm. 'We have to hurry.'

She stands her ground. 'I'm doing no such thing. Three people crammed into that thing is hardly going to make the Guinness Book of Records.'

Ollie's close to tears. 'Daddy won't be able to find us unless we go there.' A stronger pull this time. 'We have to. Pleeease, Mummy.'

Something about his urgency persuades her to follow him across the road – no sign of any casualties, thank God. It's a relief to see Mr Tanner on his feet and being slowly shepherded up his garden path by his carer.

She looks back at the pub sure she'll spot Tom but there's no sign of him. Before they reach the phone box, she can see it's empty. Just as well. Except Ollie's not deterred – not for a second. 'I tried before, but I couldn't open the door,' he tells her.

Playing along, she yanks it open with an effort. No wonder he struggled. 'See there's nobody inside. I expect Daddy got fed up with waiting for us. Let's hope he's gone back to the bar where he bloody well ought to be at this hour instead of mucking about out here.'

Before she can let go, Ollie steps inside. To humour him, she does the same and the heavy door closes on them both. 'Okay, you've got your wish, what now?'

He holds up his arms. 'We need to hold hands very tightly.'

His little palms are unusually sweaty. Glass already steaming up around them, the stale air is beginning to turn her stomach.

'It's not working.' He frowns. 'I think we need to close our eyes. You have to do it too, Mummy.'

'Are we meant to make a wish or something?'

'Shhh! No talking. I need to concentrate.' She's surprised he's familiar with a word like concentrate.

'You haven't shut them yet,' he says without opening his. How on earth could he tell? She does as she's told to placate him. About to rebel at how ridiculous it is for the two of them to be standing in an old phone box, she opens her eyes to find everything is as black as the darkest night.

When it comes, the light is blinding. So intense it forces her eyes shut again. When she opens them, Ollie is still there, his small hands gripping onto hers. She hears a pulse inside her head. No – it's outside. Drums. And now fiddles. A merry tune. And movement. Against the steamed-up windows, shadows pass by in a never-ending stream.

Head reeling, nausea rises in her throat once more. Without letting go of Ollie's hands, she leans against the glass for support. 'Are you okay, Mummy?' It takes a few more seconds for the worst of it to pass.

Freeing one hand, Beth wipes away a circle of condensation to discover the village green is swarming with people. Children are skipping and dancing to the music. Ollie is now swaying to the same beat, his cheeks rosy with heat and excitement. The air inside the phone box is stifling and stinks of the amassed cigarette butts under their feet.

Clearing a larger spy hole, she sees there are trestle tables laid out in front of the pub. On them is a row of five wooden casks. A queue of people are lined up to be served. Not a face mask in sight, even amongst the elderly.

'Oh Ollie,' she wails, 'what have you gone and done?'

He looks up beaming in triumph. 'It's alright, Mummy,' he says, 'Don't worry, Daddy's here.'

'No, you're wrong Ollie.' Angry now, she lifts him up to tell him face-to-face. 'Daddy is back home where we belong; where the two of us should go right now.' Any minute someone could wrench the door open and reveal their presence to the crowd. 'Daddy's not here,' she tells him again.

Distracted, Ollie looks on past her, his smile slow and sure. 'He's just over there by the pond.'

Not bothering to look, she shakes her head. 'No Ollie. You're mistaken. Whoever that is, whoever you've spotted is not your daddy because right now he's back at home working in the pub.' In desperation she adds, 'In the proper year – the one we belong in, which is 2022. Most definitely not this one – whenever this time is.'

With him in her arms, it's hard to turn around because the space has narrowed. Curious, she notices that the phone is black with a round dial on the front. It's attached by the cord to a separate box with buttons marked A and B on it. There are shelves on either side holding directories. Controlling her voice, she says, 'Ollie, we need to go back to our own time and we need to do it now, d'you here me?'

'But Mummy–'

'No buts, d'you understand what I'm saying? None of

this is good. In fact, us being here could be dangerous. Who knows…' No, she'd better not scare him too much. 'You need to do whatever you just did to get us back home where we belong. This second. Are you listening to me, young man?'

Finger wavering, he points. 'But I can see Daddy over there.' He wipes at the glass to clear it. 'Look!'

So many people milling about it's hard to see through them to prove him wrong. 'It might look like…' The crowd momentarily parts giving her a clear line of sight to the pond and there he is – not some long-dead doppelganger but her Tom dressed in his black jeans and wearing the same blue shirt he had on when he left the flat earlier today.

Only this isn't today. God alone knows what year they've all ended up in.

Breathless, she cracks open the door to let in some fresh air. Nearby, someone is talking through a loud hailer – their deafening words indecipherable. Why and how did Tom get here ahead of them?

Grabbing Ollie's hand, she decides it's time to bloody well find out.

Chapter Twenty-Three

Ollie

'Don't you dare let go of my hand. Not for one second, d'you hear me?'

'Yes, Mummy,' he says. She's walking so fast his legs can't quite keep up. He pulls on her arm because he wants to dance to the music along with the other children. Mummy drags him on across the green. There's so much happening around him his head is dizzy with excitement. And there's bunting everywhere – just like in the story book, but with smaller triangles made up of different colours and patterns. He reads signs saying, Guess the Weight of the Lamb and Homemade Scrumpy and Three goes for 1d and … Finally, Mummy picks him up so she can go faster.

They reach the pond but Daddy's not there anymore. Ollie can tell he's nearby. The ducks have sensibly gone over to the tiny island in the middle away from the noise and excitement. He spots mallards and some white ones he doesn't know the name of. No Mandarins.

Mummy's heart is beating fast against his chest. She keeps

calling out, 'Tom! Tom where are you?' but doesn't get an answer back. People are turning to stare at her. A man with a spotty red cloth round his neck says, 'No need to get so worried, my dear. Chances are you'll find him wetting his whistle somewhere.'

The man he's with says, 'I shouldn't wonder at it. Hot day like this drives a man to drink.' They both laugh as if this is a clever joke. Why would his daddy wet a whistle?

Instead of a smile, Mummy shows them her angry face. She's not happy to be here. Ollie is thrilled to see all the people laughing and smiling and wearing pretty clothes, flowers on hats or stuck in their hair. For some reason none of the men have flowers in their hats but some have them on their jackets.

A group of excited girls run past, ribbons flying, daisy chains around their necks and wrists. The smaller boys have shorter trousers than the older ones – his must look odd to them.

It's a good job Mummy is wearing a flowery dress with a pale blue cardigan and not her jeans. She keeps on calling and calling for Daddy. Ollie can't see him, but he has spotted a man in a straw hat and pale suit who hasn't moved for some time and seems to be staring right at them. When they turn around, Straw-Hat man is still standing by the Win a Goldfish game. He doesn't look like someone who would want to win a goldfish.

Ollie stares back at him. The man doesn't look away – which is something most people do. Instead, he takes his hat off and runs his hand through his messy blond hair. It's a hot day, but Straw-Hat isn't carrying his jacket over his arm like the other men.

Ollie shivers. Before he can tell Mummy, someone calls out, 'Beth?' And then his daddy is pushing through the crowd towards them. 'Beth. Wow – you're here. And you've found Ollie.' He hugs them so hard it hurts. Ollie's glad when Daddy finally lets them go.

Standing still they're in the way. Mummy has stopped calling but people are still staring at them. 'Sorry folks.' Daddy pulls on her arm and together they walk over to some trees on the other side of the pond. Before he speaks, Daddy checks no one is near them. 'I can't believe it … I didn't expect to find *both* of you here.'

'We came here looking for you,' Mummy tells him. 'I mean, I wouldn't have known you were stupid enough to pull a stunt like this, but Ollie knew. He practically dragged me over to that phone box and–'

'Wait.' Daddy holds up a pointy finger. 'Hang on just a bloody minute – that's bullshit. I followed Ollie here not the other way around. He'd disappeared. Old man Tanner told me he'd been describing this fair to him, and I realised that, despite everything we've told him, Ollie must have wanted to see it for himself.'

She frowns. 'What made you think he'd disappeared?'

'Because I looked everywhere and couldn't find him. Or you, for that matter.'

'Not *everywhere*,' she says. 'I was only in the car park.'

'And I was hiding under the bench so you wouldn't see me,' Ollie tells them. Seeing their shocked faces, he starts to cry.

'It's okay, little man.' She lifts his chin. 'It's not your fault. Tell him Tom.'

'But I don't understand,' Daddy says, 'Why would you deliberately hide when you must have known I was frantically searching for you?'

'I wanted to leap out and make you jump.'

'Oh my God.' Daddy holds his head with both hands like he's in pain. 'I can't believe it. So, this was all a mistake – a stupid misunderstanding.'

'Hold on a minute,' Mummy says. 'I know how we got here but how did you manage it? Is that old phone box a time portal?'

'Not usually,' Tom says. 'I was so desperate to find Ollie, I thought if I concentrated incredibly hard, I might be able to open a portal and follow him here. Obviously it worked.'

'So,' Mummy says, 'that means you can both do the whole jumping-through- time trick.'

'Yes, I suppose we can,' Daddy says.

She makes an angry noise in her throat. 'There's no need to look so effing pleased with yourself, Tom Brookes. You of all people know this wasn't supposed to happen. Already we could be in danger.'

No one speaks. After a minute Mummy says, 'It won't have gone unnoticed. We could be really in the shit now.'

Daddy says, 'Look around you. We haven't caused any problems or disruption here. No one's paid more than a passing interest in us. Once we've gone, we won't have changed a thing.' Daddy rubs at his chin. 'And I suppose you could look at this another way.'

She glares at him. 'Which is?'

'Well, you could argue that, collectively, it gives us another string to our bow. I can follow Ollie through time – obviously only if it proves to be necessary. And, in extremis, he can also follow me.'

'Hmm.' Mummy looks around. 'So, what do we do now?'

'Can we watch the piglet competition before we go?' Ollie asks.

Daddy is about to say no but instead he chuckles. 'Shouldn't think that'll ruffle any feathers. Either way, might as well be hung for a sheep as a lamb.'

Mummy smiles at last. 'Or a hog for a piglet.'

Ollie checks. 'Does that mean yes?'

She nods. 'We'll stay just for a bit.'

A sign near them reads: 2 toffee apples for a ½ d. When he asks, Mummy tells him they're just ordinary apples covered in toffee and spiked with a stick. 'The toffee is really hard. Tricky to eat if you don't have many teeth yet. Besides, we have no money – at least none they would accept.'

People have gathered around a group of men dressed in white costumes with black hats. One man starts to play an instrument that goes in and out and then the other men dance and leap about and wave white cloths at each other. Ollie notices they have bells tied to their legs. 'Why are they doing that?' he asks.

'A very good question,' Daddy says. 'They're known as Morris dancers.' He nudges Mummy. 'I think it was Thomas Beecham who said, "You should try everything once except Morris dancing and incest".'

'What's incest?'

'Let's move along,' Mummy says.

Ollie is about to ask again when a man starts speaking through a cone-shaped thing that makes his voice sound really loud. 'Ladies and Gentlemen, the judging for the finest piglet in the village competition is about to commence.'

They follow the crowd to a line of men in waistcoats with their sleeves rolled up and a wriggling pink piglet wedged under one arm. Each man comes forward to place his piglet on a table where a pink-faced man in a straw hat and blue-striped apron examines it. Ollie feels sorry for the poor things. He hates the way they squeal when the pink-faced man grabs hold of their tail so they can't run away. Every piglet looks the same. Once he's examined them all, the man whispers something to a man in a brown suit who's standing next to him.

Brown suit man holds up his hand and everyone stops talking and waits. 'I'm delighted to announce that this year's winner is... Mr Edward Tanner.' The winner is delighted. Everyone stood around claps and says "well done". Then the chosen piglet is lifted high in the air making it squeal even louder. They put it in a pen made from lots of woven branches so that everyone can admire it.

Now the winner's been decided, people get bored and move on. The brown-suited man slaps Mr Tanner's daddy on the back and hands him a shiny coin and then they head off towards the pub. Ollie stares at the skinny boy standing next to the piglet's pen and looking sad. As far as Ollie can tell he looks nothing like the old Mr Tanner. Whoever he is, he's not very happy.

They go over to look down at the winning piglet, which is like the others except it's a bit fatter. 'I fear the worst,' Daddy says. Ollie can't see any way for the poor thing to escape.

He's about to say something when Daddy slides a foot under the bottom branch, lifting it up a just a bit. The piglet's twitching nose appears underneath the branch and then the rest of him squeezes out. Someone tries to grab him but he races away through the crowd. People are shouting and trying to catch him, but he dodges past hands and through legs and shoots up into the woods. Most people are laughing but some have serious faces. A group of men and boys run off into the trees calling after the piglet as if he would be stupid enough to come back like a lost dog.

'I'm guessing roast suckling pig is off the menu tonight,' Daddy says with a smirk.

When Ollie looks up, Hat-man is standing a few metres away openly staring at them. Daddy leans across. 'Yes, I've spotted him too,' he whispers. 'We should try to lose him before we go back to the phone box.'

They hurry through the crowd. 'There it is,' Daddy says, 'our very own Tardis, so to speak.'

'What's a Tardis?'

'We'll explain later.' Mummy looks around. 'There's too many people about. We need to wait until the right moment.'

He can't see Straw Hat Man but he can hear lots of shouting. A different piglet with two black spots on its back is running towards them. People are throwing themselves on the ground trying to catch it. 'I seem to have kicked off the great escape,' Daddy says. Squealing, the piglet dodges across the road with a noisy trail of men and children following behind.

'Perfect,' Mummy says. 'Quick, let's go.'

Chapter Twenty-Four

Lana

Lana's not expecting visitors. Hair wild and in her scruffy cleaning outfit, she's tempted not to answer the door. The knocker goes again. Meanwhile the dog's barking and turning circles in the hallway, creating such a racket it forces her hand. Still clutching a duster, she opens the door to find Matt on her doorstep. Poppy rushes past her to make an absurd fuss of him.

Dressed immaculately, he has her at a disadvantage once again. Like a priest giving a blessing, as soon as Matt raises a hand the dog instantly calms. 'Hope you're not planning to use the same trick on me,' she says. And then, with more edge, 'Two visits in one decade – I'm honoured.'

'It's good to see you too.' His ready smile disarms her. He takes off his fedora and smooths down his dark hair with that annoying small quota of grey. In the pale sunlight, his features seem to light up – larger than life. Unlike her own, his skin is smooth except for a few crinkles around his eyes. 'I think we should talk,' he says. 'Just the two of us this time.'

'Then in the great British tradition, I'll make us a pot of

tea.' She stands aside to let him in. 'That's if you've got time. I suppose that's an odd thing to say to someone who spends his life fliting about in different eras. I see you remember the way to the kitchen?'

Behind his back she puts down the dusty cloth to rake her hair into some sort of order. 'So, you couldn't keep away then,' she says. 'I tend to have that effect on men.'

Wisely perhaps, he doesn't respond. Poppy is still slobbering over him. When he strokes her head, the dog's eyes close with pure pleasure. Lana wishes her own emotions could be so easily quelled. Her hands get the jitters as she puts the kettle back onto the Aga's hotplate and lines up a couple of mugs. 'Tea okay?'

He nods. 'Fine by me.'

To the dog he says, 'Calm.' Instead of settling down, Poopy slinks off towards the back door to be let out. Knowing the weakness of her aging bladder when she gets over-excited, Lana goes to let her out into the back garden.

Returning to the kitchen, she half expects Matt to have disappeared but he's still there. In fact, he doesn't seem to have moved an inch. She hears him inhale. 'Believe me, I really wish this was merely a social call.'

'But it's not.' She swallows her disappointment.

'You haven't heard yet, but there's been a development.'

Legs trembling, she remembers to put two teabags in the pot. 'A worrying one?' She can guess the answer.

'Potentially.' He places his hat on the table then moves it further to one side until apparently satisfied with its position. Turning his head, he scans the chaos of her kitchen shelves. In the past, if she left him alone, he would subtly impose more order on her household. This need for precision was one of the first things she'd noticed about him – one of many differences that marked him out from other men. Matt always stood out – stood apart. Of course, she hadn't known at the start how spectacularly true that was. "Far too good looking" one of her friends had remarked at the time. But of course what distinguished him most was that he'd saved her life one terrible night during what they euphemistically called the Baby Blitz. The destruction of the building she'd been living in didn't feel especially minor. How could she not to fall for the handsome rescuer who emerged from the dust cloud to carry her to safety moments before the rest of the roof collapsed? March 1944 – a whole other lifetime ago. The everyday act of falling in love had led not only to an unplanned pregnancy, but an undreamt-of new life five decades in the future.

The kettle's whistle makes her jump. Off the heat, it dwindles to nothing leaving a heavy silence. While she pours water into the pot, he comes over to stand beside her. 'You're right.' His voice is gentle, seductive. 'Although sometimes it only seems like yesterday.'

'Better leave it to brew,' she says, backing away to a distance where she can more easily control herself. 'We both know you can't stay long, so you might as well get straight to it and tell me why you've come.'

He clears his throat. 'Because, despite my earlier warnings, Tom, Beth and Ollie attended a spring fair being held on the village green in–'

'That hardly sounds serious.'

'It wouldn't be but for the fact that this particular fair occurred in April 1936.'

'Christ almighty!'

'Exactly.' He shakes his head ruefully. 'Although the saving grace this time is that it occurred due to an unfortunate misunderstanding. Tom imagined Ollie had travelled to the fair and went there to bring him back. Aware of his father's absence, Ollie subsequently set off with his mother after Tom.' A twitch of a smile. 'Farcical in some ways, but still a serious breach of the bargain we struck.'

Robbed of speech, Lana finds she needs to sit down.

'I have to say Tom surprised everyone. We hadn't thought him capable of creating a portal. The power of a father's love, I suppose. I'm inordinately proud of him.'

Matt looks at her like he's guessed what she's thinking, then he looks away. 'Needless to say, the opening of two unscheduled portals brought the situation to the highest attention.' He grimaces. 'Whilst they were at this fair, they were shadowed by Nikolai – Ford's current attack dog. Rather predictably, his subsequent recommendation is for immediate and coercive intervention in order to avoid any future reoccurrences. I pointed out that, this time, they all returned relatively promptly, and the consequences were limited. Admittedly, they were instrumental in the introduction and then proliferation of a colony of escaped domestic pigs. These were soon hunted to extinction by hungry villagers. I of course argued that these were extenuating circumstances and, of course, stressed Ollie's enormous potential should he learn to fully control his actions.'

'His potential for what exactly?' She can't contain her

anger. 'I certainly wouldn't wish my grandson to lead a kind of half-life unable to make any kind of commitments to people and be forever estranged from those he loves.'

'Like me, you mean.'

She looks straight into those dark eyes. 'If the cap fits.'

Looking rattled, Matt spins round on his heels. 'There was general acknowledgement that Ollie is beginning to show encouraging signs of self-restraint. I'm relieved to say any further intervention has been ruled out for the time being. But only because of the boy's future promise.'

He finally sits down next to her. When he reaches out, she lets him take her hand. His skin is too smooth against hers. 'The matter is settled for now, but I fear I've made some enemies today.'

She reads the concern in his eyes. 'You mean Ford,' she says. 'Him and this Nikolai chap.'

He smirks. 'He'd hate to be called a chap.'

'But you're worried the two of them could still intervene?'

He gently rubs her palm with his thumb. 'No. They know better than to go against what's been decided.'

'But?'

'Like conspirators, Ford and Nikolai shroud their thoughts far too often for my liking. History repeatedly teaches us that where there's a ruthless will, anything is possible.'

His grin doesn't fool her for a second. 'But I'm probably overstating things.'

Under his caresses, her palm has become sweaty. 'It wasn't my intention to frighten you.'

His words have the opposite effect. She searches his eyes.

'Why did you come here to speak to me and not Tom and Beth?'

'Discretion – if you like. Currently a great deal of attention is focused on Tom and Ollie. Besides, the truth is I wanted to see you again. You may not believe me, but I care about you more than – well, more than anyone I've ever known.' He shakes his head. 'And yes, I know words are easy. I just want you to know how I feel – how I will always feel…'

'Now you're really frightening me,' she says. 'Tell me you're not in danger.'

He squeezes her hand once more before he lets it go. 'I doubt either of them would be stupid enough to risk harming me. At least not directly.'

Matt stands up so abruptly, the lilies she'd just bought slide off the table, glass shattering on impact.

The crash echoes on. Lana surveys the broken shards, sharp edges protruding above the spreading pool of water like traps for the unwary. 'Clumsy of me,' Matt says, 'I didn't foresee…' He continues to stare at the mess it's made.

'No big deal – it was only an old jar,' she tells him. 'Nothing more precious.'

'I'm so very sorry.' He bends down to pick up the lilies and hand them to her. 'And not just about the flowers. Take care of yourself, Lana.'

He retrieves his hat. 'I know they'll be anxious after this. You should tell Tom they're safe. For now.' Though he's smiling, his dark eyes remain sad. 'Tell him to be vigilant. And to trust the boy's instincts. And now I should go before I'm missed.'

She clutches her bedraggled bouquet. 'But you can't go,' she says. Instead of anything meaningful, she adds, 'You haven't drunk your tea yet.'

'Another time, perhaps.' He's already in the hallway.

'If there is one.' Lana doesn't follow, refuses to wave him off. 'Bye then,' she calls out like he's a normal departing visitor and not the love of her life. She hears the front door open and close behind him.

Chapter Twenty-Five

Beth

The heat rising from the kitchen below is less welcome now the weather's turned warmer. She's opened every window but the flat still feels stuffy. Tired of playing chess against himself, Ollie is cross-legged on the rug working on another elaborate Lego construction. It's hard to make out what he's building because her vision is currently blurred due to the onion she's chopping. 'Mummy,' he says, 'why do you and Daddy tell fibs about me?'

Eyes smarting, Beth wipes the tears away with the back of her hand. 'I'm sure we do no such thing.'

'But I heard you pretend I've got something Daddy called Custos Lucis – which I know he made up.'

Busted. She shuts her eyes hoping it will make the sting go away. 'Well now, that's only what you might call a *white lie*. And before you ask, that means a lie which is sort of allowed because it doesn't do anyone any harm.'

'Like when you told Granny you liked her new blouse.'

She laughs at that. 'Exactly. I didn't want to hurt her

feelings.' She puts down the knife. 'How do *you* know I don't like it?'

He goes quiet for a moment. 'I just do.'

Now the tears have gone she can see he's building what appears to be a townhouse on four floors. He's made a perfect little chimney pot which he carefully secures to the roof. He says, 'So, is telling people I've got a pretend illness a white lie?'

'We never said it was an illness – only a rare medical condition.' A lame excuse even to her own ears. After wiping her hands, she goes over to sit on the sofa next to him. 'The thing is, Ollie, you must have noticed you're able to say and do all sorts of things other children of your age can't – well, not yet anyway.'

There's a pause before he nods.

'We don't want people to see you as different. Not the same as them. And so that's why we thought it wouldn't do any harm to pretend you're a bit older than you look so that, to them, the things you say and do won't seem so peculiar... No, *peculiar* isn't the right word. I should have said *unusual*.'

He looks up frowning. 'But why don't you want them to think I'm unusual?'

'Well...' Those ever-questioning brown eyes demand a proper answer. 'Because we both think it's better that other people don't see you, you know, as a bit odd.' This isn't going well. 'We lied for your own good – because Daddy and I want you to make lots of friends and lead a normal life like everybody else.'

'But I don't have any friends.' His words hit her like a slap. He'd said it without a trace of self-pity, his attention already back on the Lego and yet Beth is mortified. How can he, or any of them, lead a normal life in this stage-set of a village so removed from the rest of the world?

Ollie is engrossed in what he's doing. Her thoughts in turmoil, Beth goes back to making the soup. In their desire not to break rules laid down by the Guardians, they've condemned him, and by extension all of them, to something close to house arrest. The truth is they've failed him.

She sets her jaw. 'It's a beautiful day,' she says. 'Why don't we have a picnic on the green?'

She sends him off to fetch the old rug from the sofa while she pours the soup into a flask and stuffs it into a backpack along with bread rolls, yoghurts, crisps and a bottle of fizzy elderflower. He comes back giggling, the rug a trailing cape.

Once they're outside, Ollie points and shouts, 'Look – there's Mr Tanner.'

The old man is ensconced on his favoured bench, thin white hair lit up like thistledown. Ollie waves but he doesn't wave back. 'I expect he's having one of his naps.'

The ground has dried out enough to spread a blanket in the shade of the old horse chestnut. It's such a relief to be out in the fresh air surrounded by birdsong. She can smell blossom and cut grass. Her Aunty Joan used to love picnicking in the park in Cheltenham. "Makes any food taste ten-times better" she'd say. Even now Beth still finds it hard to accept her aunty must be long dead.

The grass is awash with dandelions and daisies. Looking at the old phone box, Beth shudders remembering how the three of them had squeezed into it praying they'd return to the right time and place. Turned out they'd arrived only seconds after they'd left. Relieved, she'd staggered outside and thrown up on the grass in full view of the pub and any customer who might have been looking out of the window. Though disorientated, Tom had risen to the challenge and completed his lunchtime shift before collapsing. Physically at least, Ollie seemed unaffected this time. He's jabbered on about the fair, hasn't stopped asking for a pet piglet since.

Something tickles her leg. She's ready to slap at it when she discovers Ollie is trailing a blade of grass across her skin. 'Got you.' He giggles. When he tries it again, she bats him away, sips the soup which tastes good – better than it deserves to be.

Out of the corner of her eye she watches him pluck another blade of grass. Playing along, she pretends not to notice he's about to tickle her arm. 'You're watching,' he tells her, throwing it away disappointed.

She picks a few daisies, shows him how to thread them into a chain. Instead of copying, he starts ripping clumps of grass up by the roots. Sensing his mood, she decides not to complain about him getting his hands dirty while he's still eating. He stops abruptly. 'When are you going to tell Daddy?'

Unnerved, Beth puts on a smile. 'Tell Daddy what, little man?'

Against the sun, his long dark lashes come together like spider's legs. 'You know.'

Shaken, she's tempted to lie but can't. 'Daddy's always so tired when he finishes work.' Ollie studies her the way he increasingly does – like he can see right through her. 'Okay,' she concedes. 'As soon as I find the right moment.'

He purses his little lips exactly like his father does when not convinced. 'Hmm!' To distract him, she gets out the crisps.

Once he's finished eating, Ollie wants to run over and chat to Mr Tanner. A simple request any mother would readily agree to. 'Please?' Head on one side, he gives her a look that speaks volumes. If they continue to deny him any kind of freedom, isn't he more likely to take matters into his own hands? And besides, over the last few months they've both grown more confident he understands the importance of not following where the old man's reminiscences might lead, or anyone else's he might speak to.

'Go on then,' she says. 'But remember...' She leaves the rest unsaid.

'I promise,' he shouts back.

Not wanting him to feel spied on, Beth averts her gaze to the sky. Lots of fluffy white clouds float on a china blue background reminding her of Magritte. How long is it since she visited an art exhibition? Or made a trip to the theatre? Or the cinema? Activities now officially fully permitted are still off-limits to them.

In 1982 she'd worked as a part-time usher in an avant-garde theatre where she could see the latest plays for nothing. She'd seen some amazing productions. Repeated viewings had helped her to study some great actors at work. An exciting time.

Beth does her best to shrug her longing away. On a day like today, who would choose to be stuck indoors anyway? She lies back on the blanket, props her head on her hand to surreptitiously keep an eye on Ollie. Yes, he's still there chatting away to the old man. She follows the path of a butterfly – a rare orange and brown Duke of Burgundy Tom will wish he'd spotted. Beth tries to relax, to simply concentrate on the warm breeze on her skin, the earthy smell of the ground beneath her.

When is she going to tell Tom?

The sound of slamming draws her attention to a man unloading things from the boot of a shiny Range Rover parked outside Jasmine Cottage. With the warm weather, like St George's mushrooms, the absent owners of the cottages have started to pop up.

A few minutes later a fair-haired woman in a floral dress emerges from the front door of the cottage holding the hand of a small child wearing a sunhat. They're dressed for the part, straight out of the pages of a country lifestyle magazine. The child – a girl of about four – breaks loose to chase a duck which promptly takes off. Surprised, she watches it fly away. Seeking alternative amusement, the child heads over to Mr Tanner and Ollie.

The girl stops short of them, checks to be certain her mother isn't far away. Ollie's all smiles. He jumps down, runs over to chat to her. The next time Beth looks he's picking daisies and demonstrating how to make them into a chain. Even from a distance she can see his face is animated like it hasn't been in a long while. Sadly, in a few days this little girl will be off back to London or wherever she's sprung from. Worse still, poor old Mr Tanner may not be long for this world.

Beth looks around her. She ought to feel grateful not to be fleeing a war zone. Many people would envy their situation wanting for nothing and living in this picture-perfect place.

For many this would be enough but not for her and, more importantly, not for Ollie. His use of language and general understanding are developing at an astounding rate. Without more stimulation he's likely to get bored. How long before he rebels? They need to do better by him. What harm would it do if, for example, they took a short trip? While clearing away their picnic things, Beth vows to have a proper sit-down conversation with Tom as soon as he's finished his evening shift.

Chapter Twenty-Six

Ollie

Daddy nudges Mummy and says, 'We've got some exciting news to tell you.' Ollie gets ready to look surprised, which means opening his eyes and mouth wide and saying things like *wow!* and *amazing!*

Daddy holds his arms up like he's about to catch a ball. 'You, me and Mummy are going to take a trip together. We're going to London.'

Not what he was expecting. 'Do you mean London the capital of Great Britain?'

'The very same.' Daddy laughs. 'Did you know there are 28 other towns or cities in the world also called London – and in 13 different countries.'

'So, some countries must have more than one London.'

Daddy claps his hands. 'Clever boy. Ah, but I bet you didn't know there are 15 towns called London in America alone? Think of all the letters and parcels that must head off to the wrong London.'

Mummy makes an odd noise in her throat, but Ollie can

see she's not choking. 'Yes well, anyway,' Daddy says, 'Fun news, eh?'

'Is Granny coming with us?'

'Not this time,' Mummy says.

'It's all arranged,' Daddy says. 'I'm due some leave and Pete – the man who owns this pub – has agreed to hire a replacement manager for four days next week.' He rubs his hands together. 'I've just booked us an Airbnb. It looks really great.'

Mummy screws up her eyes. 'How exactly did you manage that, Tom?'

'Does it matter? The point is we're all set. Oh, and my old friend Davy – who's just moved to a new part of London – has invited us round to a barbecue party he's having.'

Mummy looks surprised. 'How did Davy contact you? I certainly don't remember him ringing here.'

'Must have been on the pub phone,' Daddy says too quickly, 'Anyway, back to the trip. Should be fun, eh?'

'A barbecue,' she says. 'Let's hope it doesn't get washed-out.'

'What does washed-out mean?'

Mummy says, 'When it rains a lot and it's too wet to light the barbecue so the food has to be cooked indoors while everybody stands outside shivering under a wobbly gazebo looking out on a wall of water.'

Daddy frowns at her. 'Which isn't going to happen because, according to the Met Office, it's going to be sunny all week. Scorchio – or so they reckon. Anyway, knowing Davy, he'll go ahead even if it's pissing down.'

Ollie gasps. 'You said pissing.'

'Yes, but Daddy meant to say pouring,' Mummy tells him.

'Unfortunate slip of the tongue,' Daddy says, 'I remember one time' – his eyeballs go up to the ceiling – 'We're all standing around under umbrellas, but Davy is determined he's going to light the barbecue. After an epic struggle, he finally gets it going but then he gets distracted by this girl and manages to incinerate the sausages in the time-honoured British tradition. All the food was ruined – I mean completely and utterly inedible. We had to order a takeaway.' He smiles. 'No one really cared. By then we were utterly rat–'

'Tom!' Mummy has her cross face on.

'I was going to say wrecked.'

Another fib. Ollie can't tell what colour this one is. 'Will we go on a train to London?'

'I hope so,' Mummy says. 'I doubt the Fiat will get us there and back without breaking down at least once.'

'Can we go to Pimlico where Granny's digs got hit by a German bomb?'

'I can't believe Granny told you about that.' Daddy looks over at Mummy and both of them shake their heads. 'Luckily she got out before the whole roof collapsed. I'm pretty sure there won't be anything left to see.'

'But...' Before he can ask, Daddy picks him up, lifts him above his head and spins him around and around until he's dizzy and might be sick.

'Careful – look out for that light fitting, Tom.'

Ollie feels wobbly when Daddy puts him down. 'Did you know Granny grew up in Paddington?' Daddy says. 'I'm not sure which street but it can't be very far from where our train gets in.'

'Did she?' Ollie pulls his surprised face.

At the train station they look for the number 4 because that's where the sign says they need to stand for the train. Some people are wearing face masks. Daddy says no one is made to anymore. 'You can choose. Beth and I are triple-vaxxed, so we won't be putting ours on unless it gets really busy.'

'Am I triple-vaxxed too?'

'No,' Mummy says. 'You're still too young to have it.'

'Triple means three of them, like triplets.' The train is coming. 'So, if I get this nasty illness, will I die?'

'Of course not.' She smiles. 'It's usually only a mild sort of thing in children.'

'Usually, but not always.'

Mummy points. 'Look – here it comes now.' Daddy lifts him up. He can see lights and then the driver in the front. 'The trains on this line run on electricity,' Daddy tells him. 'D'you see that funny-shaped thing sticking up on the roof – that's called a pantograph. It's designed to move up and down so it can pick up the electric charge running through that wire up above it. That's what powers the train.'

'For goodness' sake, he's only a toddler,' Mummy says, 'Don't keep filling his head with all that technical stuff. He needs to enjoy himself, stare out of the window dribbling or bouncing up and down on the seat while trying to poke a cheesy-puff into his ear.'

A woman is now standing next to them. Under her arm

she's has a tiny dog with a sparkly collar and a pink ribbon tied to the hair between its ears. Ollie wants to ask her why she's done that.

'Did you actually bring some cheesy-puffs?' Daddy asks.

'No, Tom – I was just, you know, making a point.'

'You must never stick things in your ears,' Ollie says. 'If they get stuck, you have to go to hospital and you might have to have an operation to get them out again.'

'You know sometimes it feels like I'm living with aliens.' Mummy gives a loud sigh. 'Anyway, let's just get on this effing train, shall we?'

'Is *effing* a rude word like fuck?' Ollie asks.

The woman with the tiny dog makes a clicking noise with her mouth. 'I've never heard such terrible language from such a small child.' She stares at Mummy and then Daddy. 'The two of you should be ashamed of yourselves teaching your baby words like that.'

Mummy's face grows red. She stares at the woman. 'I suggest you mind your own business, madam.'

The woman stares back. 'Ah, but it is my business. We all, as a society, have to put up with the anti-social, unruly thugs they grow into.'

'That's quite enough,' Daddy tells her. 'I can assure you, madam we're not about to take parental advice from someone who clearly infantilises her dog. I've got news for you – that thing under your arm is not a human being and never will be. It's a dog – an animal – and it needs to be allowed to behave like one.'

'Is there a problem here?' It's a big-bellied man in a tight black waistcoat with a whistle hanging from a yellow ribbon around his neck.

'Are you the Fat Controller?' Ollie asks.

The man opens his mouth really wide. Mummy pulls on Daddy's arm. 'Why don't we walk along to the next carriage?'

Chapter Twenty-Seven

Tom

Once they've settled into their seats, Beth says, 'So here we are again – you and me on a train together just like old times.'

Remembering, he smiles. 'Let's hope this journey is less eventful.' Finding her hand, he gives it a squeeze. 'And there's one big difference – this little scamp here.'

Standing on her lap, Ollie is already bobbing up and down making old-fashioned train noises. Tom ruffles his son's hair but gets no response. 'Shame there's no cheese puffs.'

Beth giggles. 'Perhaps they'll have some on the trolley.' And then, 'I'm joking of course – he'd do a much better job with Twiglets.'

'God forbid.' Tom laughs along though in truth he's distracted. Instinct makes him turn away to check out the other passengers in the carriage. It's much easier to scan faces now the majority are mask-less although, heads down, they're mostly already glued to their phones or laptops and don't look up.

Living without those devices has made him aware of the

hours he used to spend on the things – half the time on utter nonsense. He would feel smug if it weren't for the fact that his contraband phone is currently hidden at the bottom of his holdall where Beth's less likely to find it. He knows Ollie knows. So far, he's chosen not to tell his mother.

The train pulls out. Ollie shouts, 'Look Mummy, Daddy, we're moving,' drawing amused attention as he bounces up and down with an enthusiasm that touches Tom's heart. Seeing his son so transfixed by the passing countryside, his sense of guilt at having denied Ollie such experiences is assuaged by the sight of two young children further along the carriage who haven't once looked up from their separate screens. Scarcely drawing breath, their mother is chatting on her phone.

Tom's about to look away when he notices the ruffled blond hair of the person sitting with their back to the woman. A man he thinks, although he can only see a sliver of them. He's taken back to the fair, is sure the man in the straw hat so obviously trailing them was the ruthless young Guardian Matt told them about. Nikolai.

He touches Beth's arm. 'Just off to the loo.'

'What already?' She leans in and whispers, 'Quite the piss artist these days. Watch out for pentagrams.'

He smiles back. 'Won't be long.'

As he stands up Ollie says, 'That was definitely a white one.'

Very deliberately Tom walks past the suspect. Further up the carriage, he pretends to stumble and grabs one of the pink handles sticking out from the seatbacks like so many listening ears. In the process of balancing, his eyes stray over towards his mark. It isn't Nikolai, just a blonde-haired girl with strong features.

Mightily relieved, he continues in the direction of the toilets, studying the passengers especially the handful with their features hidden behind face masks. Their suspicious eyes follow him as he goes past. He's pretty sure he doesn't recognise anyone.

The tunnel is on them without warning. Heart pounding in his chest, Tom freezes. Surely not. The lights flicker though this time they stay on. He checks all the obvious signs – people's clothes, actions, official notices, what he can see through the window. To his enormous relief nothing's changed.

In the sanctuary of the toilet, he fights to regain his equilibrium, telling himself nothing's happened – he just needs to calm the fuck down. Tom knows the train they're on is an electric 800 built by Hitachi with diesel generators for non-electrified lines. It was only introduced in October 2017 so there's no way it could suddenly appear in the past without causing complete pandemonium.

It's all good.

And of course the two of them are exactly where he left them. Returning to his seat, his walk is as jaunty as a fast-moving train will allow. Nose pressed to the glass, Ollie is mesmerised by the wider world beyond. He sits down beside Beth who is pointing out a herd of llamas. They're actually alpacas, but for once he lets it go.

She gives him a curious look. 'Everything alright, Tom?'

'Course.' A baffled frown. 'Why wouldn't it be? I only went to the toilet.'

'You were gone so long I started wondering if you might have, you know, accidentally slipped back a few years while you were in there.' For some reason she seems amused by the idea.

'Don't even joke about it,' he tells her.

They reach Paddington only a couple of minutes behind time. Instead of diving down into the Underground network, Tom steers them through the crowd towards the outside entrance. 'It's a lovely day,' he says pointing at the blue sky. 'How do you fancy a stroll in Hyde Park?'

Beth looks uncertain. 'But what about our bags?'

'I'll carry them as long as you don't mind having Ollie on your back for a bit.'

'Okay,' she says. 'Hyde Park it is.'

'We can grab something to eat in one of the cafés by the Serpentine.'

'Considering what happened last time we were in Hyde Park are we really going to chance a walk down memory lane?'

Ollie swings her arm to get her attention. 'Is Memory Lane near here?'

'In a way it is,' Tom says. Despite his questions, neither of them elaborate.

After so long in a tiny country hamlet, Tom is quickly overwhelmed by the city. He's not alone – in his backpack carrier Ollie's head keeps swivelling from one side to the other, dribbling from his open mouth. A road drill starts up and he shrieks with fright, blocks his ears with both hands.

The roadworks seem to be never-ending. Snarled-up traffic crawls past it all. Through open windows resigned drivers tap their fingers to competing soundtracks. Dua Lipa restates her "New Rules"; Ed Sheeran duets with a rapper hoping some of his cool will rub off; Adele wails about a failed relationship. So much noise. It's a fine day but mostly Tom tastes diesel fumes.

Turning to Beth, he shouts above it, 'Is it good to be back on home turf?'

'Yes and no.' She looks around. 'Remember this isn't *my* London.'

At a crossing, she addresses Ollie over her shoulder, 'See that green flashing man up there?' He nods. 'That means it's safe for us to cross.' Reaching the pavement, she says, 'Now look back – see how the man's turned red. That means you mustn't cross. Remember that sweetheart – it's important.'

Ollie looks confused. 'But why did that man just run across the road when the light was red?'

'Because he's a stupid idiot who enjoys dicing with death,' Tom tells him. 'We would never do a dangerous thing like that, would we?'

'No.' Ollie shakes his head with vigour.

Once they're in the side streets it quietens down. They pass shops offering all manner of specialist foods and bargain goods. Shisha bars vie with independent cafés and gaudy chain restaurants. The next street's once-grand buildings have been converted to budget hotels. Amongst them stuccoed Victorian villas sport signboards offering Ensuite B'n'B Accommodation while proudly declaring they have No Vacancies. Rounding a corner, the buildings shrink a little in scale.

For a minute everything blurs together but he keeps walking.

'Tom wait – you're going the wrong way.' Beth grabs his arm to pull him back. 'Tom! Hyde Park's the other way. If you don't believe me, look at that sign over there. See?'

He puts down the bags, holds up a hand to plead for patience. 'Give me a minute; okay?' His head's reeling. 'I just need to think for a sec.'

'Why? You feeling dizzy or something? I mean, we could go back to one of those cafés and get some water.'

'No,' he tells her. 'I'm not ill. Nothing like that. I just know… Trust me – we need to go this way.'

'But why?' She forcibly turns him round to look at her. 'Tom – you're not making any sense.'

'Daddy's right,' Ollie pipes up.

Beth frowns. 'Right about what, sweetheart?'

'Granny's house – it's that way!' He points his finger in the same direction Tom feels compelled to go in.

'Wait!' Beth demands. 'What exactly is going on here? I mean how do you know that?'

Behind her back he shrugs his little shoulders. 'I just do.'

Tom leads the way while she reluctantly trails him down the next road and into a quiet street of tall, red-bricked houses. Everything seems familiar though Tom can't recall ever coming this way before.

Ollie starts to whine and wriggle, demanding to be put down. He's squirming and trying to climb out of the backpack. 'Stop that,' Beth says to no effect. As there's no passing traffic Tom lifts him out. As soon as he's set down on the pavement,

Ollie rushes off so fast they're forced to run to catch him up. Two-thirds of the way down the street he comes to a halt in front of one of the houses. 'Here,' he says. 'This one's Granny's.'

'You mustn't run off like that,' Beth says scooping him up. 'Not ever.'

Tom puts down the bags and straightens up. Number 23. Studying the façade, a creeping sensation steals up the back of his neck. He knows without a shadow of a doubt his mother once lived in this place. Though it makes no sense, he's convinced that right now she's at one of the windows on the second floor looking at them. When he checks, there's no one there.

If only there was a phone box. He has his mobile. Hiding it from Beth isn't nearly as important as checking his mum's safely at home where she belongs. After fishing around in his bag, he locates the phone and pulls it out.

'You've got to be kidding me,' Beth says. 'You kept your mobile.'

'Only for emergencies.' He holds it up like it's no big deal. 'I need to call Mum.'

Beth shakes her head. 'You're unbelievable. Literally.' Face like an assassin, she walks away, leaving him to make the call.

He holds his breath, releasing it only when his mum answers. 'Tom? I thought you were up in London.' He switches to speaker mode so Ollie can hear her.

'I am. We are. Thought I'd just, you know, give you a quick call, just to check everything's alright.'

'Yes, of course it is.' Then with suspicion, 'Why wouldn't it be?'

'No reason. None at all, in fact.'

'Tom?'

Beth has stopped twenty metres away. She's still giving him daggers.

'Guess what – we're all standing outside your old flat.'

'Really? Which one?'

'Number 23 something-or-other road. In Paddington.'

'Ah yes.' She goes quiet. 'I don't remember it all that well. They weren't happy times, Tom. I was only six when we moved away.' There's a change to her voice. 'How did you know?'

'Listen – I'd better go,' he says. 'See you when we get back.' Before she goes, he quickly adds, 'Love you.'

'I love you too.' The suspicion is back. 'What's this…'

'Bye, Mum.' He cuts her off.

Though it's a warm day, Ollie is shivering. Tom picks him up. 'Hey, no need to get upset, little man. You heard her yourself – she's absolutely fine.' The tremors run through his own chest. He knows they share the same lingering unease.

Beth comes back to have her say. Mouth open ready, she pauses and then a gasp escapes. Staring up at the house, 'Oh my God, I've only just noticed that chimney has three pots. And look at the steps, that funny-shaped overhang above the front door. I can't take it in.'

'Sorry?' Tom shakes her arm until she turns to face him. She leans over, hot breath in his ear, her voice barely audible, 'This house – it's identical to the one Ollie built out of Lego.'

Chapter Twenty-Eight

Ollie

'It's okay,' Daddy cuddles him, strokes the hair back from his face. 'Hey, everything's alright – no need to cry. You heard yourself she's absolutely fine; nothing bad has happened to her.' Ollie's eyes hurt and dribbles of snot keep running down his nose making him sniff.

Mummy holds a tissue in front of his face and says, 'Blow.' He does as he's told. 'Now calm down,' she says. 'This isn't Granny's house anymore. Which is fine because she's very, very happy living in Stoatsfield with Poppy.'

'But Mummy…'

'Uh-uh.' She waves her finger from side to side. 'Buts aren't allowed.' The finger points at the house. 'Can you see those buzzers by the door? Well, they're there because this house is divided into lots of flats and lots of *other* people live here now. D'you understand?'

He nods. 'Good. So, we're done here and Daddy's now going to lift you back into the carrier, aren't you, Tom?'

Daddy does as he's told.

'Are we sitting comfortably?' she says. 'Right, then let's go.' She starts to walk back towards the sign that said Hyde Park. 'Like any *normal* family we've been a bit upset, but now that's finished with and we're going to go off to the big park and sit by the lake and have something to eat. And maybe afterwards, if we behave really well and try to remember we're supposed to be on flaming holiday, we'll all have an ice cream to cool us down a bit.'

Her head swivels towards Daddy. 'Agreed Tom?'

'Agreed,' he says. 'Next stop Hyde Park – no deviations or hesitations allowed.'

In the park there are lots and lots of people everywhere – more people than Ollie's ever seen in his life before. Some are running, some walking, some sitting on benches or in special stripey chairs. 'You have to pay to sit in them,' Mummy says.

More people are out on the water in little blue boats. There are also lots of ducks. And swans. And geese and seagulls. And some other birds he's never seen before. 'A bit bigger than the pond on the green,' Mummy says.

'You shouldn't call it a pond if it's more than an acre,' Daddy says. 'The Serpentine's way bigger than that so it easily qualifies as a lake.'

'What's an acre?'

'An area of water or land that's roughly 4,000 square metres. Do you remember how long a metre is?'

'One of your big footsteps.'

'That's right. And a square metre is one of my big footsteps this way and then one that way.' Daddy steps forward and back like he's doing a dance. 'So just imagine 4,000 of those and you have an acre.'

'Or you can call it a big lake,' Mummy says.

'You can, but remember this one is really big,' Daddy says. 'Around 40 acres in total. And over five metres deep in places. It was created in 1730, so nearly 300 hundred years ago by…'

'Enough.' Mummy must have her angry face on again. 'Lift him out,' she tells Daddy. 'He can walk by himself now.'

'It's amazing how blue the water looks today,' she says. 'Almost Mediterranean blue. And no, don't ask any more questions for now, Ollie. Just take it all in. This light – it's so clear today. Feels like we've stepped into that painting by Seurat.'

'Bathers at Asnières,' Daddy says.

'That's the one. Doesn't it make you want to dip your toes in the water to cool off?'

'I don't think that's allowed in this section,' Daddy says. 'There's a place further along where you can swim. I think you need to book in advance though I'm not sure.'

'Finally, something you don't know,' Mummy opens her shoulder bag and gets out her sunglasses. Ollie doesn't like her wearing them because when he looks at her all he can see is his own face looking back at him.

'Don't know about you two but I'm ravenous,' Daddy says. 'Why don't we head for that café over there. I seem to remember they do pretty good wood-fired pizzas.'

'What does wood-fired mean?'

He can't see Mummy's eyes behind her dark glasses, but he hears her sigh.

The pizza tastes good and he's hungry. It hurts when he chews on one side of his mouth where his gum feels big and a bit hot. When he opens his mouth to show her, Mummy says, 'Looks like you'll soon have a new tooth.'

A funny squirrel comes right up to their feet looking for any food they might drop. It keeps twitching its tail. 'Bad luck, mate,' Daddy says. 'No picky-eaters on this table.' Which isn't true because Mummy's only eaten the crust on hers.

Some people stand up to leave and right away seagulls dive down and carry the food they've left off in their beaks. When it's all gone, they circle above the tables making strange noises like they're laughing, or they've just stepped on something sharp. Ollie finds seagulls big and scary. He doesn't like their beady eyes or their sharp yellow beaks always ready to grab things off you.

There are lots of other families sitting at the tables. Mummy wants them to be a *normal family*. Normal is one of those slippery words. The families he can see are all different so that doesn't help much.

Some children get up and begin to throw bits of the pizza they don't want towards the ducks. 'We've got to stop them,' Ollie says, 'or the ducklings might choke.'

Daddy catches him around the waist. He tries to break free but can't. Daddy whispers, 'Stop wriggling. I think we're being watched.' His eyes go sideways. 'Let's not draw any more attention to ourselves, eh?' When Ollie looks sideways, he sees a person in a white shirt with yellow hair sitting on a bench holding a newspaper up in front of their face.

Daddy stands up. 'We promised you an ice cream didn't

we, little man.' He holds his hand out to stop Mummy getting up. 'Why don't you stay here and finish your meal while we go and get them?'

'I'm not really in the mood for pizza,' she says.

'Then just sit here and people watch. Look after the bags until we get back.' He rubs his hands together. 'I fancy chocolate or maybe salted caramel if they've got it.

'Can I get you anything, Beth?' Daddy asks. 'How about a 99? Or a mint Magnum? Or a Cornetto? You name it – no expense spared for my girl.'

'No thanks.' She shakes her head. Ollie can't see her eyes, so he can't tell if she's happy or sad at being left behind. 'I'm not feeling hungry at the moment,' she says.

'Ah but then ice creams don't really count as food,' Daddy says. 'It slips down without you noticing.' She shakes her head again. 'Okay, well we won't be long. P'raps a few minutes peace and quiet will help restore your appetite.'

Daddy takes hold of his hand and they walk away like nothing is wrong. They pass some people kicking a football around. It runs away and Daddy kicks it back to one of them and he shouts, 'Cheers, man.'

When they're further away from the café, Daddy stops and points to some bright green birds twittering in the trees. 'Those are parrakeets,' he says. 'Foreign invaders. Shouldn't be here by rights, but they are.'

'I'm glad they're here,' Ollie says. 'They're really pretty.'

Daddy's looking sideways again. 'Yep, there he is. Thrown his newspaper away. Yep – now I've looked his way, our man is pretending to tie his shoelace. Rookie tactic I'd call that. If I turn around, can you tell me if he's still following?'

'He's walking this way,' Ollie tells him.

'Let's go,' Daddy says. And then, 'Do you recognise him? He's dressed a bit different today but I'm pretty sure it's the same man we saw at the fair on the green.' Ollie's not as sure.

'I thought they weren't going to trouble us so why is he here?' Daddy kneels down and says, 'Climb up on my back,' and then, 'Okay, hold on really tight now.'

Ollie likes piggybacks. Daddy starts to jog. After checking behind, he goes faster bumping him up and down until Ollie feels a bit sick and can taste pizza again. He runs right on past the ice cream hut. Ollie looks back and sees the yellow-haired man. He must be running fast too because he's right behind them. Frightened he might catch them up any minute, he shuts his eyes and makes a wish.

When he opens them again, they're back by the café. Delighted that it worked, Ollie laughs out loud.

'Hell's bells.' Breathing hard, Daddy spins him around. Around them people are walking and sitting and running just like they were before. 'Oh my God, Ollie – what the hell did you just do?'

He doesn't have an answer.

'Thank God we're in the shade here. I don't think anyone noticed. At least no one who's normal.'

'I got us away from that nasty man.'

'Yes, but now we're really in the shit.' Daddy lowers him to the ground. On his knees, he says, 'Listen Ollie, that was a very clever trick you just did. An amazing one in fact, but you really shouldn't have done it. And you must never do it again.'

'Why?'

'Because it's against their rules.'

He frowns. 'Whose rules?'

'I think you know.' Daddy stares at him so hard he thinks he might cry. 'It's okay, little man.' He messes up Ollie's hair with his hand. 'We'll talk about this later. Shall we go and find Mummy?'

Ollie nods. They walk around to the front of the café and when Mummy looks up she sees them and smiles. 'Goodness that was fast.' She takes off her sunglasses and stares at them. 'Where's the ice cream then?'

'Oh, there was a long queue,' Daddy tells her. 'So, you know, we changed our minds. Couldn't be arsed to wait.'

Ollie likes to see her laugh. He whispers in Daddy's ear, 'You must always protect your queen.'

Daddy whispers back, 'This isn't a game, Ollie. It's life.'

Chapter Twenty-Nine

Beth

Eleven o'clock in the morning and she's already exhausted. A nightmare woke Ollie up screaming and kicking in the small hours. He took ages to settle and was wide awake again at some ungodly hour. They'd cuddled and reassured him hoping he'd go back to sleep but no such luck.

For the last hour it's been mercifully quiet since Tom took him off to the little play park across the street. Their rental flat – or swanky apartment – is part of a converted warehouse building in Bermondsey. The whole area's gone through an amazing transformation from the empty, vandalised warehouses she remembers. It seems interior bare brick walls and "industrial-look" furnishings are now trendy – though according to Tom, no one says *trendy* these days.

Beth's trying to summon up some enthusiasm for this barbecue even though she won't know a soul and hasn't met Davy or any of Tom's London friends. Given a choice, she'd rather visit the new Globe theatre she's read about. New to her that is – apparently it opened 23 years ago.

She sighs at her mirror self. The flowery frock she's brought to wear today seems faded and frumpy under the judgemental glare of industrial-style lights. She's considering a change of outfit when the two of them rush in. If anything, Ollie seems more hyper than before. He bounces on the bed while Tom comes up behind her, his reflection smiling.

She says, 'Ollie still seems full of beans.'

'I guess everything is new to him.' Tom's smile seems a bit strained. When it drops, he looks worried. Apprehensive even.

She says, 'If this Davy bloke can afford to buy a big house in Tufnell Park, he must be doing alright for himself. What's he do for a living?'

'To be honest with you I'm not entirely sure.' Tom puts his arms around her waist and leans in to kiss the back of her neck. 'He started off buying and selling classic motorbikes then branched out a bit. Whenever I've tried to pin him down, he's vague – just talks about needing to have lots of irons in the fire.'

'Sounds like he's a bit of a Del Boy.'

'Maybe.' Tom chuckles. 'You know I never got into Fools and Horses. It was of its time – and certainly before mine.'

'Bullshit!'

'Bullshit!' Ollie echoes as he jumps up and down. 'Bullshit!'

'Mummy shouldn't have used that naughty word,' she says. 'Please stop repeating it.' He carries on whispering it under his breath.

She frowns at Tom. 'Don't give me all that *my time* nonsense. Lana told me you were actually conceived in 1944, so, by rights, you should be about 78.'

'Mirror mirror on the wall.' He turns his head this way and that. 'Not looking bad for my age, eh?' He goes quiet the way he does when he's calculating. Finally, he comes out with it. 'If we're playing that game, you were born in 1962 – so you ought to be 60. And, as you may well recall, Ollie was conceived in 1983, so he should be 39.'

'I'm not sure we should *play that game*.' She looks down at her dress. 'Although mostly I'm not sure about this outfit. D'you think jeans and a t-shirt would be more appropriate? Don't want to give the impression I'm trying too hard.'

'You'd look beautiful in a bin bag. They're going to love you whatever you're wearing.'

He kisses her neck absentmindedly. 'You know, at uni me and my mates started out as equals. Although, to be honest, academically I could have run rings around them. Had to rein it in so I didn't come across as a total geek. Since then, they've all done way better than me.' He gives a heavy sigh. 'Apart from seeing as much of the world as possible, I've never had a game plan. Now most of them have moved on to better things, while I'm working all hours in a pub that's miles from anywhere. For different reasons, I stick out like a sore thumb – or possibly a webbed one.'

'Come off it, you're not some freak.'

His smile drops. 'Ah but I am though, aren't I? Let's face it. No wonder you get heartily sick of me at times.'

'If going to this party isn't going to make either of us happy, perhaps we should give it a miss and do something else.'

'They're expecting us. Besides, Ollie's never been to a barbecue – he told me he's really looking forward to it.'

'Glad someone is,' she tells him.

The music is loud enough to piss off most of Davy's neighbours. A homemade sign on the side gate instructs them to *go through to the garden*. They follow where it leads. Ollie looks nervous, probably wishing he hadn't left his precious Bobbity behind.

The smell of cooking meat turns her stomach. Tom almost drops Ollie when they collide with a rampaging gaggle of children armed with pump-action water pistols spraying each other. Twenty or so adults are choosing to studiously ignore their collective offspring. Everyone's laughing and chatting – Beth's surprised they can hear each other over the pounding beat. It's a relief when someone turns down the volume. More so when they change the track. She recognises the intro to *Summer in the City* – one of her Aunty Joan's old favourites.

Most of the guests are a good ten years older than them and dressed in what they used to call *smart casual*. From the prominence of logos, she guesses smart in their eyes means designer-label, accessorised with expensive watches and jewellery. Once again Beth looks down at her dress in dismay.

Davy comes over to greet them sporting an unnatural tan and a sideways smirk. 'Hiya mate, glad you could make it.' An elaborate double-handed shake worthy of a freemason.

'Nice shirt,' Tom says. The Hawaiian pattern could induce a migraine if you looked at it for too long.

'Bought this on a trip to Miami back in January,' Davy pointedly reveals. 'First time it's been warm enough to wear it here.' He takes off his aviator sunglasses – a style that's apparently come round again. Exposed to the sunlight his eyes are a nondescript colour. She bristles at the patronising way he keeps slapping Tom's back, his lascivious tone when he says, 'So, this is Beth – good to finally meet you *in the flesh*, as it were.'

The music segues into *Billie Jean* – a new discovery for her. At home she'd be tempted to dance and sing along.

Davy holds his hand out to her. His thumb casually strokes her palm before he lets go and turns to Tom. 'Full marks for snagging this one, mate.' Pupils more dilated than they ought to be, Davy's breath is so laden with alcohol he might set himself alight if he breathed on that barbecue. 'You know,' he says, 'at one point when Tom here was all "Beth this" and "Beth that", I started to wonder if you were real or some avatar off a nerdy website he was getting his rocks off to.'

With an edge, she says. 'In the flesh, you're *exactly* what I was expecting.' Those thin irises fail to react. She looks away, threads her arm through Tom's and leans into his embrace.

Davy puts on a smile. 'So, who's this little rug-rat then?' Scowling, Ollie silently stares him out.

'Our son,' Tom says a note of pride in his voice. 'His name's Ollie.'

'My sprog's a few years older. Byron – his mother's choice. He's running around here somewhere; they tend to get a bit feral when they're hunting in a pack.'

Extravagantly waving at the latest arrival, Davy's already moving away. 'Grab a drink,' he instructs them. 'Mi casa su casa and all that. Help yourself to anything you fancy.'

Narrowly sidestepping a couple of battling soaked-to-the-skin kids, a dark-haired woman is making a beeline for them, her smile revealing teeth so perfect they could be false.

'Tom – good to see you again. Won't kiss you – we're still elbow-bumping,' she says proving the point. Her heavy dark eyebrows look like escapees from a child's dressing-up kit.

'This is Cherry,' Tom says. 'Davy's partner.'

'Davy's *wife*.' As proof she waves her left hand, and a cluster of diamonds catch the light. 'Oh, you didn't know?' Her face clouds, eyebrows forming a monobrow. 'Thanks to the bloody pandemic, we were forced to limit the guest list – ended up being just close friends and family.'

'Well congratulations.' Put in his place, Tom raises his glass along with a false smile.

She flashes a dazzling one back. 'You must be Beth.' Singling her out, Cherry grabs her by the elbow and forcibly steers her away. 'Let me introduce you to a few people.' Their hostess awkwardly propels her into a nearby circle. 'Everyone,' she announces silencing the group, 'This is Beth.'

'Hi Beth,' they chorus. The stocky silver-haired man nearest her makes a point of drawing out the word, 'He-llo.'

Wine of different shades is circulating courtesy of a couple of bored teenagers. Hard to resist under the circumstances. A few drinks would certainly make the next few hours more bearable.

Silver-Hair gestures towards the hedge. 'I live just next door.' He nods towards the enormous house towering over the hedge. And then, 'Tell me Beth, how do you know our hosts?'

'I don't,' she says. 'They're old friends of my partner.'

He grabs a glass of white from a passing tray replacing it with his empty one. 'And what do you do, Beth?' he asks like she needs to justify her existence.

Though tempted to answer, *Oh, I'm a full-time mum and an occasional time-traveller*, she says, 'I'm an actress.'

'How fascinating.' He raises one wiry eyebrow. 'Films or television?' Before she can reply, he adds, 'You're not in one of those ghastly soaps, are you?'

Beth shakes her head. 'I work in the theatre, mostly.' She hadn't meant to make it sound quite so lofty.

'Really? Are we talking RSC, West End…?'

'Mostly fringe productions,' she admits. 'So far, anyway.'

'Hmm.' A sigh. 'Still, you're young and very pretty – plenty of time I imagine.'

Insulted, Beth turns to the forty-something woman on her other side. Her jet-black hair has a single white strand near the front putting Beth in mind of Cruella de Vil. 'Are you a neighbour too?' Beth asks.

'Good Lord no. We live in Hampstead,' the woman says as if she ought to have guessed. 'My husband's a business associate of David's.' It takes Beth a moment to connect David with Davy.

Turns out Cruella is something called "an actuarial consultant". That topic doesn't get them very far.

'Did I hear you say earlier you're an actress?' Cruella demands.

'Yes, that's right, I am.'

The conversation runs along much the same lines as before. No, she hasn't been in a film or on TV. No, not the West End either. It concludes with Cruella saying, 'So do I gather you're what is euphemistically called *resting* at the moment?'

'I wouldn't describe looking after a toddler as restful,' Beth says though the woman's attention is caught by a new arrival.

The conversation moves on. 'If you ask me, we're letting in too many ruddy refugees,' Silver-hair opines to general agreement. Out of politeness and in no mood for an argument, Beth excuses herself.

Tom is talking to a couple of younger blokes over by the barbecue. Ollie clutches his leg as a stream of frolicking children race past.

Beth heads inside looking for the sanctuary and somewhere to pee. A helpful arrow with *Ladies* written above it points her up a glass and steel stairway. At the top another sign sends her along a walkway that looks down on a fancy, open-plan kitchen. She comes to another door with a crude, verging on pornographic, drawing of a woman pinned to it. Raucous laughter is coming from inside.

Instead of knocking, Beth crosses her legs and waits. Ten minutes later she finally bangs on the door. 'I'm really sorry, but I need a pee.' A few seconds later it swings open and a group of women emerge giggling and sniffing. One of them wipes away some tell-tale white residue from under her nose. Shocked, Beth's tempted to run ahead and block their path, point out the trail of human misery their apparently harmless social habit leaves across the globe, not to mention communities closer to home.

Instead, she lets it pass, lets them pass by to presumably re-join men who might well have been doing the same thing behind a different, appropriately marked door. Is this what passes for normal family life in 2022?

Once Beth's finished in the loo, she reluctantly heads back

to the garden. Tom has moved – he's now standing on his own near the gate like he's keen to make an exit. His hair is dripping. Ollie is still plastered to his now sodden leg. As soon as he spots her, he shouts, 'There's Mummy,' and runs to her. 'I'm all wet. They kept spraying me.'

Tom looks relieved to see her. 'I don't know most of these people,' he tells her. 'Davy's clearly moved on. Moved *up* in the world, as I expect he sees it.' He looks about him. 'Most of these people seem to be bankers or lawyers or hedge-fund managers.' He shrugs. 'Not much common ground to be had.'

She says, 'I think I can guess exactly how Davy fits in – what he brings to the party. Or should I say he *supplies*?'

'You could be right.' Tom drains the beer he's nursing and puts the bottle down. 'Mum always said he was dodgy.' A bitter smile. 'There's only one way this party is like the old days: he's let Jake and Max take charge of the barbecue. Predictably, they're now totally off their tits and incinerating everything.'

Ollie tugs on his trousers. 'You said *tits*, Daddy.'

'I did, didn't I? But you know *tits* isn't really a rude word. I mean there are bluetits, long-tailed tits, great tits, *really* great tits…'

Beth laughs out loud. 'You know if this is the alternative, I'm quite glad you're such a loser.'

'Thanks for the compliment.' Tom's expression turns serious. 'I was watching you earlier – you kept passing on the wine, which is most definitely not like you. It was stupid of me not to clock you've lost your appetite.' He looks into her eyes. 'I think there's something you need to tell me.'

'There is,' she says. Ollie gives her a look that says, *Finally.*

Chapter Thirty

Tom

'Not now. We'll talk when Ollie's asleep,' she promises. The three of them stroll back to the flat hand in hand – Ollie in the middle. When space allows, they swing him up in the air and down while he giggles and shrieks. Eventually the pavements become too narrow, and Tom is forced to let go of his hand.

Ollie's curious about almost everything, peering into shops and cafés, reading the signs in their windows out loud. His little finger points out landmarks, passing buses and taxis, unusual people and dogs; with each new observation there's a torrent of questions to be answered.

Tom hasn't told Beth about Ollie's transgression in the park the previous day. Any minute a Guardian might step out of a side alley and confront them. He rehearses their defence in his head. No one had even noticed. It was a momentary lapse due to unnecessary and unreasonable provocation by one of their own. Can Matt smooth things over again or might there be repercussions? Unpleasant consequences?

He's trying not to look over his shoulder every five minutes.

Thankfully, there's no obvious sign of either Ford or his blond acolyte. Is it good or bad that he hasn't spotted anyone else following them? The sun's shining but Beth is pale, worn out in a way someone her age really shouldn't be.

Once they're back in the flat he does his best to cheer her up. He makes beans on toast for them all though she hardly touches hers. When he offers to put Ollie to bed, she doesn't object but doesn't join in either. The warmth of the day has been quick to dissipate; high ceilings, brick walls and hard floors mean the heating struggles to warm the place up.

Freshly bathed, he brings Ollie through in his thickest pyjamas to say goodnight. She strokes his forehead, sweeps his hair to one side and kisses him goodnight. Her eyes are elsewhere. After all that walking, Ollie's worn out and drops off to sleep without a fuss.

Tom goes to the window and checks the street outside. It's well lit. Plenty of people are coming and going but he can't see anyone lurking under a streetlight or looking up at the building.

He makes tea, carries two mugs into the living room where Beth is reclining on the giant sofa, her legs wrapped in a tartan throw that momentarily puts him in mind of Mr Tanner. He puts her drink on the glass-topped table in front of her and she reaches for it, cupping her hands around the mug. 'I'm sorry,' she says. 'I know I should have told you a lot sooner.'

He sits down by her feet. 'I don't understand how it could have happened. I mean, I thought you were on the pill and everything.'

'I was.' She shakes her head, gives a bitter laugh. 'I certainly didn't plan it if that's what you're thinking.'

'So how…?'

'It might have been when I had that stomach bug after eating those mussels. I suppose the pills couldn't have been in my system for long enough to do their job properly.'

'But that was some time back.' He rubs his chin, the stubble catching on his fingers. 'So, you've known for quite a while.'

Beth pulls a cushion out from behind her and puts it on her lap before pulling her knees up to meet it. A defensive position. 'I didn't tell you because I needed time to think.' A loaded sigh. 'Though I love Ollie to bits, you must admit it's hard with him being – well the way he is. And on top of everything else, we have those evil fucking Guardians breathing down our necks waiting for Ollie to slip up so they have an excuse to do something terrible to his little brain.'

'Hold on. Not all Guardians are evil. Granted my father – I can't call him dad – he never showed up for me when I was growing up. And while he must be pretty ancient, he's weirdly youthful in appearance. Even so he did manage to persuade the others to hold off and give Ollie a chance.'

'You know as well as I do it's been horrendous trying to stop our son from disappearing off wherever he chooses at the drop of a hat. For ages we've had to live with this sodding sword of Damocles hanging over us night and day.'

Tom can't deny it.

She runs a hand across her stomach. 'What if this one turns out to be exactly the same?'

'A baby, you mean?'

Beth gives an ironic snort. 'Ollie's never been just a baby. If that's all he was, those bastards wouldn't consider him a threat to mankind, or whatever it is he's supposed to be endangering.'

'I think they're concerned he may accidentally create some sort of catastrophic interference in the space-time continuum that could destabilise the universe. Or possibly the multiverse.'

'Well, is that all?' She throws up her hands. 'What if this next baby comes out the same – or worse? Or better – whatever that means? How are *they* going to feel about the potential chaos our little dynamic duo would be capable of wreaking?'

'Ollie understands the risks now. Okay, I admit there's been the odd slip, but he's learnt to control his impulses.'

'Has he really?' She stares at him, her blue eyes demanding the truth. He wonders if she's aware of what happened only yesterday.

He says, 'Okay, not entirely, but he is getting there.'

'Possibly.' She shakes her head. 'You have no idea what it's been like stuck in that flat every day, not even being able to listen to the radio or turn on the bloody telly to watch daytime crap, or whatever, just to hear another adult's voice. I can't even read a book in case Ollie picks it up and it sets him off.'

'I know. I've tried to do what I can. It's been hard with my shifts and everything.'

'Okay, but remember, *you* get to talk to other people every single day. You can listen to their daft jokes and stories without having to worry that your son might be eavesdropping and about to launch himself off to a completely different time and place. I mean, if he needed to use some sort of time-machine to do it, we could lock it up. We can't lock up his brain.'

'I take your point.' Instantly, he regrets his choice of words – this isn't some theoretical debate. 'Believe me,' he says, 'I know this has been especially hard on you.'

'Hard doesn't even cover it.' She hangs her head; he suspects she might be crying. When he leans over to touch her shoulder, she doesn't respond.

Tom leaves it a minute or two. Finally, he breaks the silence. 'This pregnancy – it's come as a bit of a shock. You know I'll support you whatever you choose.'

'Thank you but I've already made up my mind.'

'I see.' He waits. At last, her fingers reach for his. 'In the end we're discussing our child – Ollie's little brother or sister.' She sniffs, wipes her nose with the back of her hand. 'I realise it's going to be tough, but against the odds he or she is here now.' Another long sigh. 'I've decided I'm going to keep it.' She squeezes his hand. 'Besides, if I had an abortion, I don't think I could face Ollie knowing what I'd done.'

He smiles at her. 'If you're sure, I promise I'll do more to help. If you change your mind and decide you can't face it after all, Ollie need never know.'

'That's where you're wrong.' She pulls a face. 'I'm afraid he already knows about the baby.'

'You told *him* before you told me?' Tom struggles to stay calm

'No, of course not.' She lays a hand on his arm. 'I didn't need to tell him. I'm pretty sure he can read our minds some of the time.'

Tom hopes she's wrong about that – he wouldn't want anyone, never mind his infant son, to know his every thought.

'I'm not sure he can do it all the time,' she says.

'Well, I suppose that's something.'

'At least not yet. But, you know, he can sense a lot of things

– way more than either of us might imagine.' She gives a thin smile. 'Matt said the Guardians recognise Ollie's extraordinary potential. I suppose we need to do the same.'

They're woken by Ollie thrashing around and screaming. 'Not again.' Beth fumbles for the bedside light switch. 'It's three in the morning.'

Tom blinks against the brightness. 'Shhh, it's okay, it's okay, little man,' he tells him. 'Just a bad dream. You're safe here with us.'

Coming to, Ollie calms down. Tom wraps his arms around him, but his eyes remain full of fear. Yawning he picks him up. 'I'll take him into the sitting room, Beth.' He strokes her hair. 'You go back to sleep.'

His little heart is racing as he carries him into the next room, puts him on the sofa and pulls the throw over him. He's shivering. The heating is off and it's surprisingly cold.

Tom goes back to the bedroom. In the half-light he manages to locate the clothes he'd worn at the party – his best trousers, a shirt and sweater. He slips his feet into the deck shoes he'd worn then grabs a jumper and some slippers for Ollie.

'This'll warm you up.' Seeing the jumper, Ollie lifts his arms up to help him. With an extra layer on, he's soon warmer and calmer. Tom warms some milk and gives it to him in his sippy cup.

'What was it this time, little man? Ghosts?' Ollie shakes his head. Tom tries again. 'Or was it ghoulies – though I think they're pretty much the same thing?' That gets another head shake. 'Then was it some sort of scaly giant lizard with a flicking tongue?' He squares his jaw, flicks his tongue in and out.

Ollie refuses to smile. Spot-lit by the overheads he looks so small and vulnerable. Tom puts his arms around him. 'Dreams aren't real, you know.' No response. 'Bad dreams can be really scary – do you want to tell me about them?'

Ollie mumbles something under his breath.

'What was that?'

'Mummy's not the queen,' Ollie says.

'Just as well.' Tom chuckles. 'Can't say I'm that keen on corgis and I most definitely don't fancy being some bag-carrying Prince Thomas.'

'No, Daddy, not like that.' His forehead falls into a frown. 'Before… when we were in the park… I thought Mummy was the queen.'

'I remember you saying. And do you remember I told you we weren't playing a game.'

'In chess you said we need to remember that the other person – your appo… appomment –'

'Opponent,' Tom supplies.

'That your op-po-nent wants to take your queen because she's the most important piece in the game.' His face crumples. 'I got it wrong.'

Tom lifts his little chin up. 'Hey, there's no need to look so upset–'

'Mummy's not the queen,' Ollie wails, 'Granny Lana is. And we need to help her.'

The room goes dark. At first, Tom thinks a fuse must have blown.

Chapter Thirty-One

Ollie

It's dark. Warm. Quiet – no cars, no people. The two of them are sitting on someone's wall. He looks along the houses, turns his head to check the ones behind. No lights on in any of them. A dog starts to bark. Further away another one joins in. Not the right street, but close. Which way? Daddy might know.

But Daddy's cross and making lots of groaning noise in his throat. 'Oh Christ… What the hell have you gone and done now?' When he tries to stand up, he goes wobbly in his legs and sits back down again. 'I thought you understood. I thought we'd made progress.' His voice gets quieter like it does when he's really angry. 'Ollie, you must stop doing this. It's not funny; it's not a clever trick to show off. It's serious and it's dangerous. Potentially *very* dangerous.'

The barking has stopped now. Daddy looks around. 'Streetlights are electric, not gas – narrows things down a bit time-wise.'

Ollie hears footsteps. Getting louder. A tall man in a hat

and a long dark coat is walking along the pavement towards them. His shadow looks like a giant's. Daddy whispers, 'What fresh hell is this?'

The man turns his head – eyes hidden in the shade of his hat – and nods. 'Goodnight.' He touches the front of his hat then lets it go again.

Daddy hasn't got a hat, but he says 'Goodnight' back.

'Hmm.' The man turns away and carries on walking to the end of the road and on round the corner.

'Shhh!' Daddy puts a finger over his mouth. They listen. The footsteps grow quieter and quieter until Ollie can't hear them anymore. 'We're like sitting ducks out here,' Daddy says.

'We're not ducks,' Ollie tells him.

Daddy says, 'That man could easily have been...' He stands up and then groans and dips his head back down for a bit. 'Shit – this time-travel stuff is seriously doing my head in.'

More footsteps. Two people this time – a man and a woman at the other end of the street. The man blows out clouds of smoke and says something Ollie can't quite hear. The woman looks up into the sky, opens her mouth and laughs out loud. She says, 'You're an old devil, Arthur Watts.'

They get closer and Daddy says 'Goodnight' to them but they only stare and don't answer.

When they've disappeared around the corner Daddy says, 'Bit of a stab in the dark but from the way they were dressed this could be the late twenties – the *nineteen* twenties that is.'

Ollie slips off the wall onto the pavement. Headlights shine in their faces as a car goes past, skinny big tyres splashing and spraying water. The roof of the car is folded back. There's a driver sitting in the front and two other men in the back with tall black hats on. The car doesn't stop but goes on past and the engine noise grows quieter and quieter until he can't hear it anymore.

Daddy says, 'Think that might have been a Crossley. British made classic. Rare these days. Made in Manchester.'

Once he stops thinking about the car, Daddy gets angry again. 'Look at us, look how we're dressed. We stick out like bloody beacons.' Daddy grabs his shoulders. 'We need to go back to where we belong right now Ollie. I'm pretty sure you'd rather be back at the flat with Mummy. Think how worried she'll be if she wakes up and finds us gone.'

'But we need to go to Granny's house,' Ollie tells him.

'No, we don't. In fact, we're not hanging around here for another second.' Feeling the tug, Ollie shuts his eyes, concentrates on keeping their feet on this pavement, in this time.

'You blocked me,' Daddy says. 'I felt it; like some sort of gravity weighing me down.' He holds both hands up like he's praying. 'Jesus! I assumed you'd be a hell of a lot older before you were stronger than me.'

After a minute, Daddy gives a big sigh like he does when he's trying not to show he's cross. 'What makes you think we need to go back to Granny's old house in the twenties? And what the hell is all this nonsense about saving the queen? Your mum's right, Ollie, I should never have taught you to play that sodding game. You're only a toddler after all. Teaching you chess strategies...' His head drops. 'I mean, what the bloody hell was I thinking?'

'We have to stay here,' Ollie says. 'To stop it.' He tries to find more words but can't.

'Stop what? Why did you bring us here, Ollie? What on earth are you so worried about? What d'you imagine is going happen?'

Too many questions. He starts to cry. 'I know it will,' he wails.

'Okay, let's both calm down. Everything's fine. No real harm done – not yet anyway.' Daddy rubs his back. 'Let's just sit back down for a second, shall we?' He does as he's told though the wall feels cold and hard against his bum.

'Now then,' Daddy says, 'as I understand it, you did this because you want us to go back to Granny's old house because you believe she's in some sort of danger.'

'She is.'

'Leaving that aside, if I'm right and this is the late twenties, Granny's just a small child at this moment in time. Okay, that's a mind-f… flipping weird idea. So anyway, am I right so far?'

Ollie nods. 'Lana's four, nearly five.'

'Four years old – wow!' Daddy's mouth makes a funny shape. 'So, let's consider the facts here, eh? We already know Granny is going to be okay because years later she's going to meet Matt, your grandfather, in 1944 when she's all grown up. Which means nothing really bad can possibly happen to little Lana. We already know how her life turns out after this. And we also know – because we spoke to her on the phone only yesterday, which was in our *proper* time in 2022 where we belong – that's she's perfectly fine and healthy and happy in Stoatsfield with Poppy. Are you following my reasoning here, Ollie?'

'But tomorrow…'

'Yes?'

'It's not the same. Something's changed.'

Daddy throws his hands up in the air. 'Logically, that makes no sense. Lana's future is determined. Any change is – well it's impossible.'

'*They* want to change it,' Ollie tells him.

'And who exactly are *they*?'

'The bad ones. The nasty ones.' He's not sure if he should say. 'The ones who hate Grandad Matt.'

Daddy's eyes go narrow. 'I don't know how you know about them, but I assume you're talking about Ford and his blond-haired attack dog.'

'He's not a dog. He's the man who chased us in the park yesterday.'

'I figured that. The dog thing – that was just a figure of speech. Anyway, even if they do hate Matt like you said, for them to interfere in the natural course of events – well it makes no sense. The Guardians are just that – they guard time and make sure there are no changes. As I understand it, that's their whole raison d'être.'

Ollie frowns. 'Those little black things Granny puts in cakes?'

'No. Raison d'être is French – it means the very reason they exist. It's their job to guard what happens.'

Ollie goes quiet. 'What if they didn't do their job?'

'Then I suppose things might get changed.' Daddy smiles. 'Like when I met your mother and you being born… Holy shit! There'd be no need for Guardians in the first place if everything that has happened is then fixed and immutable.'

217

'What does im…?'

'Never mind.' Daddy jumps down, spins around like he's going to do a dance. 'I remember now. I've been so stupid – so fucking dense. When your granny was four years old something terrible happened.'

'You said fucking.'

'And I shouldn't have but some things are a lot worse than using bad language.' He looks up and down the road. 'If you're right, we're not safe here. In fact, we need to go this minute.' He rubs at his face. 'Although we also need to look like everybody else, so we don't draw attention to ourselves like you and Granny on the village green that time.'

Ollie shudders. 'You need a hat,' he tells him.

'I agree. Sadly, I'm not likely to find one lying about.' Daddy looks around. 'Stay here for a second, little man.' He points his finger. 'I mean it. Don't you dare move a centimetre. Promise?'

'A centimetre is only tiny. I might need to scratch–'

'Just stay where you are. Can you do that?'

Ollie nods.

Daddy runs all the way to the end of the street, looks around and then runs back past him all the way to the other end and then comes back again. 'I think I know the way to Granny Lana's house,' he says panting a lot. 'Climb up on my back. Make sure you hold on tight.' He coughs. 'Not quite as much as that or you'll end up strangling me.'

Chapter Thirty-Two

Tom

They need to get off the street before they arouse any more suspicion. Darkness is an advantage. He has no idea what time it is. If only a convenient clock would ring out the hour. If he could pin down the date it might help. Sniffing, he thinks he can smell blossom. Flowering cherries? Lilacs maybe. Could be late May or early June. Ollie's instincts have brought them here at this particular point in time, which in turn suggests a defining moment in Lana's young life is looming large.

If he's going to see this through, he needs a plan. Tom looks around trying to take stock. What now? The big picture is too much to take in, better to concentrate on the next step. He'd spotted a narrow pathway behind the houses leading to a row of backyards.

Ollie is certainly a lot heavier than he used to be. Reaching the end of the street, he turns into it, follows the path along. They're heading roughly in the right direction as far as he can tell.

A clear sky – various constellations are visible with far less interference from light pollution. Away from the lights, the moon – waxing gibbous stage – is bright enough to show him the way forward. The path gives access to a row of small, brick-built outhouses. From his reading of Orwell, he guesses these serve as privies, coal stores and washhouses combined. The unmistakable smell of sewage confirms the first part. Next to each there's a small yard just big enough to dry clothes. The ground is pitted and rough; walking fast, he does his best to avoid the bigger puddles – fortunately the moon's reflection picks them out. He takes care to duck low under the empty washing lines strung out ready to garrot the unwary trespasser.

Ollie whispers in his ear, 'Someone's coming, Daddy.' Up ahead Tom sees a wondering light – a torch beam he guesses. Most likely someone heading for the privy. He hangs back in the shadows, gives the person – a man by their dimensions – time to go about his business. As soon as the privy door shuts, he hurries on past.

Tom is brought up sharp by a dark shape blocking their path. It moves from side to side as if getting ready to spring. He almost laughs out loud when he realises it's only a waistcoat pegged up by the shoulders on one of the washing lines. A fan of Peaky Blinders, he has a rough idea of what ordinary people wore in the twenties and waistcoats were definitely a thing. This one is designed for a bigger man. Even so, putting Ollie down, Tom takes off his sweater and tries it on over his shirt. It's roomy although probably not suspiciously so. Tom pegs his favourite jumper up in its place. 'A fair exchange isn't stealing,' he tells Ollie.

The drying clothes have been arranged in descending order of size and so he follows the line along as it zigzags. They must have an awful lot of kids. Besides a little girl's dress, there's a small pair of dark trousers and a pale shirt. 'Let's try these on you for size,' he whispers.

'But they're still wet.'

'Only a tiny bit damp. It's a warm night, they'll soon dry out.'

'But they don't belong to us. Taking other people's thing is naughty.'

Exasperated, Tom says, 'Look, you're still in your pyjamas for heaven's sake. First off, let's just see if these fit you, shall we?'

Ollie doesn't make the task any easier for him. Predictably, they're way too big. Tom rolls up the bottoms and then the sleeves. With his own jumper on top the outfit is passable.

His son looks at himself in disgust. 'Okay, not ideal,' Tom concedes, 'but you know lots of people wore hand-me-downs in those – these days.'

'They're itchy and smelly.'

'We could look for something else, but I have to warn you boys of your age often wore dresses in this era.' Ollie pulls a face. 'Does that mean you'd rather wear this?' He nods. 'Okay then.'

He pegs his son's pyjamas up in their place wondering how the owners will respond to these overnight swaps. Will it be put down to pranksters or some sort of mischievous night spirit?

The two of them will probably pass muster in a crowd if no one looks down at their footwear. Through a gap in the houses, Tom thinks he recognises a church spire from the other day.

If he's right, his mum's house is only a couple of streets away.

Eventually they're forced to leave the relative safety of the warren of back passages and enter the main streets. At last, they turn into one that looks familiar; with its tall brick houses, the street has altered very little since yesterday. Or was it the day before? Either day is now about a hundred years in the future. His mind reels when he tries to get his head around that idea. A faint glow on the skyline suggests dawn won't be long. In the semi-darkness, the houses seem to merge into one.

He puts Ollie down on the pavement. Hand in hand they walk towards what he hopes is his mother's childhood home. His son points an unwavering finger at one of the houses and declares, 'It's that one.'

Tom can't decide if it's a good or a bad thing that there are no lights on inside. 'Seeing's you're the one with the vision,' he says, 'what do you suggest we do now?'

There's a rustling sound in the hedge separating the gardens. Next second a black and white cat rushes out. Seconds later a ginger cat sets off in hot pursuit. The first cat turns to face its enemy and they begin to yowl and spit at each other. Soon the caterwauling quickly escalates to fever pitch. A light goes on two storeys up. He hears the scrape of a stiff sash window being lifted.

Tom pulls Ollie into the shadows. A face appears at the open window. The only feature he can make out with any certainty is a sizable moustache. The moustache seems to quiver and then the man shouts and waves his arms about. 'Get out of it you noisy little varmints,' is thankfully aimed at the fighting cats not at them. 'Shoo!' the man shouts. 'Go on – bugger off!'

During a lull in the fighting, a woman's voice floats out into the night. 'For goodness' sake, Harry, you're making more racket than them cats. Come away back to bed.'

Undeterred, the cats continue their rivalry – ears back, swipes and opportunist nips are accompanied by more wailing and squalling.

'Bugger off the pair of you.' The man lobs something which hits the bushes. The animals instantly take flight and run off into the back gardens.

The man's about to close the window when the woman says, 'Leave it open – we need some fresh air in here.' A minute later their light goes out.

Tom thinks back over the details his mother had supplied over the years. If Ollie's right, somewhere in the building he's looking at, his grandmother Celia Brookes is asleep alongside her four-year-old daughter Lana. At some point, possibly this very morning, Celia's sister Kathy is due to arrive. She's agreed to babysit young Lana while her mother catches the train to Bristol to surprise her husband – Able Seaman Reggie Brookes – when his ship docks. She must have imagined being there on the quay ready to throw herself into his open arms. Tom knows this touching reunion is destined never to take place.

'We can't possibly stay here in the street,' he tells Ollie. He opens the gate that leads through to the back garden hoping there might be somewhere they can shelter until daybreak. With the moon's aid he locates a shed. The door is unlocked.

'I'm not going in there.' Ollie folds his arms defiantly. 'Bad things happen in woodsheds.'

Tom recognises the silhouette of a couple of deckchairs. With some relief he sits down in one and pulls Ollie onto his lap. It's early; nothing is going to happen for the next few hours at least. They might as well settle down for a nap.

A good idea in theory but he can't relax, and neither can Ollie. All they can do is wait. Tom can only sit and ponder what might be about to happen to change the course of events. More to the point, if Ollie's right – and it certainly is a big if – what can he and his toddler son possibly do about it?

Chapter Thirty-Three

Ollie

The sky is turning from red to pink and yellow. Ollie remembers Mr Tanner tapping his nose and saying, 'Red sky in the morning – shepherd's warning'. A shepherd is a person who looks after sheep; he doesn't think there are many shepherds or sheep in London.

The birds in the garden are singing really loudly, which is called the dawn chorus. Mummy said it's their way of telling other birds to stay away from their bit of bush or their special tree. At home it sounds like the singing makes them happy; here they sound frightened. Perhaps they're scared of the noise – the cars going past, that man shouting out something over and over, the clippity-clop of horses' hooves and a low grumbly sort of noise which might be a train somewhere.

More lights are coming on in the back windows of Granny's house. A door slams and someone's baby starts to cry and now the drainpipes are all swishing and gurgling with water and other stuff. If someone was to look out of their window, they might wonder why a strange man is sleeping in one of the deckchairs in the garden.

The sky begins to turn blue with a few tiny white clouds that look like they're lined up and waiting. After a bit he goes over to examine Daddy's face. Both his eyes are shut and he's breathing with his mouth open. When he shakes his arm, Daddy only mumbles. He puts a finger on each side of Daddy's eyelid and lifts it open.

Daddy jumps up and hits his hand away at the same time. 'What the hell?' He blinks a bit and then rubs at his eye. 'Christ, I didn't mean to fall asleep.'

'We need to go,' Ollie tells him.

Daddy nods a lot. 'Yes, yes you're right.' He runs his fingers through his hair like a comb. Then he does up the buttons on his shirt and the nasty brown waistcoat that doesn't belong to him. 'Okay. What next?'

'We knock on the door and ask to speak to Mrs Celia Brookes.'

'No – I think that's far too direct. We mustn't interfere with events unless it's absolutely unavoidable.'

Daddy stares at the ground for a bit. 'I think we'd be better off finding a spot where we can watch the front door without looking like we're a couple of would-be thieves casing the joint.'

'What does–'

'Never mind that now. The point is, we don't want people to notice us, but we need to find out what's going on – if anything's changed like you believe it has.'

'It has.'

'We need to be certain before we act. Promise me you'll do that?'

'I promise. Cross my heart and hope to die.'

'Who taught you to say that?'

'Mr Tanner.'

'Hmm.' Daddy pulls a face. 'We need to find some sort of vantage point where we can watch who comes and goes from Granny's house. It's important we don't arouse suspicion. We need to blend in. Blending is all about acting like you're just going about your everyday life as normal. Nothing to see here, so to speak.'

Daddy opens the gate and bumps into a man in a white coat carrying lots of bottles. 'Watch it,' the man says. And then less grumpy, 'A fine morning for it.' He touches the black peak of his white hat.

'A fine morning indeed,' Daddy says touching his hair in place of a hat.

People must get up earlier in this time because there are lots of them everywhere. A horse is standing to one side of the road. It has round black things like slipped sunglasses attached to its head. Behind the horse there's a cart with lots more bottles piled up on it and a sign at the back in curly, old-fashioned writing. *E Evans & Sons* and then *fresh milk delivered daily to your doorstep*. Ollie wishes he could have a cup of warm milk with a spoonful of honey like Granny makes it.

'Shit! Shit!' Daddy says scraping his foot to get the horse poo he's stepped in off his shoe. 'Damned animal has no right to be here in central London.' The horse carries on staring straight ahead. 'At least I smell like a local now.' Daddy is hiding something inside his waistcoat.

There's a sound that might be a goose but instead is coming

from a funny-looking red car. 'Wow – that's an Armstrong Siddeley Coupé,' Daddy tells him. 'Great little car.' Ollie's reached the pavement on the other side, but Daddy is back where he was in the middle of road – which is something Mummy says you must never do. He's staring after the car. An angry bell rings and Daddy steps back to let a man on a bicycle go past. Another bicycle wizzes by him before he runs over to Ollie's side of the road. Ollie decides not to remind Daddy that it's safer to walk and not run when you cross a road.

'Morning.' A man in a flat hat goes past with a spotty black and white dog trotting next to him. His 'morning' wasn't for them but a woman in a long dark coat and black boots pushing a pram with enormous wheels. In his stolen shirt and trousers, Ollie's already warm. Most of the people are wearing heavy jackets and coats. They must like being hot.

The houses on this side of the street have steps leading from the pavement to another lot of doors and windows. Daddy grabs his hand. 'Quick, this way.' He stops halfway down the steps. 'This is perfect,' he says. 'We can keep watch on the house without being seen.'

He reaches inside his waistcoat and pulls out a bottle of milk. 'Breakfast,' he says taking off the shiny little cap. 'I'll let you go first.'

Ollie shakes his head. 'You stole it.'

'Yes, technically you're right. Under normal circumstances I wouldn't dream of doing such a thing. However, we have no money, and it looks like it's going to be a long hot day and we need to stay hydrated, or we won't be able to rescue Granny Lana. That milkman won't notice one bottle's gone missing.'

When Ollie takes a sip, the milk tastes odd because it isn't cold or hot but in between. And really creamy. A woman in a tight purple hat stares down at them as she goes past. Ollie stops drinking. 'She saw us. She'll tell the police about the milk.'

Daddy smirks. 'There's no way she could tell we didn't pay for it.'

Ollie looks at the windows below them. 'The people who live here will get really cross with us for being here.'

'Their curtains are still pulled. Looks to me like no one's up yet. Don't look so worried, little man. We're not doing any harm here.' Daddy lifts his hands up to show he's not worried. '*If* someone comes out and makes a fuss about us standing here, we'll move on. Until then, we stay where we are.' He smiles. 'Now give me some of that milk before it's all gone.' He takes a long drink. 'Delicious.' He wipes his mouth with the back of his hand. 'So far so good, eh?' He finishes the rest of the milk and then puts the empty bottle on the doorstep below. It looks odd next to two full bottles. Ollie says, 'Won't they wonder–'

'Forget everything else,' Daddy tells him. 'We need to concentrate now.'

He can't see the house so he climbs up a few steps until he can. Holding his waist, Daddy moves him over to one side. 'That's better; now we can both keep watch. You're Watson to my Sherlock, so to speak. Actually, forget I said that – just focus on that door there.'

They stare at Granny's house for ages; Ollie's not sure what they're waiting for. Finally, the front door opens and a man with a walking stick and a round black hat walks down the steps. He looks both ways, lights a cigarette and then strolls off swinging his stick. Ollie can't think why people are wearing hats when it's not raining or cold. And why are so many of them smoking when it's bad for their lungs?

Ollie's tummy is rumbling so loud he's surprised no one comes out to complain about the noise.

A man in a smart uniform walks up the steps of Granny's house and posts several letters through the letterbox. He moves on to the next house and then the next one. 'Looks like a genuine postie to me.' Ollie's eyes follow him down the street just in case.

He's getting a bit bored when a woman and two boys come out of the house. The boys are wearing flat hats and short grey jackets with grey shorts. One of them is making a round thing on a string go up and down as he walks. After them, an old man with a white beard comes out. A lot of other people must live in Granny's house.

A tall van – Hillier's Superior Pork Pies – has to wait while some people cross the road in front of it. The van blocks their view of the door for a bit. Ollie doesn't know what a pork pie tastes like but he's so hungry he's beginning to feel sick.

The van moves on. 'Look,' Daddy says. A woman in a tight flowery hat and matching blue coat is walking down the steps. She's holding the hand of a little girl with curly fair hair. 'I'm pretty sure that woman is Granny Celia. I recognise her from a wedding photo Mum has. It's mind blowing to think that little girl in the red coat is my mum – your Granny Lana.'

From where he is Ollie can't see the girl's face properly

to tell. He frowns. 'But Granny's hair is darker in the photos from when she was younger.'

'Ah, but children's hair often gets darker as they age,' Daddy says. 'This might sound odd, but I just…I know in my heart it's them.'

Ollie shuts his eyes. He's learnt that what he sees isn't as true as what he feels. When he opens them, the woman and the girl have moved on down the road. 'Yes,' he says, 'it's definitely them.'

Daddy's face changes. 'Which means that, for whatever reason, Celia's sister Kathy hasn't shown up for babysitting duties yet. Unless they're planning to meet up on the way there or at the station, it looks like Celia is taking Lana with her today.' He starts breathing hard. 'Christ almighty – this is a disaster. We need to stop this – stop them before…'

Daddy picks him up and hurries into the street. Ollie can feel his heart beating really fast. Daddy looks up and down the street. 'If we had any sodding money, we could hail a cab. I suppose at least we know she must be heading to Paddington.' He looks around. 'It's possible there could be a shorter route. If only I had Google Maps.'

'Don't worry,' Ollie says. 'I know a really quick way.'

Chapter Thirty-Four

Tom

They're standing in Paddington station on a busy platform lined with people and bizarrely, a load of milk churns. He's struggling to process what just happened. His senses are assaulted by the echoing sound of steam trains and footfall. The air is laden with smoke and smuts – when he swallows there's an acrid taste in his mouth. Around him numerous conversations are going on. A suitcase nudges his leg; 'I do beg your pardon' – a man's voice.

Smiling up at him, Ollie looks pleased with himself. Against his expectations they're not confronted by shocked onlookers. In fact, there's no sign any of the people waiting have clocked their instant arrival amongst them. Thank God for the numbing effect of travelling by public transport.

'Damn it, Ollie,' Tom says, 'you might have warned me before you went and did that.' He doesn't admonish him further – how can he since they're now in a position to intercept Celia and Lana?

Tom goes to pick Ollie up, then stops when his head spins.

He pinches the bridge of his nose, tries to focus on the dozens of cigarette butts littering the concrete floor and thrown casually onto the rails. His eyes travel up past the crush and clatter of people to the magnificent cast-iron and glass dome above them. Apart from being blackened with soot, Brunel's masterpiece has stood the test of time and looks remarkably like it did when they arrived two days ago.

They've gained an advantage that he needs to use wisely. Ollie is distracted – wide-eyed as a steam train pulls into the opposite platform hissing and belching smoke. Its brakes screech before it comes to a halt against the buffers. Dressed in his rag-tag borrowed outfit, his son looks like a diminutive street urchin. Tom is astounded at how lightly he carries his extraordinary powers. Fascinated by the activity accompanying numerous trains coming and going, you'd never guess Ollie had just transported the two of them from an ordinary London backstreet to this precise location.

Thank God he'd listened to his son's warnings. The boy is absolutely right – Lana *is* the key, the pivotal piece in the deadly game someone is playing. If she boards the train due in any minute, it will put their whole family in jeopardy.

No wonder the Guardians haven't been concentrating on them. Ford and Nikolai only needed to prevent Kathy from arriving today to change the course of Lana's life. In this new reality, if she shares her mother's fate, she won't meet Matt and so he will no longer exist. And neither will Ollie or the baby growing in Beth's womb. If he's not around to bump into Beth on that fateful train to Cheltenham, she'll live out the life she would have led in 1982 and be none the wiser. A simple and yet ingenious move – he gives them that much. Matt's bothersome family will cease to be an issue. Problem solved. Revenge exacted. Ford and Nikolai will no doubt congratulate themselves on achieving the ultimate victory.

In "Back to the Future" when it looks like Marty's mom isn't going to get it together with his dad, a photograph of their family begins to fade. Tom looks down at his own hand and then at his son. Both appear solid enough – for the moment at least. 'Daddy.' Ollie pulls on his trouser leg, wordlessly looks up at him in expectation as if to say, 'What next?'

First off, they need to be sure they're in the right place. Tom turns to a fellow traveller – a brown-haired man smoking a foul-smelling pipe. 'Is this the right platform for the Bristol train?'

Brown suit, brown shoes, brown moustache – the only thing that isn't brown is the man's unhealthy pallor. A cloud of smoke accompanies 'I believe so.' The man checks his wristwatch. 'She's been held up outside Reading according to one of the porters. Should be here in the next ten minutes.'

He picks up Ollie and the two of them scan the crowd for any sign of Celia and Lana. Nothing so far. He tries not to panic though in truth Tom hasn't figured out exactly how he's going to stop his infant mother boarding the ill-fated train. He can't simply abduct a four-year-old child in front of dozens of witnesses and expect to get away with it. Celia would rightly scream blue murder and he'd be set upon by the mob.

What if he were to jump in front of the incoming train? It's an idea but not a good one. The subsequent pandemonium might possibly save his mum, but that would leave Ollie traumatised and alone a hundred years before his proper time.

The question, 'What are we going to do now?' is in his head. He's not sure if Ollie spoke or not.

Tom looks around at the men, women and children casually waiting to board a train for what they must think will be a pleasant uneventful trip to Bristol. The children are all well behaved, their faces lit up with excitement. Surely, he should warn them.

How? If he starts to rant and rave like some unhinged doomster, they'll dismiss him as a nut job. And what if they believe him – what then? By changing the course of so many lives, who's to say that the future consequences won't be far worse? If you could go back in time and murder a despot, the unintended outcomes could be far more disastrous – or so the theoretical argument goes. This must be the moral dilemma the Guardians have to confront all the time.

'Daddy?' he definitely spoke then. Putting all other thoughts aside, Tom now has less than ten minutes to come up with a plan to save his whole family. Fuck! The clock's ticking. Abduction is out of the question. What if, with Ollie's help, they go back in time and sort out whatever it is that prevented his great aunt Kathy from showing up today? His knowledge of family history is vague; he has no idea where Kathy lives and can't guess what might have occurred to stop her arriving to babysit today. All the same, it might be worth a go.

'Daddy.' This time Ollie sounds panicked.

'What is it?'

'They're watching us.' Tom follows the direction of his pointing finger to an ordinary looking man in a wide brimmed hat that conveniently hides most of his upper face. His mouth offers few clues to his identity.

Before he can decide if he recognises him, there's a sudden and growing commotion around them. As if by some shared signal, people begin to peel away from the packed platform. The leaders of this breakaway movement are hurrying with some urgency. They're marching across the concourse in a stream that becomes mixed up with all the other people coming and going. The words, *platform change* reach them almost by osmosis. Damn it – how is he going to pick Celia and Lana out in such a muddle of bodies and faces?

When Tom checks again, the man in the hat has vanished. However, the solid, middle-aged woman who'd been standing right next to him hasn't followed the crowd; she's still rather aimlessly lurking by the milk churns. He whispers, 'Did you mean her?' but gets no answer. Tom pictures the woman crouching like some forward prop or sumo wrestler ready to intercept them as they pass.

To avoid a direct confrontation, they keep to the centre of the pack, weaving from side to side and yet following the general urgency of those keen not to be left behind.

On the new platform, people are milling about, disconcerted by the change in the pecking order they now find themselves in. Increasingly desperate, he asks, 'Can you see Celia and Lana anywhere?'

'No – not yet,' Ollie tells him.

In the general commotion, Tom hears the unmistakeable sound of an approaching train. Shit – he's lost the advantage and now they're almost out of time. A man in a smart GWR uniform spreads his arms wide. 'Stand aside please, ladies and gentlemen.'

Tom scans his fellow passengers. He doesn't need to tell Ollie to check in the other direction. Meanwhile the solid bulk of the engine comes into view. The grimy-faced driver is making last adjustments as the train comes to a slow squealing halt. 'Stand aside folks,' they're reminded by the same GWR man. 'Make room for departing passengers to alight from the train first, please.'

They're forced to comply.

With the aid of two others, an elderly man finally steps down from the carriage nearest him. 'Look,' Ollie shouts. 'There they are.' He's pointing to the spot further along the platform where a woman in a blue outfit is in the process of helping a fair-haired little girl up the step and onto the train. The carriage they've just entered is of a much older design than the ones at the front of the train.

'Damn it, we missed them,' Tom mutters. 'Shit a brick!'

'Here, you'd better watch your language,' a burly man tells him. 'There are ladies present.'

Tom runs along the platform. Ignoring yet more protests, he squeezes through to the front of the crowd and, possibly due to the persuasiveness of having Ollie in his arms, manages to scramble up onto the train.

They've made it. That's something – a small victory at least. They're standing in a narrow corridor that runs along past a number of separate, half-glazed compartments labelled THIRD CLASS. Celia and Lana could be in any one of them. The windows are all open but it's still stiflingly hot. Impatient passengers hard on their his heels, Tom sets about checking each compartment in turn. People are reaching up to stow luggage on the racks, taking off jackets and generally blocking his view of the interior. It might be easier to give them a few minutes to settle down in their seats. This has the advantage of allowing him more time to think because he still hasn't the faintest idea what he's going to do once he's located them.

Tom moves away from the clouds of smoke some bloke's pipe is giving off while attempting to piece together the scant information his mother had divulged over the years. For obvious reasons, she never liked to dwell on what happened. A few years back, armed with his curiosity and the sparse clues he'd gleaned, Tom had carried out an internet search into what happened that day. This day, in fact.

Due to previous disasters, it had become standard practice to put the newer steel-framed carriages with electric lights at either end of the train – points considered more vulnerable in the event of a collision. The older carriages– like this one with its mainly wooden construction and gas lights – were acknowledged as far less rigid and, crucially, highly inflammable, and so they were sandwiched in the middle like this one is. Or was.

He knows the derailment will take place after a glancing collision with a freight train on what they call the Up line. The other train will be largely undamaged while this train will come to rest under a bridge just outside Bathampton junction. When flames begin to engulf the central carriages, the bridge will reflect the heat back and so it will intensify the fire.

Fortunately, there will be many more scheduled stops

between Paddington and the crash site – each one representing a possible escape route well before Bathampton.

'Daddy,' Ollie whispers in his ear, 'what are you planning to do now?' A very good question.

Chapter Thirty-Five

Ollie

'Don't look so worried.' Daddy puts him down. 'The situation is totally under control.' Ollie can tell he's fibbing. There's a long whistle and then he feels the train start to move. He can't see out of the windows because of all the smoke and steam.

'We're off.' Daddy rubs his hands together. 'Once we find out which of these compartments they're in, we'll be able to sort all this out. We may not be able to do it with any finesse. I think we're just going to have to go in there and, at the right time, I'll find a way to grab little Lana and get her away to safety.'

Ollie doesn't think his plan is a good one though he doesn't say so. The train is now making clickety-clackety noises. With the buildings whizzing by faster, he leans against the side of the carriage to keep his balance and not fall over.

'Remember to stay close to me at all times,' Daddy says. 'If I'm forced to pick Lana up and bundle her off the train, I don't want to have to worry about you being left behind.' He does that sideways thing with his mouth. 'There's plenty of time. I'll do it before we get anywhere near Bathampton.'

'But her mummy will chase after us.'

'Hmm – I suppose you're right. And then that will alter everything – and who knows what the consequences will be.' Daddy rubs at his chin. 'Kidnapping her is a bit old-school. Maybe we need some diversionary tactics.'

'Excuse me.' They have to flatten themselves to let a grumpy-looking woman in a green jacket and skirt squeeze past them. Her hat has green feathers sticking out of it that must have come from a dead bird. Looking down, she peers at Daddy's shoes and his slippers, and hurries on.

Once she's walked through into the next carriage, Daddy says, 'I think we'll have to try something more drastic. Or rather *you* will, Ollie. Listen, I know we've been trying to stop you using your powers, or whatever you like to call it; and believe me I have no idea how you managed it earlier on. The question is – God I can't believe I'm asking this to a toddler – do you think you might be able to transport the three of us back to Paddington station?'

Ollie asks, 'But what are we going to do with Lana when we get there?'

'We can worry about that then.' Ollie frowns at him. 'Well, we certainly can't take her back to our time,' Daddy says. 'I mean, obviously, she's already there – as an old woman. Two Lanas would be pretty hard to cope with.' He gives a snorty sort of laugh. 'We'll hand her over to someone who'll look after her for a bit.'

'Poor Lana,' Ollie says. 'What will happen to her then?'

'If we're sure to tell them exactly who she is and give them her address, the police, or someone else in authority, will eventually get her home safely.'

'But no one's at her home. Who's going to look after her?'

Daddy sighs. 'That great aunt Kathy has an awful lot to answer for.' He rubs at his forehead. 'Look I'm sure she'll be fine – probably one of the neighbours won't mind looking after her.'

'Not Mrs Healey – Lana's frightened of her.'

Daddy stares at him. 'How on earth would you know that?'

Ollie shrugs. 'I just do.'

Daddy shakes his head. 'Under any other circumstances I wouldn't ask this of you, but like they say, desperate times call for desperate measures and all that.'

'Pardon me.' Touching his straw hat, a thin man in a pale flapping suit squeezes past them. It isn't Nikolai. They wait for the man to go through the door at the end of the carriage.

'Remember,' Daddy says, 'Lana's dad's ship is due into Bristol docks in a couple of hours. I happen to know your great grandfather will quit the navy not long after the accident so he can spend more time at home with her.'

Seeing his face, Daddy throws his hands up in the air. 'Look, for the moment let's just concentrate on making sure we get her and ourselves out of this carriage and off this damned train before it goes up in flames.'

'But she's not in *this* carriage,' Ollie tells him. 'She's in the next one'

'Is she now?' Daddy smiles. 'Then lead the way, little man.'

Once he's sure he's outside the right compartment, he signals for Daddy to stop. 'Pick me up.'

'You forgot to say please,' Daddy tells him. And then,

before he can say it, 'It's okay – that was a joke.' He lifts him up so he can see into the compartment.

The girl – his granny – and her mummy are sitting opposite each other. The red seats and wooden walls make it look really cosy in there.

'Whatever you do,' Daddy says, 'try not to look like you're staring at them, or they might get suspicious.' Ollie's not sure of the exact difference between looking and staring. He thinks looking might be a bit quicker.

'There she is. Pretty little thing, wasn't she?' Daddy's been looking at them for so long Ollie thinks he might be staring.

He turns away. 'We can't go in there yet. All the seats are occupied – there's nowhere to sit. We'll have to wait here and hope a few of them get off well before Bathampton.'

In his own quick look Ollie could see that his great grand-mother Celia has a nice friendly face. She's spread a hanky out on her lap with a peeled orange sitting on it. Little Lana was holding up one of the segments and laughing. The two of them looked so happy together. An older couple in the carriage were smiling at them like people do when they watch children and remember when their own were young. There were two more passengers in their compartment – both men. One was reading a book called "A Passage to India", the other was reading The Times newspaper.

Ollie's heart starts to race; he wants to stop the train, stop this terrible thing that's going to happen to Celia and all the other people on here.

Daddy lifts him up again so he takes another quick peek and this time his eyes are drawn to a small notice near the window. ALARM. Below that it says: TO STOP THE TRAIN IN CASE OF EMERGENCY PULL DOWN THE CHAIN. *Penalty for improper use £5.* 'Daddy look,' Ollie nudges him and points. 'If we pull on that chain, they'll stop the train and everyone will be saved.'

'And yet we mustn't.' Daddy tightens his hold on him. 'I know it's a hard thing to comprehend but that would alter too many people's futures. Who knows what the knock-on consequences would be?'

Daddy walks away a few steps so they can't be seen by the people in the compartment. He kisses his head like he used to do to calm him down when he was younger. It's not going to work. 'But we have to do something to save them,' Ollie wails.

'We can't take that risk. It's only natural you want to help them, and believe me I feel it too, but we mustn't interfere. The Guardians would go ape shit if we did. Remember, lots of these people will get off the train well before it happens and be thankful for their narrow escape. The stronger carriages will survive the impact and I happen to know that led them to speeding up the replacement of these old wooden ones. And so, in a roundabout way, the crash will save lots more lives after it happens. I read that miraculously some people were thrown clear and they survived with only minor injuries.' He takes a deep breath. 'Right now, the only thing you and I can do is change things back to the way they were meant to happen, and that means getting Lana off this train before she… comes to any harm.'

A howling whistle makes them both jump. They're heading off in a different direction. Trails of smoke fly in through the open window, the smell is making him feel sick. Great clouds of steam and smoke are spreading out over the fields they're leaving behind like a blanket. 'Damned smuts,' Daddy pokes at one eye then wipes it with the back of his hand. 'I can't think why steam trains are thought to be romantic. Look at all that pollution for a start.'

When Ollie glances over his shoulder, a big man in a dark suit and a black hat is striding towards them. 'Excuse me, folks.' Unblinking, the man's face comes close enough for Ollie to smell his stale breath as he pushes past.

'Thank God for that.' Daddy watches him go. 'For a minute there, I thought he might be the ticket collector.'

'He's been watching us,' Ollie tells him.

'Are you sure?' Daddy frowns. 'I mean, granted his manner seemed a bit brusque to say the least, but he struck me as in a hurry to be somewhere else. Seemed pretty harmless.'

'He's still watching us.' With both hands, Ollie pulls Daddy's face down so he can look straight into his eyes. 'You don't understand,' he says. 'They're already on this train. That man is one of them. Another one – the one with blond hair who chased us in the park – is hiding behind a newspaper in there.'

'You mean Nikolai?' Daddy puts his hand over his mouth. 'Christ – it would be him.'

Ollie points to the compartment. 'He's sitting right next to her.'

'Shit a flaming brick.'

Daddy's about to check for himself when Ollie stops him. 'Don't look,' he says. 'They think we don't know.'

Chapter Thirty-Six

Tom

The train begins to decelerate, ready for its scheduled stop at Reading. They stand off to one side, out of sight of the passengers in Lana's compartment. Taking a couple of steps forward, he ventures a quick glance inside. All six passengers are still in their seats – no sign of anyone getting ready to leave.

They remain where they are in the corridor even though they're soon in everyone's way. People tut-tut and mutter excuse-me as they're forced to squeeze past them. Possibly deliberately, some even step on his toes – an experience made more painful by the fact that he's only wearing deck shoes.

Reading station is busy. Through the window Tom studies the streams of passengers disembarking. Uniformed porters mill about eager to assist people with their luggage. He watches couples and family groups reuniting on the platform with hugs and chaste kisses. Their public show of affection might be more restrained than the twenty-first century, but the warmth in their faces is just as obvious. It's heartening to witness all those untroubled people escaping this doomed train to carrying on with their lives as before.

Tom's instincts scream at him to get his son off this damned thing while he still can. The logical part of his brain accepts this would be utterly futile; Ollie will only survive if they can find a way to save his four-year-old grandmother. Besides, he might be just a tich, but without his help Tom won't stand a chance of succeeding.

It's a comfort that fewer people are climbing aboard than have just left. A sign saying GWR and REFRESHMENTS catches his eye. The sign is attached to an elaborate and capacious tea trolley complete with cakes, snacks and a highly polished tea urn. It's parked right by the platform and presided over by a man in a white overall and peaked cap bearing the company's initials.

As the train pulls away, Tom struggles to fight back the panic that might otherwise overwhelm him. 'What are we going to do now?' Ollie demands.

'Nothing for a bit,' he tells him. 'We'll need to time this right. If we make a move too early, it'll give them more chance to come back at us.'

Instead of arguing, Ollie nods, looks up at him with a trust that hits him in the chest with the force of a sharpened spear.

He remembers what happened in Hyde Park before Ollie was born, how the Guardians had been determined to separate him from Beth. In an extraordinary demonstration of his powers, Ford had been able to freeze the people, the traffic, and even the animals around them mid-motion. Time itself was put on hold while they had shepherded him away onto the waiting train and out of her life. Or so they thought.

Despair takes hold of him – what chance could they have

against such awe-inspiring power? He shuts his eyes wondering if prayer is their only hope now.

When he opens them again, Ollie is still looking up at him – a living reminder that he and Beth had won through; they'd found a way to be together against all the odds.

Putting on a confident smile, Tom takes a long breath in and a slow one out. Even for someone from the so-called snowflake generation, there are times when a man needs to gird up his loins ready to do battle. He can do this. He's Bruce Willis barefoot and bleeding in that tower block; he's Tom Cruise throwing his motorbike around on an impossible mission; he's Harrison Ford, a tiny force about to strike back against an evil Empire…

He feels a tug on his trouser leg. 'Daddy I need a wee-wee.'

The journey seems interminable and at the same time miles of countryside seem to speed past in a heartbeat. They're pulling into Chippenham station when the door slides open and the middle-aged couple emerge from Lana's compartment. Without fear or hesitation, Tom grabs Ollie in his arms and, brushing past them, rushes inside to claim their vacant seats before anyone else can. Firmly and deliberately, he deposits Ollie right next to his grandmother. Side by side, being of a similar age, the resemblance between them is remarkable – so much so that he worries Celia might wonder about it.

Except Celia appears to be dozing. Chin on her chest, the flowers on her blue hat tremble a little with every breath. It seems an unnatural position for a nap but there's no way of knowing if she's genuinely asleep.

The window's open but the air smells of stale tobacco. The man next to Tom looks up from his book. 'Were you out in the corridor just now? I do beg your pardon – I would have offered you my seat if I'd noticed you had a youngster with you.'

'Not a problem,' Tom tells him. 'We were just stretching our legs, enjoying the view.'

On the other side of Lana, The Times is still providing the prefect shield. Ollie must be right about the identity of the reader; even the most avid news fan would have looked up by now.

Ollie appears to be wriggling in his seat, but Tom can see he's manoeuvring himself into position ready. As subtly as he can, he nods, trusting in his son's ability to understand that he should go for it now before they run out of time.

So quick he hardly catches the movement, Ollie grabs Lana's hand. The two of them grow faint and then disappear altogether.

Elation overwhelms Tom. Though he remains seated, he's tempted to stand up and cheer. His relief is only marginally tempered by the fact that he's been left behind on a train speeding towards its own imminent destruction.

He finds it remarkable and then suspicious that Celia is still asleep. The man reading "A Passage to India" appears to be so thoroughly engrossed he hasn't once looked up.

At first, Tom can't interpret the sound he hears. As it grows louder, he identifies it as distorted laughter coming from behind The Times. The newspaper shakes as if sharing the joke before Nikolai lowers it theatrically to reveal himself. Could it be ironic laughter – a defeated foe acknowledging another's victory? The man's blond hair is swept back from his face, those startling blue eyes focus only on Tom. Something in them suggests triumph not defeat.

There's a ripple in the red velvet seats where the children had been sitting and then the two of them materialise still in the same position they were in when they disappeared. Tom can only stare at them, appalled.

'Permit me to share this quote...' The Guardian's voice is inside his head, twisting his thoughts. Without looking up, Nikolai folds his newspaper in half as if merely reading from an article. 'A slogan I believe in. "He who controls the past controls the future".'

'George Orwell's 1984,' Tom says out loud. 'Though that particular book won't be published for another twenty years.'

'And yet how pertinent his words are to our present situation.'

Tom looks at his son hoping he can read his thoughts. Jeremy Paxman style he says, 'An apt observation, I grant you. I believe the quote continues, "He who controls the present controls the future".' As the train sways he lunges at Nikolai, brings one knee up to the man's chest and grabs him by the throat. Shutting his eyes, Tom concentrates all of his thoughts on keeping Nikolai where he is for as long as possible.

'I say, steady on there.' Reading-Man is on his feet attempting to restrain Tom and, in the process, helping to pin them both down. In the maelstrom of thrashing arms and kicking legs, Tom glances sideways and is elated to see the seat where the children had been sitting is once again empty.

Reading-Man is tenacious and has managed to get hold of

him by the shoulders. Determined not to be defeated this time, Tom finds the strength to throw him off with one hand while continuing to throttle Nikolai with the other. Reading-Man comes right back at him, but he holds on for dear life – not his own but his mother's and through her the life of his son and unborn child.

Chapter Thirty-Seven

Ollie

They're not in Paddington station like they should be. Something's gone wrong because they're still on the train. Not in the compartment they were in before but another one.

Ollie takes a big breath like Mummy's taught him to when he's upset. Squeezing Lana's hand, he shuts his eyes and has another go. As soon as he tries to picture where he wants them to be, a dark shape forms in the red world under his eyelids. Small at first, the more he tries the more it grows bigger and bigger until he can't see the station or anything else except darkness.

He can't breathe. It feels like a monster has hold of his legs and is pulling him down.

There's no escape. Panting, he opens his eyes to find they haven't left the train – the same one that any minute is about to come off the rails and crash.

Except it hasn't yet because all the clickety-clacking under his feet hasn't changed. He can see fields and trees whizzing past at speed. The breeze from the window smells of smoke and coal.

The two of them are standing in a corridor. Ollie jumps as high as he can to look through the glass of the nearest compartment. It's completely empty. He looks around. Windows, doors, lights – everything looks shinier than in the other part of the train. This must be one of the newer carriages – the stronger ones they put at the two ends like Daddy explained. He thinks they're a bit safer in here.

The air's really hot but Lana's shaking like she's just stepped out of freezing cold water. He can sense her fear. And confusion. Her face is so white Ollie wonders if she's going to be sick. He's much shorter than her so he has to reach up to put his arm around her waist. 'It's alright,' he tells her, though it isn't.

Her bottom lip wobbles and she starts to cry. 'I want… my mummy.' Ollie doesn't know what to say about that because her mummy is about to be killed and he can't stop it happening. He wants to cry but he knows you mustn't give in if you want to work out a way to save the queen.

Footsteps. People are running towards them. He puts his other arm around Lana's waist and pulls her down onto the floor because he can't tell if these are going to be the good or the bad people.

The first one through the door is Daddy. 'Ollie!' He runs up to them, bends down and scoops them both up into his arms. 'Oh God. I'm so sorry. So sorry.' Daddy has blood on his cheek. 'I thought at least you two were safe. Everything's gone wrong.' Horrified, he thinks Daddy might be about to cry. 'I've let you both down and now it's too late…'

The two men behind him have stopped running and

instead are walking towards them. Taking their time. The one at the front – that horrid blond one called Nikolai – has blood on his nose and a smirk on his lips. Ollie notices he's lost his hat. 'Well, well, well. What a touching little family reunion.'

'You evil fucking bastards,' Daddy says.

A fake frown. 'I really think you should moderate your language in front of these impressionable young people. Although – I suppose there's little point; it's not likely to scar their future since they won't have one.'

'You can't get away with this. My father–'

'Is totally out of the picture. Such a shame he's all tied up trying to prevent a war.' Nikolai wipes at the blood under his nose. He tries to do up his shirt, but the buttons are missing. Instead, he smooths his yellow hair back into place. 'I'm surprised you haven't learnt by now that our friend – I should say our *associate* – Matt, can't be relied on.'

The man behind him is the one who was reading in the carriage. He takes a silver watch on a chain out of his waistcoat pocket and nudges Nikolai. 'These crude devices are somewhat unreliable, but this one is more accurate than most. It suggests the local time is now 11:31. Oh wait, I tell a lie – 11:32.'

'So – less than four minutes to go.' Nikolai pulls his jacket sleeves back into place. 'You know that phrase reminds me of those four-minute-warning days. The sixties are such a fascinating era – wouldn't you agree, Seth?'

The other man says, 'I've only visited once but I wouldn't mind another trip. The Cold War – the phrase has such a ring to it. Though the threat of mutual assured destruction never really goes away. A delightful conundrum to wrestle with.'

'Damn you all.' Daddy pulls them into a tight huddle on the floor. Ollie shuts his eyes.

Nikolai gives a fake laugh. 'Oh I see – we're bracing for impact, are we? Well then allow me to relieve the suspense. In a few minutes this train will be nudged off the rails by the freight train currently on what they call the Up line, whereupon this carriage – which I grant you is stronger than many of the others – will be thrown up in the air and, later, to the puzzlement of accident investigators, somehow end up wedged under the bridge.'

Opening his eyes, Ollie sees him mime an explosion with his hands. 'The rest of the train will burst into flames causing the trapped occupants of this carriage to be rendered unconscious due to smoke inhalation.' He opens his hands. 'I doubt you'd like me to elaborate on what happens after that.'

'For Christ's sake have a heart,' Daddy yells. 'These two are harmless – they're only children.' The train's whistle is long and sad.

'That's true.' Seth looks at his watch. 'But then children do have an unfortunate tendency to become thoroughly meddlesome.'

'Try to see things from a wider perspective,' Nikolai says. 'This solution will be considerably neater all round.' He chuckles. 'We're about to kill *three* birds with one stone, so to speak. A very troublesome trio taken out of the game in one fell swoop.'

Seeing a big tree in the middle of a field, Ollie shuts his eyes and tries to picture them huddled underneath it. No matter how hard he concentrates, it doesn't work.

'You know I'm rather fond of the word fell,' Seth says. 'I believe Shakespeare coined the phrase "fell swoop" to describe how his rival Macduff's wife and child are murdered much like a determined kite swooping down to grab its prey.'

There's a strange sound – or did he feel it? Ollie looks in the other direction. Another man is now standing there. He touches the front of his hat then slowly walks towards them clapping. Clap, clap, clap his hands go. 'I congratulate you Seth on such an apt comparison.'

'Ford,' Daddy says. 'I was wondering when you'd show up.'

Chapter Thirty-Eight

Tom

Still looking remarkably like Liam Neeson, Ford stops clapping and lifts one hand like a priest about to bestow a blessing on proceedings. 'Bravo!'

'So, you've come to gloat over your handiwork.' He clutches the children to his chest; if only that was enough to protect them. 'You lot must get your rocks off on all that power.' He looks from one to the other. 'Dominance – is that what it's all about? A base motive considering your positions. You'd better savour your victory while you can because I promise you it will be short lived once my father and the others find out what you've done.'

Without seeming to move, Ford is now standing beside the other two Guardians. 'Now, now, Tom – I believe in giving credit where credit is due; and these two have put on quite a remarkable performance today. Although possibly you might want to rethink your analogy Seth, since eventually Macduff gets his revenge by decapitating Macbeth.'

Brakes are screaming for dear life. There's an echoing

whale-song of twisting metal as the world and everything he knows tilts sideways. All noise and movement stops. Outside the windows there is only the sky. They must be airborne, floating still and tranquil. This is it. The moment before impact. Enfolding his family, he shuts his eyes and waits for the crash.

Nothing.

Opening his eyes again Tom finds the whole carriage is titled at an angle – disobeying every law of physics. They appear to be static, suspended in mid-air. Tom is sitting at a weird angle. He checks the children and they appear to be unhurt – at least at this precise moment. Their regular breathing suggests they're sound asleep. A signature Guardian trick.

Clutching them awkwardly to his chest, he shuffles on his arse amongst all the accumulated dirt and cigarette ends until he and they are more upright.

Further along the wall – which percentage wise is more the floor – Ford's attention has moved away from them and is focused entirely on the other two Guardians. Viewed from such an odd angle, Tom observes the three with a weird sense of detachment.

'It pains me greatly that I defended both of you against the others,' Ford says – although perhaps his voice is only inside Tom's head. 'Today you've demonstrated that my faith in you both was entirely misplaced.'

'But all this is exactly what you asked for.' Nikolai attempts to touch Ford's shoulder, but his hand hovers a few centimetres from its target as if an invisible forcefield surrounds his boss. Giving up on this would-be friendly gesture, Nikolai withdraws his hand. 'I have to say I'm surprised you're not impressed by our ingenuity. Our initiative.'

Misreading the mood music, Seth adds, 'We were only following your orders.'

'Which is precisely the defence used by those who fail to be guided by their own inherent sense of right and wrong. Without that, such individuals *should* have no place in civilised society whatever the era.'

Seth bends down to pick up his hat. 'I'm sorry, but I mean really, you can't be serious.' After wiping the dust off, he puts his hat back on his head – a defiant gesture. 'What some call ruthlessness has been shown to be a powerful driving force throughout history. Think of all the great world leaders – what would they have achieved without a driving sense of purpose whatever the consequences? It's in the DNA of every leader of every race that has ever existed.'

'Guardians are not permitted to violate the natural course of events,' Ford thunders. 'That is *the* fundamental and immutable principle that must guide us.' He sighs. 'I regret that is precisely what you two have attempted to bring about here.'

Looking less confident now, Nikolai says, 'But you said yourself the boy and his father should never have existed.'

'The fact of their existence might well be irksome, but it is fixed and therefore undeniable. I certainly didn't expect them to be erased from all time.'

'Then we stand corrected,' Nikolai says. 'Our sincere apologies for overstepping the mark a tad.' He does his best to look humble. 'Let that be the end of the matter.'

Ford's voice rises to fill Tom's head. 'We are never permitted to expunge humans from existence.'

A heavily pregnant pause follows. 'However,' Ford says,

'when it comes to rogue and dangerous Guardians, we *are* permitted to expel them. And what's more it is our duty to ensure they can no longer pose a threat.'

As if they're wearing jetpacks, Nikolai and Seth rise into the air. Instead of crashing against the opposite wall of the carriage they simply disappear. When Ford turns around his eyes appear to be glowing.

Tom cowers in front of him. Hardly daring to speak he finally asks, 'Where have they gone?'

'I sent them into one of the central carriages,' Ford says. 'They will not survive.'

'Bloody Hell!' Tom is tempted to add something about Ford's own ruthlessness but thinks better of it. Hardly the time to poke this particular bear.

Towering over him, Ford focuses those terrifying eyes on him and says, 'Now for the remaining loose ends.'

'Believe me this particular loose end doesn't want to cause any trouble. You name it, I'll do it as long as you find a way for these two kids to survive.'

'Quite so,' Ford says. Before he's aware of it, Lana is torn from his grip. The next second she vanishes.

'What the–'

Against his will, Tom's mouth is firmly closed. 'I'm in no mood for further arguments or discussions,' Ford tells him. 'Rest assured Lana will be found by the trackside unharmed and apparently thrown clear. Her rescuers will discover a letter I removed from her mother's handbag in the child's pocket. This will lead them to her father and the two will then be reunited. Their lives will go on as before. I assume this meets with your approval.'

Tom tries in vain speak.

'You may nod,' Ford tells him. He does as he's told.

'Good.' Like a child in class, Tom raises a questioning hand. Since he can't speak, he's certainly not about to embark on a bizarre game of charades.

'Ah yes,' Ford says. 'Suffice to say your mother will have no memory of today's journey except for a lingering sense of unease whenever she boards a train. Amnesia is a common response to tragedies children are unable to fully process and so it will be. Doubtless you yourself will have previously noticed her reluctance to talk about what happened to her mother.'

Tom nods again. He tries to insert a finger to force his lips apart but fails.

Ford shakes his head. 'To answer your other question – the charred remains of Nikolai and Seth will never be identified leading to all manner of colourful, dare I say romantic, speculation.' A sardonic smirk. 'My personal favourite is that the pair were a couple of White Russians – possibly displaced minor royals fleeing the wrath of undercover Bolshevik sympathisers.'

Feeling a slight tingle in his lips, Tom finds he can open his mouth at last.

'I must fly.' Ford smiles – an expression that sits uneasily on his face.

'But what about us?' Tom cries. 'This fucking train's about to crash. You can't leave Ollie and me sitting here for God's sake.'

'Do you suppose I've forgotten?'

'I agree that would make no sense, seeing's you've gone to so much trouble to rescue us.'

'Exactly so. Bon voyage. I hope this hasn't put your son off trains – statistically it's a very safe means of travel. Although less so in the 1920s, I grant you.' Ford touches the front of his hat. 'Until we meet again.' He clicks heels together in a curious parody of Judy Garland in the Wizard of Oz before he vanishes.

His lap is vibrating because Ollie is giggling. 'That was really funny,' he says – his last words before the carriage dissolves in front of Tom's eyes.

Chapter Thirty-Nine

Beth

Yawning, Beth stretches both arms wide in the king-sized bed. She frowns when her right hand finds only empty space. According to her watch it's not even 7:00 and yet Tom and Ollie are already up.

A shaft of sunlight is making moving patterns on the ceiling. She gets out of bed and pulls back the curtains. It appears to be another fine day out there. Odd to watch the tops of so many heads – streams of people and vehicles going about their daily routines in the capital.

Beth rubs the back of her neck. She has a vague recollection of Ollie waking in the night, screaming blue murder about something. His sudden night terrors are worrying. They need to get to the bottom of what's causing them.

Turning around to face the room, she listens. In the background there's a constant drone from the traffic as well as a low plane that sounds like it's directly overhead.

Once it's passed, she listens again. There's no sound inside the flat except what she assumes is the fridge cooling itself down. No one's moving about or chatting or playing music. Possibly Tom's taken Ollie over to the park again so as not to disturb her – which is really sweet of him. Tom may have his faults but then who hasn't?

Drawn towards the stylish en suite bathroom, she decides to take a soak in the free-standing copper bath while the opportunity presents itself. A small collection of nice smelling toiletries are arranged in height order on a stool beside the bath, along with a hand-written notice telling them to help themselves.

She sniffs the bath essence. Sweet and delicious. Beth adds it to the running water and a layer of foam begins to creep up the sides of the tub. Citrus notes fill the room. When she lowers herself into the water, her whole body disappears under a thick layer of suds.

Pointing her toes, she lifts one soapy leg, pretends to be a starlet in one of those old films her and Aunty Joan used to watch when there was nothing else on telly. They were so coy about nudity. By the eighties all that had gone by the board – as an actress you had to be prepared to bare all for your art.

Any minute she expects Ollie to run in and disturb her. In anticipation, she begins to sculpt a dog in foam to amuse him. When he doesn't appear, she lets it sink and then drown.

Her hands are starting to go wrinkly – a reminder of her real age. No longer feeling like a starlet, she decides to get out before the rest of her follows suit.

Wrapped in a snowy bath sheet – Tom must have paid a fortune for this place – Beth picks up the dress she'd worn to the party then casts it aside remembering how miserable and out of place she'd felt when she was wearing it. She wraps her long hair in a towel turban, pulls on clean underwear, her jeans and a t-shirt. In the mirror she looks happier – more like herself.

Beth wanders into the sitting room and is shocked to discover the two of them flat-out on the sofa with their mouths half-open and their heads close together. A beam of light falling through the skylight above illuminates them like an old master tableau of a devoted father and son. On closer inspection, she notices the effect is enhanced by the old-fashioned clothes they're wearing, clothes that most definitely don't belong to them.

She sniffs, tries to locate the unpleasantly acrid pong before she realises that they are the source. The smell puts her in mind of a coal fire half-lit and badly smoking.

Maybe Tom found the clothes in one of the cupboards and decided to keep Ollie entertained by them dressing up. Beth pulls a face. She's tempted to wake him up and tell him off for taking liberties with what must clearly be the owner's personal property. But then the two of them look so happy and peaceful she decides not to disturb them. Sleeping dogs and all that. Instead, she'll nip out and buy some of the croissants they'd seen in the artisan bakery along the street. When Tom had pointed them out – marvelled at so many varieties – she'd had no appetite. This morning she finds she has a craving for the ones with the almond filling, so much so she can almost taste that sugary, nutty mix.

Before she leaves Beth writes a short note and props it up on the kettle where Tom can't miss it.

Down in the street, she looks up into a clear blue sky and finds she's feeling better than she has in a long while. Uplifted by the weather she starts to hum and then realises it's the tune they played at the barbecue – "Summer in the City".

Taking in the sights she walks along in time to the beat in her head. Every frontage offers more temptation to buy things she can't afford and doesn't really need. Would it be so bad to take advantage of the shopping opportunities London has to offer? They'd passed a "pre-loved" designer clothes place the other day. It had some great vintage stuff in the window. With luck it might be open this morning.

Letting herself in, Beth hears them chatting. They're up then. The tone of their conversation seems quite earnest. For a change the smell of coffee doesn't turn her stomach. She finds them sitting at the table, hair wet from the shower, both smelling a whole lot fresher. 'You two were totally out for the count when I left,' she says depositing her shopping bags on the kitchen counter.

Before she can ask about the strange clothes they'd been wearing, they rush over to envelope her in a tight hug. Ollie squeezes her legs so hard she almost topples over.

Beth laughs. 'What's all this fuss about? I only nipped out for a couple of hours to do some shopping.' She wriggles free. Looking past them to the table, she says, 'Oh – you've already eaten.' Boiled eggs and toast by the look of it. 'That's a shame; I just bought a whole load of croissants. Still warm from the oven, would you believe. Guess I'll have to eat them all by myself.'

'Pretty sure I can find room for one or two,' Tom says. 'How about you, little man?'

Ollie gives an enthusiastic thumbs-up. Addressing her son, she repeats something her mum always used to say, 'I see you've lost your appetite and found a donkey's.' They both laugh long and hard as if she'd just made the cleverest joke in the world. Something is definitely not right.

Before she can quiz him, Tom grabs her by her shoulders, pulls her to him and kisses her in a way he hasn't done in ages. Certainly not in front of Ollie. Afterwards he hugs her. 'God, you're such a wonderful sight for sore eyes.'

She pushes him away to study his face. 'Why the sudden passion?' She tilts her head to one side though changing the angle fails to make things any clearer. 'Did you both think I'd done a runner or something?' When he doesn't answer she says, 'What – you thought all it would take is one sniff of an artisan croissant and I'd be seduced by London life and run off and join a troupe of struggling actors.'

'No – course not.' When Tom laughs Ollie joins in like he's taking his cue.

'You know, I thought I'd love being back in London,' she says, 'but I have to tell you that, especially on a sunny day like today, I'd far sooner be at home in the fresh air.'

'I know what you mean,' Tom says. 'This apartment is very swanky but I can't wait to leave.' His face turns serious. 'On that note, I thought we might catch the Megabus back instead of a stuffy old train.'

Again, father and son share a look. Co-conspirators. There definitely is something they're not telling her. 'Didn't you see my note?' she asks.

'Course,' Tom tells her. 'We could hardly miss it, could we?'

'So why are you behaving strangely? Like you're surprised to see me or something.'

Dreadful actor that he is, Tom shrugs his shoulders and pretends to be baffled. 'If by *strangely* you mean affectionately, why shouldn't I be? Overlooking the fact that you were born sixty years ago, you're a beautiful woman and I adore you.'

She narrows her eyes at him. 'I can always tell when you're avoiding a question.'

He holds up both hands. 'I realise I don't tell you nearly as often as I should how much I love you.'

'I love her too,' Ollie declares.

'And I love you both back,' she says, softening more than she lets on. 'But you're keeping something from me. Whatever it is, you'd better spit it out.'

Tom searches in his pocket and pulls out a ring-pull from the top of a can. Looking into her eyes, he crouches down as if he's about to tie his shoelace. Instead, he gets down on one knee and says, 'Elizabeth Catherine Sawyer will you marry me?'

'Hmm,' she says, 'Possibly.' A smile tugs at her lips but she fights it, pulls her face back into a more serious expression. 'I want you to promise to be honest with me whatever happens. Always. And right now, I need to know what's brought on this big show of affection from both of you.'

'We missed you,' Tom says.

'Bullshit – I only popped out for an hour or so. What's more, you were asleep when I left.'

'The thing is…' He holds the ring-pull up in front of her

268

and it catches the light like some dazzling stone. 'Seeing that you're pregnant with our second child, I thought it really was about time I made an honest woman of you.'

'So, are you suggesting it was perfectly acceptable for us to have one child born out of wedlock but not two?'

Ollie pulls on his trouser leg. 'What does wedlock mean?'

In response to the tugging, Tom wobbles, loses his balance and falls over. Sprawled out on the marble checkerboard flooring, he says, 'Okay, I give in. Look at me, Beth– I'm down here grovelling at your feet. The least you could do is promise to marry me.'

She's about to give him an answer when Ollie says, 'Daddy and me just–'

'Just want to show you how much we love you by officially becoming a family.' Tom gives him another long look. 'Isn't that right, Ollie?'

Not waiting for an answer, Tom stumbles forward on his knees and kisses her trainers one at a time. 'Oh, for goodness' sake get up you idiot.' She pulls at his shirt laughing. 'How d'you know I haven't just stepped in dog shit?'

He shakes his head. 'Be totally worth it if you say yes.'

Laughing properly now, she says, 'Okay, okay.'

'So, was that just a yes?'

She nods. 'Yes, it was a yes.'

While Ollie dances around with Bobbity, Tom raises both fists in triumph – the gladiator pose. 'I knew I'd wear you down eventually – what sane woman could resist me? Second thought, don't answer that.'

Back on his feet, he takes her in his arms and is about to kiss her when Ollie says, 'Can I tell her now, Daddy?'

'Tell me what exactly?'

Stroking her hair away from her face, Tom looks deep into her eyes. 'It's a very long and very complicated story.'

'Yours usually are,' she says.

'Yes well, at least this one has a happy ending.'

Chapter Forty

Marshy Bottom

Lana

At short notice, it was an easy and practical decision to hold the wedding reception at the Pig and Piper. They've certainly been lucky with the weather; all their elaborate contingency plans can be safely forgotten now.

The thirty or so guests have naturally spilled out onto the village green with their drinks. She doesn't know most of them though Lana spots a few of Tom's old university friends. It's hard to recognise some of the pub staff in their civies. Lots of people are taking snaps. Instagram-ready – that's how the young see things these days. Several times she overhears envious remarks about living in such an idyllic rural setting and looking around on a day like today it would be hard to disagree.

Tom and Beth appear happy and relaxed. In better spirits than they have been in a long time. Ollie is running around chasing the ducks. It's quite a relief to see him behaving like any normal, high-spirited toddler for a change.

The invitation made a point of stressing that the dress code was "informal". All the same Lana's treated herself to a new outfit for the occasion. A flower strewn cream dress – matching cashmere cardigan in the car in case it gets chilly though there's no sign of that. Before they set out, Olek had told her in his faltering English that she was "dressed to stun". She'd instantly pictured a would-be assassin lying on their belly in a floral dress hoping to blend in with the scenery. If she did that now, it might work. Would anyone notice her absence?

Bending his arm, Olek had made a show of escorting her to the car before he nipped round to the passenger side. A man in his seventies, his manners are old-fashioned – she likes that about him. Despite his limited vocabulary in English, he's happily chatting to all and sundry. Charm can get you a long way in this world. It's taken a bit of adjustment, but over the last few months she's found that, on the whole, it's very pleasant having a man about the house again.

Her son is now a married man. Though he'd put the cart before the horse by having a family first, the fact of it still requires some adjustment.

They'd wanted her to bring Poppy – to tie a big bow on her collar for heaven's sake. 'She's part of the family,' Tom had argued. Ollie had suggested she could be a ring bearer with some sort of bag slung round her neck with the wedding rings inside.

Lana had put her foot down and she's glad she did. It would have been too much for the old girl in this heat. Right now Poppy would be hoovering up as much dropped food as she could only to throw it all up in the car on the way home.

No, the dog is better off where she is with Sylvie making sure she's okay.

Informal would also describe today's catering arrangements. In order to give the kitchen staff a day off, Tom's hired a couple of Australian blokes who specialise in hog roasts. She's guessing they didn't ask permission before digging out a firepit on the green with a skewered carcase rotating above it, the meat slowly turning a deep caramel colour. Beside it a converted classic Citroën van, bears the legend: "Hog in the Limelight". The drop-down counter displays bowls of salads for guests who aren't quite so red in tooth and claw. Fluttering above the van a faded string of bunting is swaying in the breeze.

For a moment, Lana recalls the patriotic bunting in the picture-book that so disastrously sent Ollie and her back to 1911. She vividly remembers those irate villagers closing in on her and Ollie on this very spot. Lana shudders, half expecting them to materialise again in front of her. There's even a fire ready to burn the witch.

The smell of roasting pork drifts across bringing her back to the present. Lana takes a much-needed sip of champagne while studying her son and new daughter-in-law. A handsome couple, for sure. Since they got back from London, they seem a lot happier. And they've made some changes for the better. Ollie's started nursery school and, by all accounts, he's learning to enjoy the company of children nearer his own age. As a child Tom had grown adept at hiding some of his extraordinary abilities and in the process had discovered the joy of mindless play. With his dad's guidance, Ollie seems to be acquiring the same skill.

Several times a week Beth swaps with Tom to work a shift in the pub. She'd hooted with laughter when Lana said something about her enjoying some adult conversation for a change. 'I get enough of that at home.'

Some time back the two of them had finally carried out their plan to go to the bank and reclaim the money in the account Beth had opened back in 1983. With accumulated interest it should have been a tidy sum. Lana had had to impersonate Beth's older self. When they searched through their records, the bank could find no trace of the account. Outside Beth had kicked at a waste bin and hurt her foot. She'd raved about 'That bitch Rachel' and how she must have forged her signature and withdrawn the lot. A harsh blow and one that might have made one or both of them bitter; and yet it doesn't seem to have.

Lana studies Beth now, the way her face lights up when she's animated. She's chatting to a couple of women who could be mothers from Ollie's nursery school. In profile, it's more noticeable Beth's expecting. It occurs to her that, in a break with family tradition, this new baby will actually be born in the same year it was conceived.

An odd sensation comes over her. Without turning around, she can sense Matt has arrived. She scans the crowd until she picks him out. No one will have noticed him appear and no doubt he'll leave unseen in the same way. He wouldn't have needed an invitation to know all about the wedding. A striking figure in his pale lightweight suit, *informal* isn't something he does. No hat at least, the sun picks out the maddeningly small amount of silver at his temples. He's making a beeline for Tom. An awkward encounter – a handshake that morphs into overzealous backslapping. Beth goes over – greets Matt with a smile though her whole body stiffens when he leans in to kiss her on both cheeks.

Arm along Tom's shoulder, Matt steers him away from the others for a man-to-man conversation. They look furtive, glancing around frequently presumably to check they can't be overheard.

Curious, and not a little put out at not being included, Lana surreptitiously moves nearer hoping to eavesdrop. She gets close enough to hear Matt say, 'I believe the catalyst for recent events was most likely an awareness that Beth was pregnant again. According to the warped logic of certain parties who shall remain nameless, with the prospect of another gifted but potentially highly disruptive infant in the offing, they decided a more radical solution was needed.'

Tom nods. 'The two of them cooked up the ultimate solution. Ingenious in its way. It still frightens me to think how close they came to succeeding.'

Matt spots her. 'Lana – come join us,' he says, extending the other arm so that the three of them are bound closely together. 'I was just congratulating our son here on the prospect of becoming a father again.'

She notes the *our*. The photographer – a pub regular charging what Tom referred to as 'mates-rates' – comes over to claim the groom. His bride is already positioned by the ancient stone bridge spanning the little river at its narrowest point. She could be an actress awaiting her leading man. In her ear, Matt says, 'Do you think he'll want us to pose alongside the happy couple?'

'Are you worried at being officially identified as his father?'

A thin smile. 'I regret that such an acknowledgement didn't happen long ago.' He takes a glass of champagne from the tray and raises it in her direction. The glass barely touches his lips before he lowers it again. 'You're looking particularly lovely today,' he says.

She meets those dark eyes. 'You know I really hate it when people keep things from me.'

'Even if, hypothetically speaking, they judge it to be in your best interest to do so?'

'How can anyone make that judgement on someone else's behalf?'

'Let us suppose they were to divulge certain things then, hypothetically speaking, it might have a detrimental effect on the person they wish to protect. On the other hand, if they decide not to disclose the information, it could lead to suspicion and mistrust. Quite a conundrum. And then of course there's the possibility the person might find out for themselves.'

Lana loses patience. 'For goodness' sake, I've already heard enough to understand we were all facing some awful threat.'

'Which with extraordinary courage and determination, Tom and Ollie successfully thwarted. I think you must hear the rest from Tom's lips. But surely not on his wedding day.'

On the riverbank Ollie is now posing with his parents along with the surprisingly contented looking duck nestling in his arms. Lana wonders if he's perfecting an ability to subdue animals.

She says, 'Of course I won't ask them now.' She's tempted

to add, *I hardly need parenting advice from you.*

'I take your point.' Matt gives her one of his penetrating stares – the sort that seem to pass right through her. 'I'm reminded of that rather hackneyed saying about not being able to teach an old dog new tricks. Seeing our son again – observing the man and the father he's become – has taught me a lot. I should have found a way to be a better parent to the boy. And a better partner to you.'

She smiles. 'I suppose it's tricky when you're always off saving the universe from itself.'

He smiles back at her, eyes shining like they did when she saw him that first time all those years ago. 'Yes of course I remember,' he says. And then clearing his throat, 'I see you've brought what I believe they call a plus-one.'

Lana wonders if she detects a tiny note of jealousy. 'Oleksander is a Ukrainian refugee who's staying with me while he finds his feet. I assume you already knew that.'

He nods. Doesn't deny it. 'As you must have guessed, we have our informants.'

'Spies, you mean.'

'I wonder if Oleksander will find his feet under your table.'

She says, 'To misquote L.P. Hartley – the future is another country. Olek and I have a surprising amount in common. I haven't forgotten what it was like to live through a brutal war and its terrible destruction. After I found safety, thanks to you, it was a struggle to start a new life in a new era with nothing to my name, away from everything and everyone I'd ever known. At least I could speak the language even if for a long time I felt like a stranger in my own land.'

'There have been many occasions when I wished with all my heart it could have been different for us; that we could have been just an ordinary family.'

'On that we can agree,' she says watching the photographer approach.

'Groom's parents next please.' Scruffy in jeans and a faded Black Sabbath t-shirt, the man beckons them with a rough gesture. 'If you wouldn't mind standing beside the happy couple.'

With no relatives by her side, Beth must really feel their absence today. As they make their way over, Matt offers Lana his arm and she willingly takes it. If they should never see him again, at least there will be this photograph to show their grandchildren.

Chapter Forty-One

Tom

He looks over at his wife and can hardly believe his luck. Yes, he'd been persistent, but all the same how had such an amazing woman ever agreed to marry him? She smiles back at him now in a way that fills him with joy. Looking more like a teenager than a mother, she's twisted flowers through her long dark hair to make a floral crown. Ollie had been right the first time – she is The Queen.

Her multi-layered dress floats around her when she moves like she's in slow motion. He's reminded of their brief trip back to that spring fair. He half shuts his eyes and could almost be back there. Except for the hog roast van parked on the green; and all the wires leading to the coloured lights and massive speakers set up for later; and those two planes leaving criss-crossing contrails in the otherwise unbroken blue sky. Today it's a sign – a giant kiss entirely for their benefit.

The sun and the booze must be going to his head. He looks for Ollie and spots him standing on the bridge – commanding it more like – where he appears to be demonstrating the rules of pooh sticks to one of the kids. More kids run over to join in the game. It doesn't take long for the competition to degenerate into a noisy argument about whose stick won.

Looking around he can't see Matt. He's probably left already – no goodbye as usual. He'd hate to be the kind of father who is here one minute and gone the next. His mother looks a bit lost amongst a crowd of people she hardly knows. Though she's a music fan, it's doubtful she'll stick around for the dancing.

He should go and have a chat with her before she slopes off. No need – Oleksander has gone over to talk to her. Surprising how at ease that man is in a crowd. A sprightly figure, he wears his silver hair swept back from his face; longer than is usual for a man of his age. You had to feel compassion for any refugee and yet, not for the first time, he wonders at the way the man has so easily found a place in his mother's life. She must have been lonely. All the same, he can't shake the feeling there's more to Oleksander. It's crossed his mind before that he could be a plant – someone sent by the Guardians to subtly keep an eye on them all.

'Penny for your thoughts.' Beth links her arm through his.

'I've been watching Mum with Oleksander. He seems to make her happy.'

'Don't go jumping to conclusions. Can't a man and a woman simply be friends? Besides, at their age…' He's relieved she doesn't finish that sentence. 'Look at you – you've gone all soppy. We've only been married a few hours and already you're matchmaking for other people.'

'Hardly that. But don't *you* think it's odd though the way he arrived here out of the blue?'

'No, I don't. It's what happens when you're a displaced person.' She shakes his arm. 'You need to stop thinking like that. Olek is simply a harmless and very charming old man who's been through a hell of a lot.'

'So he's Olek now, is he?'

'Tom.' She gives him a sharp look.

'You're right,' he says. 'I need to be less suspicious of new people.'

'Exactly.' Her attention wanders away from him. 'Talking of which, I should go and have a word with Noah's mum. Did I tell you Ollie's been invited to Noah's birthday party?'

Tom laughs. 'You might happen to have mentioned it a couple of dozen times.' He gives her a kiss and then watches her walk off to the other side of the green.

For the first time he notices a "For Sale" sign in the garden of Mr Tanner's house. Delores comes over to congratulate him. For the occasion she's piled her flaming red hair on top of her head putting him in mind of a matchstick ready to strike, which is odd because she's not exactly skinny.

He nods towards Mr Tanner's house. 'I only just noticed the sign.'

'Yeah – they were hammering it in when I left yesterday. Quite a turnip for the books.' She laughs at her own joke. 'Shame really,' she says, 'he was the last of the old families that used to live 'ere back in the day.' Spect some London lot with too much money are already circling. The agents will call it something like "Cotswold cottage with potential" and pretty soon they'll smash down the old fence and a skip will appear. Next thing you know a team of heavy-handed, radio-playing

281

builders will arrive to rip the heart and soul out of the place.'

'You paint a vivid picture,' he tells her.

'Seen it all before, haven't I?' She takes out a cigarette. 'D'you mind if I..?' He does really but as they're outside he can't really object.

'So, what's happened to Mr Tanner? Did they put him in a home?'

'Kicked his toes up, didn't he. Best thing to happen really. He'd have hated being uprooted and stuck in some home miles away.'

'I really liked him.' Tom finds he's close to tears. 'When did he die?'

'Months ago. They couldn't put it on the market due to some hold up with the probate – least that's what I heard from one of the neighbours I do for.'

Tom frowns. 'Hold on a minute – you just said he died months ago. Exactly how long are we talking about?'

'Hard to be exact.' She takes a drag on her cigarette, has the decency to blow the smoke well away from him. 'To be honest, I'm surprised you even knew him. Poor old bugger pegged out well before you got here.'

A cold prickle runs up Tom's back. 'So, you're saying it happened – that Mr Tanner died months ago?'

'Best part of a year, I shouldn't wonder.' Her eyebrows narrow to form a line of suspicion. 'How come you knowed him then?'

'You forget I've lived in these parts most of my life.'

Apparently satisfied with his answer, she says, 'I see they're already queuing up for that spit-roast. Smells bloody amazing, don't it? Reckon I should go and join the queue in case it runs out.'

'I'll be along in a minute,' he tells her trying to process what he's just learnt. Mr Tanner had seemed as solid as any person could be when he told stories about what happened here in the past. Tom's never believed in ghosts but he's the last person to deny that certain individuals can travel forward or backwards in time. In this case, exactly who did the travelling?

'Everything alright, Tom?' His mother. 'You look a bit shellshocked.'

He rubs at his eyes. 'Yeah – I'm a bit, you know, over-whelmed at the moment, that's all.'

'I'm not surprised; it's your big day after all. And a long one at that. In my time, the bride and groom left straight after the wedding breakfast for their honeymoon – if they could afford one that is. They called it a breakfast whatever time of day it happened. These days, the bride and groom stay to the last. I was going to say the bitter end but that's hardly appropriate.'

It occurs to him the Mr Tanner he knew might not be the same Mr Tanner who died a year ago but an imposter. The carer would have had to be in on it. Maybe he didn't even look like the late Mr Tanner – the real one. That way, if Delores or anyone else spotted him, they would only see a random old man who could be the elderly relative of any one of the weekenders.'

'Tom are you listening?'

'Sorry. Miles away.'

'I just told you I'm keeping an eye on Ollie in case he's tempted to demonstrate that so-called magic trick of his where he disappears.' She nudges him. '*You* should make sure Beth gets a chance to put her feet up. We don't want this baby coming early like the last time.'

'God no. I doubt either of us could go through that again.'

His mum lingers like she's got something on her mind. He almost tells her to spit it out. 'You know,' she says at last, 'I used to think you were a bit irresponsible. Typical snowdrop and all that. I was wrong – in fact you're remarkably steadfast, if one can still use such a word these days.' She squeezes his hand. 'It's surprising what we can and do endure for the sake of our family.'

She gives him an enigmatic look – a look that makes him wonder what Matt must have told her. 'And on that note,' she says, 'I think I might stay for the dancing. You only live once, after all.'

Chapter Forty-Two

Ollie

Mummy and Daddy have gone over to Noah's mummy and daddy's house to eat. He doesn't understand why they can't just eat in their own houses. 'We won't be late back,' Daddy tells him. He wasn't pleased when Oleksander arrived with Lana and Poppy. He never said it out loud, but he knows Daddy suspects him of being a spy for the Guardians.

'No need to rush back,' Granny tells them. After climbing up all the steps, Poppy is still panting and looking dead tired. Her breath smells of meat and something much nastier. Straight away she flops down on the rug and goes to sleep.

'I've brought us a shepherd's pie for supper.' Granny unwraps a big white dish. 'Made with lamb mince not beef, just like you like it.' She puts it in the oven to heat up again. Ollie doesn't much like her shepherd's pie – it's too salty and runny but he knows he mustn't say so.

Olek likes to play board games with him, which is fun because Ollie can't tell what move he's going to make next. Olek always calls him *small one,* never little man.

They usually play snakes and ladders or draughts but without saying anything, Olek starts to set up the chess board. 'Soon you will have little brother or sister to play games with.' When he's finished arranging the pieces in the right places, he holds a white pawn and a black one behind his back. 'Choose side,' he says.

Ollie taps his left arm. 'I like the white ones better.'

Olek looks behind him and then nudges Granny. 'Do you see mirror somewhere, Lana? P'raps we should take him to casino.' Granny laughs more when he's with her.

'What's a casino, Granny?'

'A very silly place where people dress up in their best clothes just to play a lot of different games for money. And before you ask, the only thing you need to know about gambling of any sort is that almost always you come home with a lot less money in your pockets than when you went out.'

'Then why do people go to casinos?'

'Good question,' she says. 'I suppose they must keep hoping that the next time they'll get lucky and come home with lots more money than they started with.'

Poppy makes a long groaning noise as she struggles up onto her feet and comes over to see what she might have been missing. They all cry out when her wagging tail knocks some of the chess pieces off onto the floor. They're scattered everywhere – Ollie has to crawl around picking them all up again. Poppy looks at him like she's trying to say something.

'She's a girl,' Ollie says.

'Yes, we know,' Granny says. 'That's why we called her Poppy and not Percy. Although as I recall your father wanted to call her Fang.'

'No, the baby in Mummy's tummy is a girl.'

'Oh.' Granny frowns. 'I thought Beth said they wouldn't know until the next scan.'

'They're going to call her Celia like your mother.'

'Fancy you remembering my mother's name.' Her eyes have gone teary.

'But Daddy wants to call her Vega after the brightest star in the summer triangle except Mummy doesn't want her being teased at school.'

'Hmm. Well maybe Vega could always be her second name,' Granny says. 'After all, no one could object to being named after a really bright star.' She chuckles. 'They could have called you Orion instead of Ollie.'

'That's a whole constellation,' he tells her. 'They named it after Orion the hunter because it's this shape.' He poses with an imaginary shield and stick.

Olek has finished putting all the pieces back where they belong. 'We play chess, eh?' he says. 'White have first move.'

'I've never known why that should be,' Granny says. 'You know I read the other day it had something to do with white privilege or so some people have argued. Funny how you can miss these things.'

Olek taps the side of his head. 'We concentrate – yes?'

When Ollie looks down at the pieces on the board, he pictures his queen with Granny's face on it; not her face now but her face when she was little. He picks her up not wanting to risk losing her again. 'I don't like chess,' he says. 'Why don't we play draughts instead.'

Ollie hears a loud intermittent beeping sound – the one delivery lorries make when they're reversing. Out of the window he sees a huge van with MOVE YOUR ASSETS written along the side. It stops outside Mr Tanner's old house. Two men in green overalls jump out of the front and go round to open the back doors.

A tall man about Daddy's age comes out of the house and soon the three of them are carrying tables and chairs and lamps and all sorts of other things in through the front door.

Excited, Ollie puts on his shoes and grabs Bobbity before running down the steps to watch them from a distance. A few minutes later Delores comes out of the pub carrying her cleaning things. She stops and waves her mop towards the van. 'I see the new people are moving in at long last. After them builders and all their banging and crashing, there can't be much of the old place left standing.'

A woman with long brown hair comes out and starts talking to the men. 'Eyup, the foreman's arrived.' Delores chuckles. The woman carefully checks the different rugs and lamps and cardboard boxes they're carrying and then points at different windows.

'I see they've finally gone and ripped the phone out of that old phone box,' Delores says. 'Shame in a way. S'pose they think it ent needed now everybody carries a mobile.'

'That bright yellow box in there is called a de-fib-rill-a-tor,' he tells her. 'Mummy said if somebody's heart stops you can use it to give them an electric shock that can start their heart beating again.'

'Handy things to have around, I suppose.' She points her

mop at the removals van. 'Builders reckon this lot are planning to live here full time, which makes a ruddy change. Apparently, after all the various lockdowns and that, they decided they've had enough of London life. Dare say they're after a bit more peace and quiet.' She chuckles. 'They'll certainly get that round here. In ruddy spades.'

'What's a ruddy spade?'

She winks at him. 'Pretend I didn't say that.'

Confused, he remembers what Mummy says about not asking too many questions. Instead, he tells her, 'They're called Mr and Mrs Woodward.'

Delores looks surprised. 'Postie tell you that, did he?'

'They have a daughter who's called Scarlett – which is a lovely colour like your hair.'

'I'll have you know, young man, this shade is what they call *fire red*.' Delores lifts a strand of hair up to check. 'Least ways that's what it says on the packet.'

A fair-haired little girl comes out of the house. 'That's Scarlett,' he says. 'We're going to be best friends.'

'Let's hope you're right.' She taps her nose. 'Best not count your chickens before they're hatched.'

Ollie frowns. 'I don't think they have any chickens. But they're going to get a hot tub.'

'You wish.' Delores doesn't look happy about that. 'Well, they'll certainly have their work cut out clearing up all the rubble them builders left in the garden.' She checks her watch. 'Will you look at the time, I'd best be getting on with my chores.'

When Scarlett looks over and waves at him, he waves back.

Delores hasn't gone yet. 'She certainly seems a friendly little thing, I'll say that much. Wonder why they called her that?'

'I expect her mummy's favourite film is "Gone with the Wind".' Delores looks blank. 'Scarlett O'Hara – that's the name of the main character. The heroine.'

'Is that so?' She gives him a sideways look. 'Fancy a lad of your age knowing something like that.'

'Knowledge itself is power – Sir Francis Bacon said that about 600 years ago.'

Delores shakes her red curls at him. 'Yer dad told you that, did he? I reckon Tom should have a go at Mastermind.' A throaty chuckle. 'Though, if you ask me, Pointless would be more appropriate.'

'D'you remember when you said I was like that old lady Miss Marple? How she was so ordinary-looking, nobody really noticed her.' Ollie taps his nose. 'It's surprising what you observe about people if you study them for long enough.'

'That little head of yours must be bursting at the seams.' Shaking her own, she walks off.

'It's Tuesday,' he shouts after her, 'you should be cleaning River View but you're heading in the wrong direction.'

Seeing her shocked expression, Ollie smiles.

About the Author

Before becoming a writer, Jan Turk Petrie taught English in inner city London schools. She now lives in the Cotswolds area of southern England. Jan has an M.A. in Creative Writing (University of Gloucestershire) and, as well as her published novels, she has written numerous, prize-winning short stories

As a writer, Jan is always keen to challenge herself. Her first published novels – the three volumes that make up **The Eldísvík Trilogy** – are Nordic noir thrillers set fifty years in the future in a Scandinavian city where the rule of law comes under threat from criminal cartels controlling the forbidden zones surrounding it.

By contrast, **'Too Many Heroes'** – is a period romantic thriller set in the early 1950s. A story of an illicit love affair that angers the mobsters controlling London's East End at that time.

Jan's fifth novel: **'Towards the Vanishing Point'** is set primarily in the 1950s and depicts an enduring friendship between two women that is put to the test when one of them falls under the spell of a sinister charmer.

'**The Truth in a Lie**' was her first novel with a contemporary setting. It is the story of a successful writer who has a complex and often difficult relationship with her mother and her own daughter as well as with the men in her life.

'**Still Life with a Vengeance**' also has a contemporary setting. Married to a famous rock guitarist and apparently living a picture-perfect life, a young woman's life begins to unravel when her husband is accused of rape.

'**Running Behind Time**' was Jan's first time-slip novel. Written during the unprecedented events of 2020 and the new social norms arising from the pandemic, she was inspired to imagine a time-hop back to the early 1980s.

'**Play For Time**' is its sequel.

Jan is a big fan of Margaret Atwood, Kate Atkinson, Philip Roth, Kurt Vonnegut and Jennifer Egan – authors who are prepared to take risks in their writing.

Dear reader,

I really hope you've enjoyed reading 'Play For Time'. Thank you so much for buying or borrowing a copy, the book means a lot to me. If you would like to help readers discover the book, please consider leaving a review on Amazon, Goodreads, Bookbub, or anywhere else readers are likely to visit. It doesn't need to be a long review – a sentence or two is fine.

Many thanks in advance to anyone who takes the time to do so.

If you would like to find out more about this book, or are interested in discovering more about my other published novels, please visit my website: https://janturkpetrie.com

If you'd like to follow me on Twitter, my handle is: @Turk-Petrie

Twitter profile: https://twitter.com/TurkPetrie

Facebook author page:
https://www.facebook.com/janturkpetrie

Contact Pintail Press via the website: https://pintailpress.com

Instagram: @jan_turk_petrie

Acknowledgements

I genuinely hadn't planned to write a sequel to 'Running Behind Time', but then an idea for an interesting new direction came to me…

Hard to believe this is my ninth published novel. As always, it was not without its challenges and moments of self-doubt and so, first and foremost I want to thank my brilliant husband, John, for encouraging me when I really needed it. As always, I'm indebted to him for reading and commenting on the various drafts of Play For Time. His feedback and enthusiasm kept me going during the long process of writing this book.

I want to thank my daughters Laila and Natalie for their unfailing love and support. Our gorgeous grandson, Leon, was safely delivered after most of this book was written. I sincerely hope his life turns out to be less complicated than little Ollie's.

Grateful thanks also to my wider family and in particular my mum, Pearl Turk, for her unwavering interest in my books and those highly prized 'Pearls of Wisdom'.

Writing is an essentially solitary occupation and so sharing detailed feedback from my fellow writers during zoom meetings and more recently face to face was consistently helpful and uplifting. I'm very grateful for all the comments and suggestions from the highly talented members of *Catchword*, the *Wild Women Writers* and Stroud's *Little George Group* – it made a world of difference.

Special thanks must go to author Debbie Young and everyone in my local Alliance of Independent Authors (ALLI) group for their impressive knowledge of indie publishing and sound collective advice. I'm also grateful for online advice from members of the Alli Facebook group.

Lastly, I'm once again indebted to my excellent editor and proofreader, Johnny Hudspith and to my highly talented cover designer, Jane Dixon-Smith, for their consistently outstanding work.

Printed in Great Britain
by Amazon

85876725R00176